S0-BJM-296

ALSO BY JULE MILLER

Non Fiction

- *Slippery Places: How the Delusions of Modern Management Destroyed an American Manufacturing Firm*
- *From an Idea to a Profit: Managing Advanced Manufacturing Technology*

Fiction

- *A Voyage Toward Vengeance*
- *A Question of Closure*

Voyages in Desperate Times

a novel

by

JULE A. MILLER

Copyright © 2011 Jule A. Miller

All rights reserved. No part of this book may be used, reproduced, or transmitted by any means or in any manner whatsoever without written permission, except in the case of brief quotations embodied in critical articles and reviews. For information contact Jule Miller via email at *Longviewtoo@verizon.net*

This is a work of fiction, although based upon real events that took place in Germany in 1936 and on the East Coast of the United States in the early months of World War Two. The characters and the plot of this story are inventions of the author and do not depict any real persons or events.

Printed in the United States of America

"**Desperate**: Involving or employing extreme measures in an attempt to escape defeat..."
—*Webster's New Collegiate Dictionary*

"My Navy has definitely been slack in preparing for this submarine war off our coast. As I need not tell you, most naval officers have declined in the past to think in terms of any vessel less than two thousand tons. You learned this lesson two years ago. We still have to learn it. I have begged, borrowed and stolen every vessel of every description..."
—Franklin Roosevelt in a letter to Winston Churchill, March 1942

"The regulations say you have to go out, but they don't say you have to come back."
—Saying dating back to the old US Life Saving Service, which became the United States Coast Guard

ACKNOWLEDGMENTS

I would like to thank Dr. Ronald Paul (the neurosurgeon, not the politician) for the advice that kept me from committing a couple of medical mistakes, one of which was hilarious. I would also like to thank Linda Morehouse, my editor, not only for bringing this book to final form, but for the witty and sometimes poetic emails she sent during the process. As always, my wife Heide was proof reader, spell checker, translator of bad sentences into English and essentially a co-author.

I began the research for this book almost fifteen years ago and kept coming back to it over the years, but could never find a way to tell the story because so many asides and explanations were necessary. It was when my granddaughter, now a college sophomore, asked me what those times were like, and why they were so different from the times in which we now live, that I found a way to hang the novel together. Thank you, Christianna.

DEDICATION

This book is dedicated to the memory of Jack Morris and all the other members of the Hooligan Navy. They went to sea and did the very best they could with what they had. No one can ask for more.

SAIL PLAN OF THE SCHOONER YACHTS
MORNING GLORY AND *TIGER LILLIE*

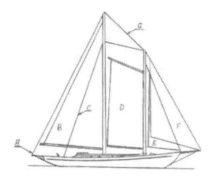

A. Boomkin and Standing Backstay

B. Marconi Mainsail

C. Running Backstays (port and starboard)

D. Gaff Foresail

E. Fore Staysails (various sizes depending on weather)

F. Jib

G. Triassic Stays

(Shrouds and running rigging omitted from the drawing for clarity.)

PROLOGUE

AUGUST 2008

THE ASSISTED LIVING FACILITY in Milford, Connecticut, where her grandfather had lived since Grandma died, was a really nice place, even if he did call it St. Peter's Waiting Room. It was laid out like a town house condominium complex and Gramps had a two-bedroom ground floor unit with a view of Charles Island and Long Island Sound. Every time she came to see him—and when she was home from college she came often— she thought of a quote from Oscar Wilde. "Is there a sailor free to choose who does not settle somewhere near the sea?"

She had a lot to do before returning to Boston at the end of the month to begin working on her master's degree in history, but she really couldn't complain about driving him to Vermont for the funeral of some old friend. She had agreed to chauffeur him when he signed over the ten-year-old, very low-mileage Buick Riviera to her.

Besides, she really liked him. They had been close ever since she was a little girl. He was sort of a classy old duck.

She parked the car, walked to his unit, and rang the doorbell but really didn't expect him to hear it. If his hearing aid was turned off, as it was most of the time, he wouldn't hear a train wreck on his front lawn. She let herself in and found him in the spare bedroom he used as a den. He wasn't working on the half-completed ship model on his workbench as she had expected. Instead, the TV was on and he was looking at some History Channel show about underwater exploration.

That was odd, because he had strict rules about not watching daytime TV other than the occasional quick peek at the news and the stock market report.

He didn't seem to have heard her come in, and when he backed the tape and reran the murky picture of some wrecked submarine she also found that odd, because Gramps had never expressed any interest in submarines. He spent his days building beautifully detailed models of sailing vessels that he donated to yacht clubs and museums.

As he once again rewound the short section of tape he was studying, she touched him on the shoulder and he looked up and said, "Oh, hi, Toots," and fumbled with his hearing aid. "Is it that time already?" He was still a slim, big-boned man, six feet tall and bald with just a fringe of fine white hair. "Here. You look at this. Your eyes are a lot better than mine. What does that thing on the foredeck, up against the deck gun, look like to you?"

She moved closer to the tube. "I don't know. It's a big lump of something. Mud, maybe? What submarine is this, anyway? Are you thinking of building a model of it?"

"It's not a submarine; it's a U-boat. I think it's U-217. You can just make out the two and the one and what might be a seven on the conning tower. The Krauts must have used some super paint. They always were good at chemistry: too good. And no, I'm not about to build any models of U-boats. I had my fill of those things a very long time ago."

He paused the tape and she peered at the image. "Yeah, I think it's 217—hard to be sure, though. And there's something painted next to the number. A person or something. Or maybe it's just a shadow."

"It's U-217 and it's not a shadow and it's not a person."

"I think you're right about the number, but I don't know what that other thing is. Hard to tell. What's the difference between a U-boat and a submarine, anyway?"

"Nothing, except that German submarines are always called U-boats: *Unterseeboote*. And they never had names, just numbers.

That always made them seem more sinister, not having names, just numbers. Sneakier, somehow."

"We really ought to hit the road if you want to be in Burlington at seven for the wake."

He stood up as he said, "My bag is all packed. Let me go to the bathroom and then we can get going."

As he limped into the bathroom, she went into the bedroom to get his bag thinking that every activity in which Gramps was involved started with his going to the bathroom. On his bed table was a photo of him and Grandma on their wedding day that had fascinated her since she was a little girl. Grandma, absolutely beautiful with her hair in that complicated puffed-up style of the 1940s, and Gramps, young and handsome in the dress blues of a Coast Guard officer. *Over 65 years ago. Almost three times longer than I have been alive. Why is it so difficult for me to believe that he was young once, like me, and that I will be old one day, like him, if I'm lucky?*

He came out of the bathroom and played the section of tape one last time. As he turned off the TV and the VCR he said, more to himself than to her, "Elise Gottlieb and U-217. Everything eventually comes full circle, doesn't it?"

ONE

SHE FOLLOWED HIM TO THE CAR and opened the passenger door for him. He sat down, swung his left leg into the car, and then used both hands behind the knee to lift his right leg into the foot well. The car had an automatic transmission and two accelerator pedals: one on either side of the brake pedal. Amy never used the left one, her grandfather's, but had never gotten around to having it removed. Although she had had the light blue luxury coupe for several years, she still thought of it as his.

As she drove out of the complex, she asked, "This lady who died in Vermont, Elise Jacobs, who was she? I don't think I ever met her."

"You did once, when you were a little girl. She brought you a huge box of crayons and colored pencils."

"Was that her? I vaguely remember her. You know, I still have some of those pencils in the beer mug on my desk. Was she an artist?"

"A gifted amateur. Elise was a gifted amateur at a lot of things. She lived in times that placed great demands on the talents of gifted amateurs." With more than a hint of wistfulness in his voice he continued, "She was three years older than I am and when we met in 1936 I was seventeen and she was twenty and one of the most stunning, and I mean that literally, women I have ever seen. Her name was Elise Gottlieb then."

She laughed, "Ah, the truth will out about the grandfather's wild youth. Was she the secret love of your life?"

"Any seventeen-year-old boy would have fallen for her on sight. But the love of my whole life? No. That was your grandmother. But for a while there . . . ." He let the sentence trail off.

"1936. That was the year you and your grandfather won your class in the Bermuda Race and got that cup that's on your bookcase next to the model of *Morning Glory*."

"I keep meaning to give those to you, Toots. I sailed with the old man from the time I was about seven or eight, and went on my first distance race with him when I was eleven, but that '36 race was the best we ever did.

"In '38 I sailed as navigator on another boat and guessed the Gulf Stream completely wrong. There weren't any satellite pictures then, or ocean-sensing buoys, or computer-generated briefings. We had celestial navigation if the weather was clear, dead reckoning when it wasn't, a thermometer hung over the side to find the Gulf Stream, and the seat of our pants—of my pants.

"In '36 I guessed right. In '38 I guessed wrong and they kicked me off the boat as soon as we got to Bermuda. The crew were all Germans and they were not very good losers, especially to Bernie Baruch, a Jew. I've been on a lot of boat races, but sailing with my grandfather in the '36 Bermuda was the best of them all and the '38 race was the absolute worst. Six days on a boat with a crew of supercilious anti-Semitic jerks. The race committee recruited me at the last minute because their navigator got sick."

"Did your father sail with you and your grandfather?"

"No. My father was a lot of things, but he wasn't a sailor. Besides, he and my grandfather had never gotten along. They finally had it out later that summer, and I don't think my grandfather ever said another word to him. Before he died he made sure my father would not inherit one thing of his through my mother."

From his tone she could tell this was a subject he didn't want to discuss. So she asked, "Is that where you met Elise Gottlieb, in Bermuda?"

"No. Elise was a fine racing sailor, but I met her in Berlin that same summer: 1936. Right after I got back from Bermuda my father and I went over for the Olympics."

"I didn't know that. The 1936 Berlin Olympics? That was the one where Jesse Owens won all those medals, wasn't it? Did you see him do it?"

"No. I played hooky that day. By then I had had enough of watching track and field while surrounded by Nazi flags and bigwigs. I never was much for spectator sports, anyway. If I can't play, the hell with it. But that was the day I met Elise Gottlieb: the seventh of August, 1936. We went sailing and then we went party-crashing."

"And you still remember the exact date you met her? She must have been some babe."

"Oh, that she was."

"Grandpa, I have to start the preliminary work on my master's thesis this fall, and I'm thinking about making it about World War Two."

"The Greatest Generation and all that. It's been done. I thought you were going to find a job once you got your bachelor's in journalism."

"Everybody has a bachelors in journalism today."

"That's why I kept telling you to get a degree in civil engineering."

"Yeah, well, I'm not cut out to be an engineer. Anyway, I've decided to get my master's in history. I thought I told you that."

"You probably did and I forgot. I can clearly remember things that happened fifty years ago but can't remember what I had for breakfast—that's if I remembered to eat breakfast."

"Grandpa, I know you were in the Coast Guard, but I know practically nothing about what you did. You never talk about it, although that's where you ..." she paused as she picked a word "...hurt your leg. I do know that the Coast Guard was involved in the Battle of the Atlantic, but there are very few books about the Coast Guard's part in it. I've read most of them in the last month and they're kind of superficial: this ship fought this battle with this wolf pack on such and such a date. I'd like to zero in on one ship and its crew. Daddy told me that Grandma once told him you were on some kind of patrol craft. I discussed this idea with my faculty advisor in a couple of emails and he suggested that if I could interview some old people in depth it might provide the material for an acceptable thesis."

"Then you'd better find some old people, Toots. I'll give you some names."

"Come on. It's going to be a long drive and we have to talk about something. Why not that? If it doesn't work or you feel uncomfortable, I'll try to find someone else or come up with another idea for a thesis."

"Wouldn't you want to record it? Isn't that what you journalists do when you talk some old fart into making an oral history?"

"This isn't going to be an oral history. Those often sound contrived because the person knows they're being recorded for posterity. This will just be you telling me stories about your youth, and then I'll do the background research to piece them all together. Ever since I was a little girl you've enjoyed telling me stories and I've loved to hear them. But you never talked about the war, or your parents or what it was like growing up. Other than mentioning the '36 Bermuda race, it's like your life began in 1946. I didn't even know you went to the Berlin Olympics. I want to hear what that was like. Besides, I don't need a tape recorder, Grandpa. I have an excellent memory."

"Well, enjoy it while you have it. When you get to be my age you'll have trouble remembering what a memory was." He rested his eyes for a while then asked, "Where would you want me to start? The story of how I wound up in the Hooligan Navy—that's what we called the part of the Coast Guard I was in—really started in the summer of 1936."

"Okay. Begin by telling me about the summer of 1936. I know you won that cup in the Bermuda Race, but you've never told me any of the details. I love sea stories. Tell me how you won your class in the Bermuda Race, Grandpa. It would be a good place to start."

"And a good way to get me talking. I had no idea you were so cunning, Toots."

She laughed and said, "Crafty. I think I prefer crafty, Grandpa. Doesn't sound so sneaky."

"You are so like your grandmother sometimes. That's exactly what she would have said."

He closed his eyes and lapsed into silence as he often did when she drove him, but she knew that he wasn't asleep. It was as if he were connected to the cruise control. All she had to do was touch the brake pedal and his eyes would open and he would be instantly alert.

After a while he said, "Okay. We'll try it. Tell me when you're bored and I'll stop." Then he paused again before saying, "What a summer. No, what a year. Not just for me, but as it turned out, for just about everyone on earth. First the Bermuda race, then I went to Germany with my father and Charles Lindbergh and I met Elise Gottlieb and the world that had started to go seriously to hell the year before took a nose dive into the pits. Is that enough for a thesis?"

"You knew Lindbergh? Tell me about him."

She let him rest his eyes for a couple of minutes, then touched the brake for a red light and said, "Come on Gramps. Lindbergh was a complex character, wasn't he?"

"No. Quite a simple man, really. A fine pilot and mechanic, personally quite courageous, and in 1927 he had been lucky enough to be in just the right place, with just the right skills, at just the right time. Lucky Lindy. But in the summer of '36 he was entering an area where he had no talent, and where he would have no luck. Where he and millions of other people would have no luck. It was an awful year. One of the worst in all of history, but no one realized it while we were living it. That's the way history works.

"You always have to remember, Amy, when you're taking those history courses, that things long in the past were once in the future, and those living at the time in question could have only the murkiest idea of what might happen in their future. The only fair way to judge them is by asking did they do the best they could, knowing what they knew then, or should have known? For example, in the early months of 1942 no one knew we would win World War Two.

"As a matter of fact, it looked very much like we were going to lose. France had been overrun. The Nazis were at the gates of Moscow. The Japs had almost wiped out the Pacific fleet at Pearl Harbor. They had grabbed the Philippines and everything west of Midway Island and it looked like they were about to invade Australia. In the Atlantic, German submarines were having what they called The Happy Time sinking hundreds of ships almost within sight of the American coast. "

"Where were you in the early months of 1942, Gramps?"

"Huh. I guess you could say I was in the thick of it. When you read those history books, try to put yourself in the place of the people living then, knowing only what they knew then, not what you know now. That's not easy."

"That's exactly what I want to be able to do. That's why I want you to tell me what those times were really like. Is that when you hurt your leg?" She knew he had lost the lower section of his right leg. She had seen him adjusting his prosthesis once in a while and he had always laughed it off by saying, "Sailors are supposed to have peg legs."

He thought about it for a moment before he said, "Yeah. That's when I hurt my leg. As to what those times were really like—in a word, desperate. They were the most desperate of times."

"My summer reading list contains a book on Lindbergh, but I haven't read it yet."

"Don't bother. I just told you everything you need to know about him."

"What should I read then?"

"Twentieth century history? Churchill's *The Gathering Storm* and *Their Finest Hour.* Were they on the list? They should have been at the top."

"No."

"I'm not surprised. Your prof probably thinks he was a warmongering has-been who should have known in the darkest days of 1940 that he was going to win and therefore should have conducted himself in a far more politically correct manner."

She was silent as she drove around the loop from Route One onto the spur road that leads to the Merritt Parkway. Then she said, "You went to Germany with your father. You never talk about him but you mention your grandfather all the time."

"My father and grandfather didn't get along. He was my mother's father. I didn't get along with my father either. I can even tell you the exact day when we started to seriously not get along. It was the same day that Jesse Owens won his medals, Joseph Goebbels threw a huge party for all the visiting foreign dignitaries, and I met that wild woman Elise Gottlieb."

"You had some summer that year."

"It started when we won our class in the Bermuda Race, and ended when I got thrown out of Germany by the Gestapo. What a summer. Desperate but nonetheless interesting times."

"Tell me about them. Start with the race."

The octogenarian Nicholas Worth closed his eyes as his granddaughter drove onto the Merritt Parkway and he vividly remembered when a teenaged Nick Worth came on deck after reducing his noon sight.

JUNE, 1936

THEY WERE ONE DAY OUT OF NEWPORT and *Morning Glory* was still close hauled to the southwest wind under her full Marconi main, gaff foresail, staysail, and jib. His grandfather, John Sloan, was steering the Alden schooner and he asked, "Do you have the foggiest notion where we are, Nick?"

"I've narrowed it down. We're probably not in the Bering Strait or the Tasman Sea. As a matter of fact there's a slight chance we're at 40 degrees, 20 North by advancing the dawn sight and 68 degrees, 40 West by the noon sight I just took. That would put us about 149 miles southeast of Newport."

His grandfather smiled. "How good a chance?"

"Not great, but considering my arithmetic ability, it's the best we've got." It was a routine they had been going through ever since Nick had started to learn celestial navigation at age twelve.

His grandfather had decided this would be the first offshore race in which Nick would do all of the navigation without anyone checking on him. He was glad that his grandson had been able to give the standard navigator's flip answers without showing just how frightening the responsibility was.

He looked around the horizon. The pleasant southwest breeze they had had since they crossed the starting line yesterday afternoon had been up and down for a while before it filled in at a steady eighteen knots or so. But the sky was starting to cloud over. Nick had been lucky to get a clear sun sight. In another hour it might have been impossible. There were only two other boats in sight.

"I see that *Duchess* is still with us." She, like *Morning Glory*, was a schooner and was in Class B with them. "Who's that boat up to weather?"

"It looks like *Kirawan*. That's the first of the Class A boats that started behind us. I imagine *Edlu* and *Stormy Weather* will be right behind her. Schooner's like poor old *Morning Glory* and *Duchess* can't go upwind with these new sloops, especially in light air."

"*Nina* stays with them upwind."

"*Nina* isn't really a schooner; she's more of a two-masted sloop. I'm glad she's not in this race. It gives us a chance. What's the glass doing?"

"Dropping. 29.91 and dropping."

"I don't think this pleasant Force Five breeze is going to last much longer."

It didn't. The southwester died off just after sunset and then it began to rain. As the fifty-four-foot schooner slatted in the short-lived calm, John Sloan had them get the jib off her and put the first reef into the mainsail. The new wind came in from the southeast and backed into the northeast as it rose, but *Morning Glory* was ready and took off like an express train. As the wind continued to increase they reduced sail by steps. By ten o'clock Nick was sure they had entered the Gulf Stream because of the rise in the seawater temperature and the way the seas were building. They were becoming more steep-sided as the gale blew harder and harder against the current. By then *Morning Glory* was roaring along under a close reefed main, a reefed foresail, and a small headsail in a windblown blackness broken only by the red of the binnacle light and the white of the breaking seas and the wake.

At midnight they took the main off of her completely and were down to just the reefed foresail and the storm staysail. The change brought her more onto her feet but didn't slow her at all. The wind was abeam and John Sloan shouted to his grandson over the noise of the wind and of the boat crashing through the seas, "Let's see any damned sloop stay with the old girl on a reach in weather like this. How she loves to pick up her skirts and stretch those lovely long legs of hers. Schooner weather." They were headed right down the rhumb line course to Bermuda. Nick estimated that the drift of the Stream and *Morning Glory's* leeway, heeled down as she was, would cancel each other. He hoped he was right.

By dawn neither the rain nor the wind had moderated and *Morning Glory's* taffrail log showed her to be barging along at better than nine knots. Nick used nine as he stood at the chart table calculating the dead reckoning position. There was no hope of getting any kind of fix in the featureless gray world that surrounded them. In the columns of the log he wrote the date and time, their estimated position, the weather, and in the comments column, "44 hours since the start".

By twilight the rain had stopped although the wind hadn't moderated at all and Nick could see both the horizon and a number of the navigational stars through the gaps in the clouds. He managed to get a three-star fix that was not as precise as he would have liked as the boat sailed up, down, and through seas that were not as square-sided as he would have expected with this wind blowing into the teeth of the Gulf Stream. The triangle formed when he plotted the positions given by averaging the best of his sextant sights explained these longer seas. It showed *Morning Glory* to be well ahead of where his DR plot said she should be. They must have stumbled onto a meander of the Stream, one of those whorls it sometimes spawns, and ridden both its southeasterly curve as well as the gale in the direction they wished to go.

They might still be riding it, and what was even better, they might be riding it alone. There had been no other boats in sight all day.

He checked the glass and it was still hovering where it had been when he checked it at 1400 hours before climbing into his bunk for four hours of what passed for sleep in a racing yacht in a gale.

When he told his grandfather that they had been averaging close to eleven knots over the ground since the last fix, the old man asked, "Are you sure?" It was not a joking question this time.

"I'm sure. I took four sights of three different stars, threw out the wildest ones, and averaged the others. They agree within a couple of miles of each other."

"What course do you want?"

"Let's hang onto this until dawn and see where that puts us."

"The wind's backing a little more. If it comes into the northwest and we have to jibe, I'd rather do it before we set the main again."

"From the way the glass is hanging down around 29.3 we may not need the main for a while."

BY NOON the next day, the water temperature had dropped so they knew they were through both the Stream and the friendly meander, but the wind held on, dropping only slowly through the afternoon and the night.

It was the middle of the following morning when they finished. When Nick saw how many boats were either anchored or rafted at the docks in Hamilton Harbor he said to his grandfather, "Well, it was a quick passage, but it looks like a lot of other boats had even faster ones."

John Sloan laughed and said, "Yup. And they're all in Class A. How does it feel to be the navigator of a boat that won its class in the Bermuda Race?"

AUGUST 2008

AMY TOUCHED THE BRAKES when an SUV swung into her lane and her grandfather said, "Yup, that was the best race I ever sailed in. We had a shotgun reach most of the way in Force Seven and Eight winds, what my grandfather called schooner weather, and I stumbled on a friendly meander in the Gulf Stream that gave us an extra couple of knots. We finished first in our class and won going away on corrected time. The very best part of it was that it was my grandfather's last offshore race. He died the following fall, the Monday after Thanksgiving. A stroke. Everybody in his family except my mother died of strokes."

"He was a doctor?"

"Yup, and a good one. He was good at anything he put his hand to."

"How did your father feel about your sailing with him?"

"He didn't like it but tolerated it." The old man thought about it for a minute before continuing. "My father was a man who could tolerate anything. If I had to describe him in one sentence I'd say he was an intolerant man who could tolerate anything."

"Grandpa, either that doesn't make any sense at all, or I'm overly dense."

"It makes sense and you definitely are not dense. I'm just not stating it very well. My father believed in the perfectibility of mankind, and thought that if he jumped wholeheartedly into the most recent -ism he could help to bring about the happy result the wild-eyed idealists like him and the hard-eyed connivers like the Nazis always promise. He was a Communist in the twenties, a Fascist in the thirties, and an Isolationist when it was fashionable before we got into the war. And all the while his own selfish, lustful, and prejudiced character gave lie to the basic premise of his life.

"Mankind is not perfectible. I'm not, and my father certainly wasn't. Individuals can strive for perfection and some can even make substantial progress toward it, but mankind, as a whole, is pretty much hopeless. Man is basically an easily led herd animal who will not only murder members of his own herd for the flimsiest of reasons, but will willingly join in the annihilation of entire other herds of humans for no reason except that some priest, mullah, or politician says they should be annihilated. No, face it, Amy, we belong to a very defective species. The Founding Fathers understood that when they wrote the Constitution."

He paused for a moment or two, then continued, "You know, I cannot think of a single tangible or useful thing my father was good at. He volunteered for the American Ambulance Service in World War One but he could not change a tire. He always claimed that an artillery barrage killed all his friends and convinced him that nothing, absolutely nothing, is worse than war. Years later one of those friends showed up and over dinner they laughed about how they had joined the ambulance corps to dodge the draft and how their cushy administrative jobs in Paris were the closest either of them ever got to the Front."

"Maybe so, Grandpa, but he was right about one thing: there is nothing worse than war."

"Of course there is. The results of accommodating international evil are always worse than the results of confronting it. If history teaches anything it's that, but it's a hard and usually expensive lesson to learn."

"It sounds like your father was just a garden variety hypocrite."

He thought about it before continuing, "No, he was a lot more complex than that—or maybe he wasn't. I have to admit that after all these years of trying, I've never really figured him out. He genuinely believed in Lindbergh and the America First isolationist cause. He was a professor at Yale, but despite his education, his intelligence, and his experience, he was one of the most politically naive people I ever met. In a sense he was even more naive than Lindbergh, because Lindbergh was an uneducated man of normal intelligence who could be expected to believe whatever his over-educated dope of a wife told him. My father was worse because he should have known better."

"Grandpa, what I've read about the 1930s is incomprehensible. What you said about judging people's actions in history by what they knew at the time, not by what we know now, makes a lot of sense. Maybe that's why the thirties are still incomprehensible. Reading about it is like watching a Greek tragedy. Everything just keeps rolling toward a bloody ending and no one knows how to stop it, even those who can see it coming. Could that have been your father's problem?"

"My father's problem was that he didn't believe in anything except that which would make him happy at the moment."

She started to say something but he waved her into silence and went on. "He could look at all sides of a question until everything became so complicated and blurry that it was impossible to reach any conclusion at all. So he would accept any conclusion handed to him by someone he thought he was supposed to respect and toss out any facts that contradicted that conclusion. That's why he joined Lindbergh and the bunch of rich, over-educated dull-normals around him. When I look back on how they played up to those Nazi thugs, it's incomprehensible to me, too. But like they say, it probably seemed like a good idea at the time. A lot of governments were doing it, too."

"Did your mother go to Germany with you?"

"No. My mother was an invalid, a shut-in."

"She was sick?"

"When it began she wasn't so much sick as sickly. Back then

people could suffer from some undefined illness and just withdraw; if that's what they wanted to do, they were allowed to do it. Now, some illness would have to be diagnosed and a course of treatment prescribed or they would be deemed to be suffering from depression and we have pills for that, too. But back then, if a person decided to just give up, stay home, and spend most of the day in bed, people just called her an invalid or a shut-in and left it at that. Nowadays it wouldn't be tolerated unless the person was very old. My mother withdrew when she was in her late thirties. She had had several miscarriages. I guess that triggered it. Later on, they found out she had a congenital heart defect they couldn't do anything about."

"How did your grandfather feel about it?"

"He blamed my father and not just for the miscarriages."

They were just south of Wallingford when the traffic that had been cruising at ten to fifteen miles per hour faster than the speed limit backed up and slowed to a crawl. The old man closed his eyes once more and remembered when he came into the living room of the suite at the Adlon Hotel dressed for another day at the Berlin Olympics.

AUGUST 1936

HE WORE A SHIRT AND TIE, a summer-weight blue blazer, and Oxford bags. Those were the wide, pleated front, gray flannel trousers that were the fashion in 1936 for young men in prep school and college. The day before he had worn the off-white bags that were called creamers, but despite the cleanliness of the city and the stadium, by the end of the day they were filthy. He had two more pairs of creamers in his trunk, but had decided to save them.

His father, Earnest Worth, was seated at the breakfast table in shirt, tie, vest, and a dressing gown talking to Frau Betzhold. He was as tall as his son and as thin. His thinning brown hair was combed straight back and held in place by a patent preparation that gave it a sheen. With his pencil mustache and silk foulard dressing gown, he looked like a movie star—George Brent, perhaps.

The Lindbergh delegation were all staying at the Adlon, the best hotel in Berlin, as guests of the German government. A number of guides had been supplied to smooth things during their stay and Frau Betzhold had been assigned to the Worths. All the guides, especially those assigned to men unaccompanied by wives, were attractive young women. Frau Betzhold was a small, very well-built woman in her late twenties with dark hair and a way of almost, but not quite, fawning over Nick's father, whom she invariably addressed as Herr Professor. Who, what, or where Herr Betzhold was seemed to be of no interest to either Frau Betzhold or Earnest Worth.

Nick greeted them as he sat down and took one of the fresh, crusty German breakfast rolls—those rolls that are so good as to be almost addictive. He split it with his thumbs and spread butter and strawberry jam on the halves as Frau Betzhold poured him a cup of coffee and asked, "And did you sleep well, Nicholas?" She was wearing a suit that in theory was rather staid, but because of the way it fitted her body was anything but. Her chair was turned sideways to the breakfast table and she seemed not to have noticed that her skirt had ridden up her crossed legs so that the tops of her silk stockings and a thin stripe of white thigh were visible as she slowly swung her leg back and forth. Earnest Worth and his seventeen-year-old son both noticed, though.

"Fine, Frau Betzhold, just fine." He was lucky that his voice hadn't cracked when he said it.

"Are you looking forward to today's events? Some think that the short and middle distance races are the heart of the Olympics."

It took all of his concentration to look at her face and not at the area above that slowly swinging high-heeled shoe as he answered, "To tell the truth, I've about had enough of sitting in the stadium and think I'd like to go out and see some of the city."

"If you wish. I'll arrange for a car and a guide."

"No, that's all right. My grandfather has an old friend who lives in Dahlem-Dorf just outside of the city center whom he asked me to look up.

I understand that I can get there on a streetcar. I think I'd like to do that and some sightseeing and shopping. I want to get something for my mother."

She started to say, "I think it would be better…"

But Earnest Worth, without looking at her face at all, said, "Come, come, Ruth. Let the boy have the day off. It's only eight-thirty and we don't have to be at the stadium until one. Perhaps you and I can find something amusing to do in the meantime." It was obvious that mention of his wife made him uneasy and that he definitely had something amusing in mind for Frau Betzhold.

She smiled and said, "Perhaps, Herr Professor. Perhaps," as she finally pulled her skirt down over her knee.

Then Earnest said, "But be back here no later than five, Nick. We have to leave at six for Herr Goebbels' party. Don't be late."

"It will be magnificent," Betzhold chimed in. "They have been decorating the island for weeks and the entertainment will be provided by the Berlin Philharmonic and the Berlin Opera and its ballet company. A wonderful evening under the stars with the very best of German culture. There can be nothing finer."

Nick finished his roll and coffee and got out of there as quickly as possible, before his father could change his mind.

The Berlin phone system was still a mystery to him, so he asked the desk clerk if he could get a phone number and place a call for him. With a big smile the clerk said, "Of course, Herr Worth." But when Nick read the name and address to him, the smile faded and he placed the call with obvious distaste.

Jacob Gottlieb had been Nick's grandfather's roommate in medical school, so when he answered the phone, Nick said, "Dr. Gottlieb, we haven't met, but my grandfather, John Sloan, asked me to contact you. I'm here visiting for the Olympics."

"How is John? I had a letter from him last spring saying he was sailing again in the Bermuda Race and inviting me to join him, but I never have the time. How did he do?"

"We won our class."

"You sailed the race with him and won? You must tell me all about it at dinner."

"I'm sorry, but my father and I are with the Lindbergh delegation and we're being wined and dined every night."

"Yes, I suppose you are. Lunch, then. Come for lunch."

"I'd like that."

"Where are you now?"

"At the Adlon."

"You have the address? Just give it to the cab driver."

"I think I'd like to take the streetcar. We've been whisked around Germany in chauffeured cars and I haven't really seen anything of the country."

"Well then, walk up Unter den Linden through the Brandenburger Tor, and take the streetcar past the Tiergarten to the Ku'damm. Then transfer to the Dahlem-Dorf Line. I think it's the number seven car. When are you going to leave?"

"Right now."

"I have to go into my clinic for an hour or two, but I'll have my daughter meet you at the streetcar stop. She will show you around the village on the way to our home."

"How will I recognize her if there's a crowd?"

He laughed, "Don't worry, Elise is recognizable in any crowd."

TWO

NICK'S PREP SCHOOL required four years of a foreign language. He had already had three years of German and intended to take a literature course in his upcoming senior year. On the way over on the *Europa,* and in the three weeks since arriving in Germany, he had taken every opportunity to practice the language. Although he was still far from fluent, he was becoming quite proficient in understanding and making himself understood.

Berlin had been a revelation. Instead of the stark, gray ugliness and humorless goose-stepping masses he had expected from what was shown in American newsreels, the city was about the greenest he had ever seen. Parks were everywhere and it was ringed by a chain of landscaped lakes, canals, and rivers. The people of the city were friendly and had a wonderful sense of sometimes-raunchy humor that his rapidly improving German allowed him to understand as he eavesdropped on the conversations around him.

AMY TOUCHED THE BRAKES as she drove off the Parkway onto I-91. Her grandfather opened his eyes and said, "Meriden already. You're making good time, Toots."

"What was Berlin like in the thirties, Grandpa? Like *Cabaret*?"

"Yeah, I guess it was in some ways." He laughed. "The music wasn't as good, though. The first morning we were there the Krauts got us up early, loaded us on a special train, and hauled us all the way to Bayreuth for the Wagner Festival. Oh God, it was dreadful."

"The train ride?"

"No, the festival."

"Wagner's music is beautiful."

"I suppose it is, in reasonable doses." He paused as a truck thundered past before continuing, "Let me put it this way, what's your favorite dessert?"

"I don't know. I had a chocolate brownie with vanilla ice cream last night that was pretty good."

"Okay. Now imagine spending eight hours a day for a week doing nothing but eating one chocolate brownie with vanilla ice cream after another, while you are surrounded by people who are doing the same thing and who, because they think it is expected of them, keep smacking their lips and saying how good it is, when they really want to run outside, throw-up, and never face another goddamned chocolate brownie with vanilla ice cream again. That's the Bayreuth Wagner Festival. Have you ever sat through a Wagner opera?"

"No. I saw La Bohème and the Barber of Seville last winter, though."

"La Bohème is to a Wagner opera, what a tennis volley is to an artillery barrage. We sat through two of them a day. Over eight hours of Wagner. German masochism at its very worst. When I think about it, it's not surprising that Hitler sat there enraptured through the entire festival. Everyone agrees he was nuts."

"Was Elise Gottlieb at the festival with you? Did she agree with your opinion?"

"No, I met her a couple of weeks after that and we never talked about it."

"Why not?"

"We had other things to talk about."

"What did she look like? Do you remember?

Again he laughed. "Oh yes, I remember quite clearly."

AUGUST 1936

SHE WAS VERY TALL for a woman, particularly for a European woman of her generation: about five-eight. In heels she was only a couple of inches shorter than Nick's six-one. Her shoulder-length hair was thick and blond with a slight reddish tint to it. Her eyes were a deep green. As he alighted from the streetcar she strode toward him with her hand held out to be shaken, and he realized that her father had been right, he needn't have worried about recognizing her. She was unique.

Speaking in English with a cross between a German and a British accent, she said, "You must be Nicholas Worth. My father asked me to meet you and show you around our village." She was dressed in a white silk blouse; loose, light blue slacks of a similar material; and low-heeled walking shoes.

"I'm very pleased to meet you, Miss Gottlieb."

"Elise, please. I shall call you Nicholas and we shall always behave together like Americans, not Germans. It takes Germans years to get onto a first-name basis and even then it always sounds stilted. I prefer the way Americans do things and I'm sure you do, too."

They started to stroll up through the village center as he desperately sought something to say that would not sound stilted. They were passing a newspaper shop and he noticed that the space in the rack outside the door marked for the *Paris Edition of the Herald Tribune* was empty. He motioned toward it and said, "Elise and Nick it is, then. I see that they've already sold out the *Trib* this morning. Does Dahlem have that many English speaking people?"

"The *Trib* has been sold out in Germany for three years now."

"It must be for just this shop. It's slipped under the door of our suite at the Adlon every morning."

"Your suite at the Adlon is not Germany, Nicholas. Not by any stretch of the imagination."

There was a wooded parkland behind the row of shops that lined the avenue, and when they passed the last shop she said, "Our home is just across the park and the shortcut is right up this path. Or would you prefer to take the long way around?"

"The long way is fine. What do you do, Elise? Are you a student too?"

"I was an aspiring painter and was at the Berlin Art Institute before I was asked to leave, although one of my professors offered to give me private lessons if I agreed to model for him. I declined. To tell the truth, I was glad to leave. It was once the finest Art Institute in Europe, but no more."

"Oh? What happened?"

"Our Fuehrer happened. He too was once a painter and he has definite opinions on the visual arts and architecture."

He thought about it for a minute and then said, "I don't understand. President Roosevelt had definite opinions on our judiciary, but that has no effect on what is taught in our law schools."

"Dear Nicolas, you are right. You don't understand." Then she changed the subject, or at least tried to. "That building ahead is my father's cancer clinic. My brother is also a doctor and works there with him. I help out with the paperwork because neither of them is very clerical. The work is actually much more productive and useful than being an aspiring painter. I'm not complaining."

It was a large stone building separated from the street by a brick wall and a strip of manicured lawn. The wrought iron gate in the wall stood open and beside it was a discreet cast bronze sign that said, *Die von Fiedler Klinik*. Nick asked, "Who's von Fiedler?"

"Oh Nick, in Germany, no matter how hard one tries, every subject eventually becomes the same subject. Doctor Ludwig von Fiedler is a funny little man who bought his *von* from some decrepit and bankrupt nobleman. Such phony arranged adoptions are a fairly common procedure among those with social aspirations. They do it by some perversion of the adoption laws that I don't understand and don't want to understand."

"Is it his clinic or your father's? My grandfather told me it was one of the most respected facilities for research and the treatment of cancer in Europe and that your father is one of the smartest men he ever met."

"It's my father's in all but name. In 1933, when the laws excluding Jews from professorships and the professions were passed, my father simply ignored them because he could not imagine that they would be enforced against a doctor of his status. Last September when the so-called Nuremburg Laws were passed, one of my father's patients was the wife of a man very close to Hitler. He still is. Another patient at the time was the fourteen-year-old son of one of the industrialists who financed the Nazi Party. Both patients recovered, incidentally. Anyway, the Nazis, who occasionally get cancer just like everyone else, thank God, do not want the clinic closed. So my father was quietly advised to sell it on paper to this Aryan nonentity and go on with his work."

"I didn't know you were Jewish. My grandfather never mentioned it."

"Oh, to live in a country where someone being Jewish is not worth mentioning." They reached the corner of the clinic's wall and she pointed down a flagstone path that led along it into the park. "Another shortcut to our home, or would you like to continue our stroll."

"What time is lunch? Do we have time to continue our stroll? I've learned more about Germany in the last few minutes than I've learned in the entire time since we arrived."

"Fine. But no more about Germany. Tell me about your grandfather's yacht. I would love to sail in a long offshore race one day. It sounds like heaven."

He laughed. "Heavenly is not a word that is often applied to offshore races by those who have done them. They can be a bit wet and uncomfortable. You're a sailor, then?"

"Oh yes. My brother and I have a little day sailer on the Wannsee not far from here, and a Star at our place on the Lake of Constance, although we have not been able to get down there in two years. The clinic is very short-staffed."

"Why? In the States we have lots more people looking for work than can find jobs. Far more. It's our single biggest problem."

"In Germany, too, there is plenty of labor, but most of it falls into one of two groups: those who will not work for Jews, and those who are afraid of what might happen to them if they were to work for Jews. We used to have a man and his wife who had been with us since I was a little girl. When they left they were both in tears but there was nothing any of us could do." She shrugged. "I'm our domestic staff now. You see? We couldn't even talk about sailing without the conversation coming right back to the same subject. Do you see how politics permeates our lives? God, I'm sick of it."

They passed two matrons, both wearing the tweed suits and feathered Tyrolean hats that middle-aged German women seemed to favor. They eyed Elise, hatless in her comfortable blouse and slacks, with obvious disapproval, and one of them made a comment about women who wear trousers that Nick did not quite catch. Elise turned to them and said, in German, "Excuse me, gnaedige Frauen, but would you be willing to answer a question for me?"

They were obviously embarrassed, but nonetheless they paused and one of them responded, "Ja?"

"Those stylish wool suits you are wearing on this hot August day, do they itch terribly? And do you enjoy the itching and get a certain, shall we say, satisfaction from it?"

Both of the women made gagging noises as they hastened away, and Nick asked in English, "You don't cut anyone any slack at all, do you?"

"Self-satisfied, sanctimonious old bats do not deserve any slack. You understood what I said, then?"

"Yeah. I get most of what is said around me if it is not said too quickly."

They had reached a corner and as she turned into it she said, "And here is the street where the Gottlieb family lives." There were half a dozen stately stone houses on large landscaped lots that backed on the park. The phone in the entryway was ringing when they entered. Elise answered it, and while she spoke for a few seconds he studied a glass-fronted cabinet that had one shelf filled with prize silverware won in boat races.

Elise hung up the phone and said, "That was my brother. He and Father are hopelessly tied up and they wonder if you could come again tomorrow or perhaps next week some time. They are terribly embarrassed but they received two new patients this morning and are anxious to finish their diagnoses and begin treatment. Time is very important in the treatment of cancers."

"I understand. Do you need to help them? If so, I'll walk you back to the clinic and call you tonight."

"No. The paperwork isn't urgent."

"In that case, why don't I take you to lunch?"

"I have a better idea. Why don't I pack a lunch and take you sailing?"

"I'd like that." He nodded at the cabinet. "The Gottlieb family seems to have won more than its share of boat races."

"Yes, but no more. The Aryans do not like to be beaten by us. There is that accursed subject again."

AUGUST 2008

As **AMY DROVE** through the complicated series of highway intersections around Hartford, her grandfather said, "The Berlin of the 1930s was a much greener and prettier place than Hartford is today, but of course the Krauts had cleaned it up for the Olympics. And they were building the Autobahns. We were building the Merritt Parkway at the same time, but the motivations were totally different. The Parkway was a make-work project at the depths of the depression; the autobahns were built to move troops around the country in time of war, but no one knew it then. We take Interstates and the Parkway for granted, but in the thirties, the idea of routing express roads so there were no cross streets or traffic lights was a marvelous innovation. I can remember going from New London to Stratford—that's what, about an hour now? Back then it took maybe three hours in good weather because you had to go through New Haven and all those little towns on the Boston Post Road."

He stared out the window for a few moments, then said, "The first autobahn I rode on was from Berlin out to Tempelhof Airdrome. Goering took the Lindbergh group out there to see a new eight-engine transport plane they had just developed. Everyone was impressed."

"You met Goering?"

"Oh, yeah."

"Was he as bad as they say? I mean not really evil, so much as ambitious and misguided. You know, a henchman."

"He had a hand in the Holocaust right at the beginning when he ran the Prussian State Police for Hitler, and he looted the museums of Europe for his own art collection, and he helped to start World War II. That's about as evil as it gets. But in contrast to some of the Nazi bigwigs who were well educated sophisticates, in person he was a fat, slimy..." He paused and searched for a word. "Creep: that's the word. The books talk about the awful things he did, but they don't really explain what a creep he was in person. My only memory of him was of an unctuous, sweaty guy in a preposterous comic opera uniform that was too heavy for the weather. He fawned over every one of us, even me, and at seventeen I was nothing to be fawned over, believe me. He had a habit of rubbing his hands together while he talked to you like the overacting villain in a silent movie."

"How did Lindbergh and the others react to him?"

"They ate it up. While he showed us the plane he went into a long spiel about how we must never allow another war to happen because then the British and the French might bomb German cities. If that happened the peace-loving Krauts would have no choice but to convert this plane into a long-range bomber and use it to obliterate

London and Paris and anyone else foolish enough to get into a war with Germany. The Germans are not noted for their subtlety, particularly when making threats."

"A creep. That's exactly the sort of first-person impressions I want for my thesis. "

As they drove under the I-84 viaduct with its hopelessly confusing maze of lane and exit signs, a BMW roadster passed them, weaving in and out and going at least twenty miles an hour faster than the rest of traffic. "Elise had a BMW convertible and she drove with all of the abandon I expected of her. A wild woman."

"You said you went sailing that afternoon?"

AUGUST 1936

IT WAS A 21-FOOT SLOOP tied to a dock in the backyard of the home of friends. While he lugged the wicker hamper with their lunch down the dock she ran ahead and pulled off the canvas cockpit cover. "It's a Sam Rabl design. Both our boats, the Star and this one were designed by Americans and they are both Olympic classes."

"Did you try out?"

"Lord, no. There is no way the Aryans would risk being beaten by my brother and me, a pair of Jews. Especially because I always steer while he does the heavy work. Can you imagine what would happen if the Herrenvolk were bested by two Jews in a boat steered by a woman? It would undermine their entire idiotic philosophy. Besides, my brother and I have far more important things to do than race sailboats for the glory of the Vaterland."

They hanked on the jib and hoisted the sails without having to discuss it at all. But when he started to drop the centerboard, she said, "Just half way. This whole end of the lake is quite shallow and the bottom mud is like glue."

The boat was facing into the light breeze so she untied the stern line as he freed the one to the bow and then pushed it off so the sails filled. They beat out into the center of the lake and then reached along the main channel. He took over the steering as she opened the hamper and removed a loaf of bread, a block of cheese, a bottle of white wine, dishes, glasses, and napkins. She looked into his eyes and anticipated him by saying, "I know, a loaf of bread, a jug of wine, et cetera."

"No, I was expecting a bottle of brew and a pretzel or two, et cetera." It wasn't original but it fitted and he was happy it had occurred to him.

She pulled the cork and then pointed ahead with the bottle as she said, "Look at that. They have that island decorated for the party for foreign dignitaries Herr Goebbels has been planning for months. It looks like the weather will be perfect. What a shame. We really could use a downpour tonight, but there is not a cloud in the sky."

The island was just a few acres of lawn with a small stand of trees near a dock on the side closest to the lakeshore. As they got closer they could see people setting up tables under the bright colored tent flies that circled a huge bandstand near the center. "Would you like to go with me?"

"Where?"

"To Herr Goebbles' party."

She handed him a plate of bread and cheese and put a glass of wine down on the thwart beside him. "You want to take a Jew to Herr Goebbles' party?"

"Sure. Besides, Elise, you have to be the most Aryan-looking person I've ever met in my life."

"That's because of my mother. She was a Jutland Dane. She died. "

It was a statement that closed the subject, so he asked, "Well, do you want to go? The food, the wine, and the entertainment are expected to be superb." He had had no idea how exciting the entertainment would prove to be.

THREE

AUGUST 2008

THEY WERE THROUGH HARTFORD FINALLY, heading up I-91 toward the Massachusetts state line when Amy asked her grandfather, "You said you went to a party the Nazi bigwigs threw that night. What was it like?"

"Like no other party I have ever attended in my life."

"Did you go with your father?"

"Not exactly."

AUGUST 1936

WHEN NICK WALKED INTO THEIR SUITE at the Adlon, it was six-thirty and his father was waiting for him already dressed in white tie and tails. "Where the hell have you been all day? You missed the games and the luncheon that had been laid on for us. Do you know how rude that was?"

Nick knew better than to say he had been sailing. "I was sightseeing and lost track of the time." He remembered something he had read in a guidebook. "Did you know that Berlin has over eight thousand acres of parks? Probably the most of any city in the world. This is a very beautiful place. And the people all seem so happy and well employed." That was a parroting of something all the members of the Lindbergh delegation were constantly telling each other.

It worked because his father said, "Get dressed. Frau Betzhold will be here with the car any minute." As if to prove him right, the phone rang and he answered it and said, "We'll be right down." Then he turned to Nick and said, "Throw on your soup and fish. I'll go down and have her wait."

"Dad, I'm filthy and sweaty. I need a bath before I can appear in polite company."

"All right. Get a cab. You know where this party is?"

"That island in the Wannsee. The cab drivers will know how to get there."

"And just this once, Nick, behave like a grown-up. Show up where you're supposed to be when you're supposed to be there and no excuses." He dug in the inside pocket of his tailcoat. "Here's your invitation. They won't let you on the boat to the island without it."

"Don't worry. I'll be there before the entertainment starts. Hurry along now. You don't want to keep Frau Betzhold waiting."

He was standing at the curb in white tie and tails when Elise drove up in her BMW convertible with the top down. When he climbed into the car, she said, "You look like a fugitive from a Fred Astaire movie. Where's your top hat?"

He looked over at her and replied in a choked voice, "And you look better than Ginger Rogers ever looked." She wore a very plain, dark blue, form-fitting gown with a more daring décolleté than anyone ever wore in a movie. It was set off by a single strand of pearls.

"This was my mother's dress. It hasn't been worn in years. I spent the last two hours taking it in so it would fit. When I sat down in it I realized that I have taken it in perhaps a bit too much. Do you think it might light a few Nazi candles?"

"It sure lit my candle."

"Oh yes, Nicholas. I can tell."

Neither Nick nor anyone else on the boat could keep their eyes off her as they rode the short distance to the island in one of the small specially-built launches that served as ferries. When she entered the area of the tables she glanced around like a duchess arriving in a room filled with peasants. His father and Frau Betzhold were seated with an overweight Chicago newspaper publisher and his Nazi-supplied guide/concubine. The men leaped to their feet and his father asked, "Nick, where did you find this absolutely flawless lady?"

Nick said, "This is Elise…"

Before he could finish the introduction Elise interrupted him. "Oh, there are flaws Herr Worth. I only hope you do not discover them too soon. My father and Nick's grandfather studied medicine together just before the War."

Frau Betzhold said, "Oh, yes. German medicine was the finest in the world before the Great War and it will soon be again."

Elise quietly replied, "We can only hope so."

A waiter rushed up and held Elise's chair while another filled their glasses with the Henkell Trocken Sekt that was being served. Betzhold lifted her glass toward Elise in toast and said, "It is not necessary to hope. It is a certainty that our Fuehrer will soon make German medicine, science, and culture as superior as this fine German sparkling wine is superior to that watery stuff the French call champagne."

Again Elise said, "We can only hope so."

Fortunately the orchestra started to play at that minute. Unfortunately, it was the Overture to Tannhaeuser, not exactly the most relaxing of dinner music.

The publisher raised his voice as well as his glass. "One of the Fuehrer's favorites and a fine example of that superior German culture Frau Betzhold mentioned."

Betzhold said, "What a lovely gown, but it does take a certain sort of person to wear it, doesn't it?"

"This? It's just something my mother bought many years ago in Copenhagen.

"I would have thought it was French. The French designers

have a wonderful way of dancing along the line of obvious decadence without quite falling over."

"Your gown is also quite lovely, Frau Betzhold. Is it yet another example of superior Teutonic culture?" Betzhold's gown was dark green with lots of complicated white lace trim wrapped around it and over her shoulders. Before Ruth could reply, Elise continued, "No, I guess it isn't. If it were it would have epaulettes instead of all that frothy lace, wouldn't it?"

Nick was relieved, as was everyone else at the table, when a waiter came over and whispered in Betzhold's ear. She stood and excused herself and as their eyes turned to see where she was going, Elise very quietly said to Nick, "We have a problem, I'm afraid." Betzhold had joined a group consisting of a Nazi functionary in a white dinner jacket, two uniformed guards, and a dumpy little man with a Prussian haircut and a monocle in white tie and tails.

Nick asked why and she replied, "You asked about Herr Doktor von Fiedler? That's him pointing at me."

"Oh, shit."

"Exactly."

Betzhold came back to the table, leaned over, and quietly spoke in German in Elise's ear so that Nick could just hear her. "Jew whores are not welcome here. Will you quietly get up and join Herr von Fiedler and those with him, or will your inferior breeding compel you to make a scene?"

Elise replied in a conversational tone that everyone at the table could hear. "No, I'll go quietly. I've had about all of the gutter aristocracy I can stand for one evening anyway."

As she stood, Nick stood with her. His father and the publisher, obviously confused, got to their feet as well. Betzhold said, "You don't have to leave, Nicholas. No one blames you for being deceived by this person. They are well known for using their sexuality to deceive."

"I haven't been deceived at all. I am undoubtedly the least deceived person here. Besides, a gentleman always leaves a social affair with the lady he brought." With that he gave Elise his arm and led her over toward the waiting group.

Fiedler scurried away as they approached as if they carried some infection. The man in the dinner jacket said to Nick, "Please excuse us, Herr Worth. This does not concern you."

The way the two guards were eyeing Elise there was no way he was going to leave her with them. "Look. If Miss Gottlieb's presence offends you people, we will leave." Then he smiled, and said as pleasantly as possible, "If I brought a date to a party and didn't see her home, my mother would never forgive me."

"This is a political matter that does not concern you."

"No, it isn't. It's a simple matter of etiquette. We have somehow committed some social error, for which I can only plead ignorance of your customs and apologize. I am truly sorry and if you will excuse us, we will now leave quietly. I'm sure you want a scene even less than I do."

The German thought about it for a second, decided not to give this ill-mannered American adolescent an excuse to make trouble, and said, "Wait here."

He went over to the two uniformed men and gave them some instructions as Nick asked, "What kind of cops are those? You people sure have a lot of cops in different uniforms."

"Goering's own cops. The Prussian State Police. Bad people."

The guy in the dinner jacket walked away and one of the cops motioned them to follow with the two-foot truncheon he was carrying.

When they were in the launch and the engine was started, one of them told the helmsman to get out, then backed the boat away from the dock himself. Instead of heading toward the landing a few hundred yards away, he turned the boat out into the lake and headed around a point of land. While this was happening the senior one, a sergeant, stood tapping his truncheon into the palm of his hand, looking Elise up and down. She leaned against the motor box and glared back at him.

When they were around the point and out of sight of the island, the cop at the helm put the engine into neutral, came aft, and pushed Nick down onto the seat that ran across the back of the boat. In German he said, "Sit down, Jew boy, and watch the fun." He too had a club that he enjoyed tapping into his palm.

The sergeant said, "Bitch, you have been caught spying on your betters and probably stealing from them as well. What have you taken?"

"You people have absolutely nothing I could ever want."

He tapped her on the shoulder with his club, not hard enough to do damage or cause much pain but hard enough to give a warning of what might come. He had obviously had a lot of practice with it. "So, we will have to search you. Take off that dress."

Elise suddenly changed character so completely that it even fooled Nick. All of her courage disappeared as she sobbed, "Whatever you wish, Herr Feldwebel. Please don't hit me again." With another sob she said in English, "Be ready, Nick."

"What did you just say?"

"I told the boy not to interfere. I don't want him hurt either."

"The dress, it's much too good a dress for a Jew bitch anyway."

"Jawohl, Herr Feldwebel."

He stepped back against the combing to get a better view as she bent forward as if to gasp the hem of her long skirt. Instead of the skirt she grabbed the ankles of his boots and with one gigantic heave threw him head first and backwards into the lake. The younger one, who was supposed to be guarding Nick, had understandably been watching Elise. Before he could react, Nick grabbed him by his thick brown leather belt and tossed him in with his comrade. They both came up together in a dripping, muddy pile. The water was only up to the pockets of their uniform shirts as they untangled themselves and stood there gasping and trying to wipe the mud and murky water from their eyes. By that time, Elise had crossed the boat and had shoved the transmission into gear and the throttle against the stop.

The only conversation they had on the trip around the point to the dock was when he said, "Oh, boy."

And she replied, "Yes. Oh, boy."

She stopped the launch beside the dock using just a touch of reverse, then, once more in her duchess mode, discreetly lifted her skirt and stepped out of the boat.

When they got to the car she said, "Let's put up the top," and he wordlessly helped her.

When they were inside they looked at each other and began to laugh.

AUGUST 2008

AMY SAID, "MY GOD, she was a wild one, wasn't she? What happened then, Grandpa?"

He thought about it in silence. *Then I kissed her and she kissed me back and my hands were all over her as she pushed her body hard against me. But then she pulled away and breathlessly said, "Danger and violence do cause a certain sexual excitement, don't they? Oh Nick, I want to as much as you do, but we may not have much time. I have to get you back to your hotel and I must get home." And that was undoubtedly the best sex I didn't have in my whole life.*

He didn't mention that interlude to his granddaughter. Instead he said, "She drove me back to the Adlon, where a message from my father was waiting. 'Stay in the room and don't go out. Frau Betzhold and I will be there shortly.'

"Well, I figured this was the end of young Nick Worth: resisting arrest, assaulting a police officer, and who knew what else? My father and Betzhold arrived right after I did, and as you can probably guess, they were just a bit pissed. But they weren't pissed about what I expected them to be pissed about."

AUGUST 1936

"GODDAMN IT NICK, how could you do such a thing, bringing that woman to Herr Goebbels' party?"

"She's a nice girl from a good family. I didn't think there was anything wrong with bringing her."

Ruth Betzhold chimed in. "She is a Jew. Bringing her to such an important social event was an insult to the entire German race. The Fuehrer is scheduled to make an appearance later. Because of your unbelievable stupidity in bringing that whore, we had to leave before he arrived."

Nick realized that they hadn't heard about the cops taking a swim. Then it dawned on him that they might never hear. The goons might not want to tell anyone what a Jew bitch and her boyfriend had done to them. He decided to test this theory. "Frau Betzhold, there may have been whores present tonight, but Elise wasn't one of them and I wish you would stop calling her that. By the way, how much are you being paid to escort my father, and where is Herr Betzhold?"

His father silenced him by saying, "That's it, young man. Not one more word. Get in the other room, get changed, and pack what clothes you'll need on the boat. You are leaving at noon on the *Bremen.*"

Betzhold now said, "And you will never be allowed back into Germany. I will personally see to that. A car is waiting downstairs to take you to Hamburg and to make sure you don't take any more of your little sightseeing trips."

"Are you coming, Dad?"

"I have to stay here and make amends to our hosts for your abominable behavior."

"Give my best to Herr Betzhold if you happen to run into him."

AUGUST 2008

"IS THAT HOW YOU LEFT IT WITH YOUR FATHER?"

"We never spoke again except when absolutely necessary."

"You know, Toots, you're only the third person I ever told about that day: your grandmother, and my grandfather were the other two."

"How did your grandfather react?"

"The next day he went to his lawyer and changed his will. His estate would go into a trust fund for my mother that would go directly to me when she died. My father had been the executor of her will. My grandfather made a bank the executor and made absolutely sure my father could never lay his hand on a penny of either his or my mother's assets. When he died that fall, my father went nuts but there was nothing he could do about it. He had his own money but it wasn't nearly as much as what was left to me and my mother. He didn't see the crash of twenty-nine coming, but Gramps had a tip from Bernard Baruch, one of his sailing buddies, and got out of the market early just like Baruch did."

"What happened to Elise? Did you ever find out?"

"I bumped into her in Washington during the war but we didn't talk about that day except in passing. Years later we visited her in Burlington and we went sailing again. Your grandmother was pregnant with your father, or maybe it was your uncle Peter, I don't remember, so she didn't want to go."

"And?"

"Oh, yeah. Anyway, she admitted that she wasn't nearly the European sophisticate she had pretended to be with me. By the time she got home she was just a scared teenager, so she told her father what had happened."

AUGUST 1936

"OH, POPPI, they will come for me any minute."

Her father paced back and forth as he thought about it. Then he said, "Maybe they won't. It will take some time for the police officers to concoct a story and then tell it, if they tell it. Even attempting to have sex with a Jewess is a serious crime and having taken you to a secluded place will raise questions at the least. Then there is the matter of having been bested by you and Nicholas Worth."

He paused and paced some more before saying, "The police officers have just as much reason to keep this quiet as you do. But we cannot take the chance. I still have your mother's Danish passport. She renewed it the year before she died. You look enough like her so that with a little makeup you can pass for her. I think you should go and visit your Uncle Jens for a while. Get changed and pack and I'll drive you to the early train."

Then he brightened. "On the way you can tell me all the details and how those two swine looked when they came up out of the mud where they belong."

AUGUST 2008

THEY HAD CROSSED THE BORDER into Massachusetts and were entering Springfield. "Did Elise stay in Denmark through the whole war?"

"No. She sort of bounced around the world doing her bit, as we used to say. We bumped into her in Washington in '42. Then, in '47 she wrote me because she needed a sponsor to get into the United States. She had already found her way to Canada."

"You sponsored her?"

"Of course."

"How did Grandma feel about sponsoring one of your old girl friends?"

"She and Elise became fast friends. Birds of a feather."

"Birds of a feather?"

"Birds of a feather. You're going to find this hard to believe, Toots, but your sweet old gray-haired grandmother was also a strong-willed wild woman in her day." He paused as he remembered. "She was also, just like Elise, quite a dish."

"So Elise didn't stay in Denmark through the war?"

"No Jew stayed in Denmark through the whole war. The Danes sailed every one of them across to Sweden in a single night, right from under the noses of the Germans."

"Did her father and brother escape too?"

"No, they stayed in Germany. Her father was beaten to death

by stormtroopers on what the Germans called the Crystal Night in November of 1938."

"Crystal Night? It was an ice storm?"

"You know, Toots, I don't know who is teaching you history, but I'm beginning to suspect that your father ought to get his money back. It was called the Crystal Night because the Germans broke the windows in every Jewish business and most of the Jewish homes in the whole accursed country. The name came from the shattered glass that littered the place. They also beat up every Jewish man, woman, and child they could find."

"Didn't the police stop it?"

"The police, and every goon that wanted to help them, did it. Elise's father died and her brother was never heard from again. He probably died in one of the death camps that were springing up at about that time."

"I have never been able to understand why the Jews didn't resist."

"Simple. The goons had all the guns and they had none. They could only do what they were told and hope for the best. I'll bet your pro-gun control professors never told you that either."

"What was Elise doing in Washington in '42?"

"Her bit. By 1940 Elise had already started to fight her own war."

"Why didn't she stay in Sweden where it was safe?"

"Elise? Stay where it was safe? Not bloody likely."

"What did you do from '36 to '41 when we got into the war?"

"Finished high school and college, then went right into the Navy."

"You were in the Navy?"

"Sort of."

"Sort of?"

"When they instituted the draft in 1940, I enlisted in the Navy but wound up in the Coast Guard for a while, then I went back to the Navy but kept my Coast Guard commission. The military never could figure out what to do with me."

"You were an officer?"

"That's another Sort Of. An enlisted Navy yeoman for a while, teaching navigation at Newport. Then a Coast Guard officer who finished his military career teaching navigation at Newport again."

They were through Springfield and the traffic was thinning out as he closed his eyes again.

JANUARY 1941

IT WAS THE WEEK before the last day of boot camp when the weathered, gray-haired retread chief who commanded his training company called him in and said, "We're sending you to Officer Candidate School, Worth, for no better reasons than you have a science degree and don't wet the bed. There you will become a little pink ensign in just ninety days. You know your way around small boats, and how to tie a bowline, but don't think that because you've been yachting," he pronounced the word with obvious distaste, "you are by any means qualified to be a naval officer. Once you graduate and get your commission, I advise you to find the nearest chief and do whatever he tells you to do. And always remember that he outranks you by a lot."

He didn't graduate and get a commission though. This time it was a weathered, gray-haired, retread lieutenant commander who called him in a week before graduation from OCS. "You're not going to get a commission, Worth."

"May I ask why, sir? I'm first in my class."

The commander thought about the question for a moment, then said, "I can only tell you this. You've been denied a security clearance. It severely limits your career options in the Navy."

He immediately realized what the problem was. "Look. I went to the Berlin Olympics with my father when I was a kid in high school. That makes me a security risk?"

"I'm sorry. I can't discuss your or your father's politics."

"What are you going to do, sir, shoot me?"

"No. This does not mean that you cannot contribute to what I am afraid will soon be the war effort. We have decided to promote you to yeoman second class and have you stay right here teaching navigation to officer candidates. You have a gift for it. We know that about a third of your class would have washed out if you hadn't tutored them on the side."

"And if I refuse?"

"We won't shoot you but we will find something a great deal more unpleasant than staying right here in Newport, Rhode Island, teaching school."

"Since you put it that way, sir, thank you, sir."

AUGUST 2008

HE WAS SILENT for a while, but Amy sensed that he was awake so she asked, "Is a yeoman second class like a sergeant?"

"More like corporal, I think."

"Then you became an ensign?"

"Probably the longest serving ensign in naval history. They thought I was a security risk but I finally found someone who would listen to me so I could talk him out of it."

"Because of your father?"

"My father and his buddy Lindbergh. The government hated Lindbergh. When he threatened to resign his commission as a reserve colonel, hoping to embarrass them, they accepted it the same day and left him hanging in limbo through the whole war. He and his wife had thought he would be elected president in 1940. Instead, Roosevelt won a third term and Lindbergh didn't even get nominated because by then he looked like an un-American anti-Semitic jerk, which was what he actually was. There is a legend that he actually flew some combat missions in the Pacific but no one knows if it was true or one of Anne Morrow Lindbergh's poetic fantasies. Anyway, being associated with them sort of stunted my military career."

"But if you didn't graduate from officer candidate school and spent the war teaching, how did you get a commission? And how did you hurt your leg?"

He ignored the second question. "The Navy wouldn't give me a commission, so I eventually became an ensign in the Coast Guard."

"You have me really confused, Grandpa. Is that intentional? If you don't want to tell me the story, it's okay. A lot of veterans don't want to talk about their war. But if you spent the war teaching navigation in Newport you shouldn't be embarrassed. You did your bit, too."

"I didn't spend the whole war in Newport. Maybe I should tell someone about it. Maybe I owe it to Roscoe Jenks and the rest of the crew. I've never told anyone about all of it. I don't know. If I tell you…" Finally he finished by saying, "It's a long story and I don't want to bore you."

"We still have a long way to go to Burlington. Halfway is the other side of Brattleboro and we're still in Massachusetts. Who was Roscoe Jenks?"

"Massachusetts is just in the way, isn't it? Maybe they should move it."

"Who was Roscoe Jenks, Grandpa?"

"Roscoe Jenks was probably the toughest and meanest man I ever met. He hated me on sight."

FOUR

THE ENTIRE WORLD may have been changed by the Japanese attack on Pearl Harbor, but Nick's life had changed hardly at all. He still spent most of his time giving classroom instruction in celestial navigation and piloting. It seemed as if he had quoted the definition of piloting from *The American Practical Navigator* to thousands of students. "Piloting is the determination of position or lines of position relative to geographic points to a high order of accuracy. It is practiced in the vicinity of land, dangers, aids to navigation, et cetera."

The only break in this routine was the occasional day spent standing on the rolling deck of an old four-stack destroyer as it cruised slowly back and forth in Block Island Sound while the officer candidates took sun sights and tried to derive lines of position from them and from bearings they took on Point Judith. He only went on these excursions when particularly dense students were repeating the trip and the warrant officer who normally conducted these practical demonstrations needed help with them.

His private time consisted of evenings spent in the base library reading all of the day's newspapers, and the occasional movie or trip into town. He was pretty much nailed to the base because the officer candidates were not allowed to have cars, and some class-conscious administrative officer had decreed that therefore enlisted instructors and staff should not be allowed private vehicles either. Again and again Nick had been surprised that the Navy could function at all under the Victorian class system that was rigidly enforced. The snow-white uniforms they wore all summer were a perfect example. If anyone had thought up a more impractical military uniform since the days of the gold-braid-laden Light Brigade, Nick was unaware of it.

He coped, but he wished he could have his car. It would have allowed him to escape from the rigidly enforced class system once in a while. It was a 1931 Ford Model A roadster that had been his mother's before she became sick. She had signed it over to him the year before she died.

He knew his war would be spent here, teaching the same things over and over again, with the only thing he could look forward to being those occasional day trips on the old destroyer. In the middle of January even that ended when ammunition for her obsolete three-inch guns and a dozen depth charges were hastily loaded and she steamed away flying the biggest American flag Nick had ever seen any ship fly.

Two weeks later the old reserve lieutenant commander who was the chairman of the navigation department called him in again. "Stand at ease, son." It took Nick a bit aback because no one, not even his own father, had ever called him son. With no further preliminaries the officer went on. "You've done a superb job here, Worth. I know it hasn't been easy teaching some of these young snobs who are convinced there is nothing any yeoman deuce could ever teach them."

"I've done my best, sir."

"You must be bored out of your skull. The same thing every three weeks over and over again."

"Sir, it's what the Navy has decided I should do."

"How would you like to do something else? Something that might even get you to sea."

"If the Navy sends me to sea, sir, it will probably be in a leaky row boat."

"Not exactly, but close. Are you interested?"

"Of course. Anything to escape from *Publication 229*."

"Well, you probably won't escape the Sight Reduction Tables no matter what you do. A request for people who are qualified navigators and have experience in sailing vessels offshore came in yesterday. I know none of the details but you sure fit the description."

"The Navy will allow me to volunteer?"

"Sure. If there is anything the Navy likes it's to get rid of anyone with political baggage. The assignment is with the Coast Guard."

"When and where, sir?"

"New London. The Coasties are across the river from the Groton Navy base. My yeoman has your temporary duty and travel orders already typed up and your 201 file in a sealed package for you to carry. I thought you'd jump at it. In your shoes, I sure would."

He got off the train in New London and asked a policeman how to get to the Coast Guard Base. The cop pointed at a gray-painted bus standing at the curb. The bus took him across the river to the Navy Base. When it dropped him at the gate, he hefted his sea bag and approached the marine on duty, who eyed him and said, "Let's see your orders. You're here for submarine duty?"

Nick handed him a copy of his orders and said, "No, I'm trying to get to the Coast Guard base."

"Sorry. I mistook you for a real swabby. Yeah, you look like you qualify for the Hooligan Navy. What are you, about six-one?"

"About. Why?"

"You have to be at least five-ten to be a Coastie. That's so that if your ship sinks you can walk ashore without getting your hairdo wet."

"Very funny. How do I get back across the river to the Coast Guard base?"

He handed back Nick's orders as he said, "Walk straight down the shore road to the small boat dock at the very end. Someone there will ferry you across the creek. And don't even think about walking down any of the other docks to get a closer look at one of the new submarines unless you want someone to give you a load of buckshot.

This is the real wartime Navy, not that finishing school for young ladies in Newport where you're assigned."

It was a cold, raw, overcast winter day with an easterly wind blowing onto the Connecticut coast and up the Thames (pronounced *thames*, not *tems*) River. Even in his woolen bell-bottom trousers and with the high collar of his pea jacket turned up to the edge of his white cap, by the time he got to the shack at the head of the launch dock he was chilled through. There were two men in the shack and although, or perhaps because, he was hoping to stay in its shelter while he warmed up, one of them put on a woolen watch cap, pulled it down to cover his ears, and led him down the dock to an open motor whaleboat, its Buda diesel idling. The sailor explained, "Can't shut the damn thing off in this weather or I won't get it started again till spring. Runs good once it's running, though." With that he dropped the short dock line fastened to a cleat beside the midships helmsman's station and left the dock so fast that it made Nick stagger. "Hang on. It's bumpy with the wind blowing right up the creek like this."

He stopped the whaleboat across the end of a dock where two forty-five-foot patrol boats were rafted on one side. An old seventy-five-footer, one of the legendary six-bit boats of the prohibition era, was tied forward of them. A much bigger and sleeker boat was moored to the opposite side of the dock. As Nick tossed his sea bag onto the dock the helmsman held the launch expertly in place with the throttle despite the wind and the opposing swift current. The sailor made a questioning gesture toward the shack at the head of the dock. When he received a negative gesture in return, he said to Nick, who was climbing out of the boat, "Take care." With that he gunned the Buda and in a cloud of blue-black smoke headed back across the river before Nick could ask for directions.

Nick stood on the dock and looked across the river to where a submarine had backed out of its slip and was turning to head downriver: long, low, gray, and lethal-looking. It was one of the new Fleet Boats that were supposedly the fastest and longest-ranged submarines in the world. A tiny American flag flew stiffly in the wind from its periscope shears, and it dawned on Nick that the Marine had been right; this was the real, wartime Navy. Everyone on the submarine's bridge was wearing a woolen watch cap and a pea jacket: no white uniforms and officer's caps. These people were not interested in distinctive uniforms, or protocol, or tradition except if it somehow aided their primary business: killing. *You wanted to get into the war; well, this looks like the place to do it.*

He walked up the dock and when he came alongside the larger boat he recognized the type. It was one of the sleek seventy-foot commuter yachts that had swiftly carried millionaire owners to their Wall Street offices from the Stamford and Belle Haven Yacht Clubs on western Long Island Sound. Now it was covered all over, even its exquisite mahogany bright work, with haze gray paint. Only its teak decks, now weathered gray, had been left unpainted. On its bow in large white letters was painted *CGR 2612*. The engine hatches in the after cockpit were open and a man in dungarees, pea jacket, and the standard woolen watch cap was changing the spark plugs in one of its big, eight-cylinder Packard engines.

Nick asked, "Hi. Could you help me?"

The man did not look up until he had turned the plug he was installing several times to make sure the threads were not crossed. Then he blew on his hand and stuck it into a glove before saying, "Yeah. What do you need?"

"I'm looking for the CDR CGPL, whatever that is. I'm supposed to report to him. I know CDR is commander but I don't have the foggiest idea what CGPL is."

"CGPL is Coast Guard Picket Line. Third building on the right from the end of the dock, counting the concrete slab for the first building."

"Thanks." *What the hell is the Coast Guard Picket line? Are the Coasties going on strike like the coal miners?* The newspapers were full of stories about John L. Lewis, the president of the miner's union, threatening to strike for more money when the country, where most of the homes and buildings were heated with coal, was in the middle of the worst winter in years and involved in a life-or-death war.

Four bundled-up Coast Guardsmen hurried down the dock and climbed aboard the commuter as one of them said to the man standing between the engines, "Jesus, Mac. Haven't you got those damned plugs changed yet? A tanker just got hit the other side of Block Island and we've got to go look for survivors."

"Fat chance of finding anyone in this." It had started to rain. A bitterly cold rain that would surely turn to sleet as the short winter afternoon wore on. "Just this plug and one more, if my fingers don't fall off first. Christ, it's cold."

"Wear gloves."

"If I wear gloves, Boats, I won't be able to feel the threads. If I cross one and honk on it with the socket wrench I'll strip it for sure. Then we'll have a real mess on our hands."

"Is the port engine done?"

"Yeah."

"Let's get the show on the road then." He motioned to the men who had come with him. "Single 'em. We'll go on one engine. Mac can finish the other one on the way downriver."

Nick wanted to go to sea, but he did not envy the Coast Guardsmen going out on a night like this in a converted motor yacht that had been designed to go fast in the narrow waters of western Long Island Sound. In the open sea it would probably roll from one gunwale to the other. While the mechanic squatted between the engines they backed away from the dock and followed the submarine down the river. Two vessels going out into a miserable winter afternoon: one on a mission of mercy and one on a mission of murder.

The first building was just a slab, as the mechanic had said. The second was under construction as a crew bolted the sections of a prefabricated Quonset hut together. He entered the third, also a Quonset hut, and found himself in a totally empty room with a bare concrete floor and sloping steel walls. It seemed even colder inside than it had been on the dock. He opened the door in the unpainted plywood wall at the back of the room and was hit by a wave of heat. A balding, grizzled chief sat on a straight-backed wooden kitchen chair behind a battered wooden desk. A potbelly stove glowed in the corner below a grate that let heat into the next room. The chief looked up and by way of greeting, said, "Close the goddamned door. You born in a barn?" Then he asked, "Did the *Number Twelve* boat get away?"

Nick scurried into the room and said, "On one engine. The mechanic is going to finish changing the spark plugs in the other as they go."

"I hope he finishes before they get outside. It's gonna be a shitty night."

"My orders say to report to the commander of the Coast Guard Picket Line. Is this the right place?"

"Can't you tell by these luxurious accommodations?"

"Is he here?"

"Nope. He's out of town. The exec is here though. Let me announce you." He got up from his desk and opened the door into the next section of the building, "There's a swabby here on orders, Lieutenant." He turned to Nick and said, "Go on in."

The lieutenant was also seated behind a beat-up wooden desk, but instead of a kitchen chair he was seated in a wheelchair.

Nick marched into the center of the room, his sealed 201 file under his arm, came to attention, and said, "Yeoman Worth reporting as ordered, sir." He didn't salute. The Navy didn't salute indoors.

"At ease, Yeoman. Let me have your personnel file." Nick placed it on the desk and stepped back as the lieutenant said, "I had a call from your boss in Newport about you this morning, Worth." He opened a riggers knife, with a round-tipped blade and a marlinespike that folded into its handle, and used the blade to slit the seals on the personnel file envelope. "He thinks you're pretty hot shit."

Nick had no idea how or if he was supposed respond to this, so he didn't say anything.

"Did you get lunch?"

"No, sir. I came straight from the train, but I'm okay."

The lieutenant said to the chief who was standing in the door, "Show Worth where he can get one of those soggy tuna sandwiches that you always bring me." He said to Nick, "The chief will tell you how to get to the canteen. Grab some lunch while I look at your file. We'll talk when you get back."

The chief pulled the office door closed behind them and Nick asked, "What happened to the Exec? Was he wounded?"

"Naah. Some drunk in a big LaSalle hit his Chevy coupe head on. Pushed the motor block through the firewall into his lap. Killed his wife. A crying shame. He was about to be promoted and get command of one of those new cutters. A damned fine officer. I'm only telling you so you won't ask him. Shut up about it."

Nick couldn't think of anything to say so he asked, "Where's the canteen?"

When he came back the chief said, "Lieutenant Nelson's on the phone with the Old Man. He'll see you when he... He just hung up, go on in."

When he entered the office, the officer motioned to a couple of folding chairs standing against the wall and said, "Grab a seat and let's talk."

When Nick was seated uncomfortably on the shaky, straight-backed metal chair, without any preliminaries the Exec asked, "Are you going to commit treason, Worth?

"No, sir, I am not."

"The Navy seems to think you are."

"Sir, when I was seventeen years old my father took me to Germany for the Berlin Olympics. He was involved with Lindbergh and the America First movement. They might have been pro-Nazi back then, but I had no politics when I went. After what I saw over there I definitely wasn't pro-Nazi. Actually the Krauts thought I was so badly behaved and disrespectful that they asked me to leave early. Getting kicked out of Germany in 1936 is one of the few things in my life I am really proud of." Nick had been rehearsing this speech for years but this was the first time he had found someone willing to listen to it.

"I think you're proud of something else: the '36 Bermuda Race. Your boss in Newport told me about it. That was a rough race."

"Were you on it?"

"I was a midshipman in the academy yawl. We were way behind you. You were in *Morning Glory?*"

"My granddad owned her. We did pretty well."

"Do you know where *Morning Glory* is now?"

"She was sold when they settled my grandfather's estate."

"She's in a yard in Fort Lauderdale with rot in her deck carlins, cabin sides, stern post, and keelson. We had her surveyed two weeks ago. Tropical downpours and warm sea water are tough on wooden boats."

Nick felt exactly as he would on hearing that a dear friend had a serious disease.

"You had her surveyed?"

"We've had just about every boat we could find that looked halfway decent surveyed. We're still at it."

"Lieutenant, what's going on here? Just what is the Coast Guard Picket Line and why is it interested in a fifty-four-foot Alden schooner?"

"OK, Worth, even if the Navy thinks you're a security risk, your boss at the officer candidate school doesn't think so and that's good enough for me. In January we lost thirty-one ships to U-boats right off our coast: nearly 200,000 tons. This month is going to be worse. We just lost a tanker off Block Island about an hour ago. The Krauts either had a bunch of subs waiting right off the coast for the Japs to hit Pearl Harbor, or they sure got over here quick. You need a small, handy vessel to hunt subs, but if it doesn't have at least eight-inch guns or a flight deck the Navy doesn't want to have anything to do with it.

"Last year the President gave the Brits fifty old destroyers and ten of our cutters, and that didn't help either. I shouldn't tell you any of this because the Navy brass seems to think you're going to swim right out and tell the Krauts everything, but we're hurting and the Krauts know it already.

"Nothing the Navy is doing seems to help, so they have come up with the perfect solution from their point of view. Since most of the sinkings are happening right off our coast, it must be the Coast Guard's problem. Only we've been sucking the financial hind tit for so long that we don't have nearly enough vessels to even make a dent in the problem. We've been commandeering every boat that might be even halfway suitable. You saw *Nightingale* down at the dock? The *Number Twelve* boat?"

"The commuter?"

"Yeah. Fast and seaworthy in reasonable conditions, except she'll roll your guts out in a seaway and those Packards give her a range of not much over a hundred miles. By the time she gets to a patrol area she has to come back. We need patrol craft that can go out there, stay on station, and handle rough weather."

"Are you telling me that you're going to send sailboats like *Morning Glory* out into the Atlantic to fight U-boats? Sir, if you don't mind my saying so, that's nuts."

"Not to fight them. To spot them, radio their position, and rescue any survivors they can find. Mainly rescue survivors. How would you like to be on a Carley float on a night like this? The hope is that the U-boats won't think some dinky sailing yacht pulling people out of the water is worth bothering with. If the picket boat spots a U-boat, we have aircraft, blimps, and our few cutters and Navy destroyers ready to come running, but they're stretched way too thin."

"Lieutenant, tell me honestly what you think of this idea."

"Other than having them out there to rescue survivors, it may very well be nuts, but these are desperate times that demand desperate measures, and I can't think of anything better. Besides, I understand that the President is behind it. The rumor at the Treasury Department—we were part of the Treasury until the first of last December when they transferred us to the Navy—is that Churchill suggested it to him because of the great job the British yachts did helping get the Army off the beaches at Dunkirk. Ignore the fact that the English Channel in summer is not the north Atlantic in winter.

"Anyway, when we started this effort we were only supposed to look at boats over eighty feet, but the 1930s were not a good time for the maintenance of big yachts. Most of them spent years hauled out in boatyards wearing For Sale signs while rainwater leaked through their decks to feed mildew and rot spores."

"Like *Morning Glory.*"

"Like *Morning Glory,* but we've found a sister ship that's sound."

"She's only fifty-four feet on deck, sir."

"Sixty-four feet with the boomkin and bowsprit. Look, the captain, my boss, is down at a boatyard in Nyack on the Hudson River right now. They built wooden sub-chasers in the last war, but after the war the government stuck them with the last three boats they had under construction and refused to pay them. He's trying to get them to build some patrol craft for us. But until something like that comes along, a picket line of commandeered yachts is the best we've got. Worth, the Japs are running riot in the Pacific and we're well on the way to losing the Battle of the Atlantic. We could lose this war. We have to get that through our heads. And if we do lose, God only knows what the world will be like then."

"I know what it will be like, sir. I had a glimpse of it in Germany in 1936. Believe me, Lieutenant, we don't want to lose this war. So where does that leave me and this *Morning Glory* sister ship?"

"Her name was *Indomitable.* She is now *Coast Guard Reserve Vessel 3114.*"

"That's better than *Indomitable*. Who thought of that name? It sounds like a British battleship."

"Her present owner renamed her when he bought her three years ago. She was originally *Tiger Lillie*. He sunk a lot of dough into her so she's in good shape. He had her thoroughly gone over by a yard on City Island. Deck canvas replaced, new keel bolts, masts pulled and gone over. The works."

"When was she built?"

"Twenty-eight. The year after *Morning Glory*. They were sisters, both built by the same yard and both named for flowers. They were really John Alden's *Malabar VII* design with slightly different cabin layouts and Marconi mains."

"Where is she now?"

"Bedell's boat yard in Stratford and the job is not going well at all. When you walked in here I could not believe my good luck. There's a lot of friction between the owner and the boatswain who's trying to get her ready." Lieutenant Nelson paused in thought for a minute, playing with his rigger's knife, opening and closing the spike. "Okay, Worth. I don't have time to beat around the bush. I just talked about you on the phone with Captain Morris. Do you want her?"

"You mean get her ready and take her to sea?"

"That's exactly what I mean."

Nick didn't hesitate. "Of course."

"The boatswain, Roscoe Jenks, was a Marine in the last war and then worked on Grand Banks fishing schooners until '38 when he joined the Coast Guard. A good sailor, but he has poor navigational skills at best. He seems to be one of those people with a mental block when it comes to mathematics. We sent him a celestial qualified coxswain, but Jenks made the guy so miserable that he asked to be reassigned. You can't send a small craft to sea unless the crew is a team."

"Why not replace Jenks?"

"The coxswain knew zip about sailing a schooner offshore.

Jenks may have no interpersonal or navigational skills but he is a fine seaman with years of experience on Gloucester schooners. He and the owner, a guy named Madison, are at each other's throats constantly. Madison is no joy either. He tried to stop us from taking the boat in the first place and he's constantly calling me to make threats and tell me that his family is, as he keeps saying, close to the administration in Washington. He's a fanatic about the boat although I suspect he doesn't know much about sailing her: He's what the Coast Guard thinks of when we hear the word yachtsman."

"Thank you, sir."

"Present company excepted. He calls me about twice a week complaining about Jenks. He says Jenks isn't preparing the boat for sea; he's destroying her. I've been trying to sort it out from here without much success. Most of their disagreements center on the rig and the sails. You've got a science degree and you smashed the mechanical aptitude tests in boot camp and OCS, as well as being an experienced sailor: just the guy to sort it out. "

"When should I leave, sir?"

"We have some administrative things to take care of first. The boss has already agreed and the chief will roll the paperwork through. Go get yourself some uniforms with buttons and be back here the day after tomorrow. He'll give you the necessary papers so you can buy them at the store at the Navy base. Some genius decided that combining our uniform store with the Navy's would be his contribution to the war effort."

"You're going to make me a chief?"

"Don't get any delusions of grandeur. Nothing that exalted. We're going to make you an ensign. We thought about giving you a warrant but it takes a lot more experience to be a warrant officer than an ensign. Since you've been through Officer Candidate School and were first in your class, we've decided to commission you. If you're not an officer you won't have a chance of dealing with Jenks or Madison."

"How should I deal with them, sir?"

"I don't care. If you have to shoot Jenks, don't do it until you're outside of the three mile-limit." Then he turned serious again. "Just do what you have to do to get *Reserve Patrol Craft 3114* ready for sea and out on patrol. How are you fixed for cash? An officer's kit will cost a hundred bucks or so and they won't give you credit because you're not assigned here yet."

"I'm okay as long as they'll take a check on the Mechanics and Farmers Bank of New Haven."

"When a yeoman deuce walks in there to buy a set of officer's duds the swabbies will try to jerk you around any way they can. If they give you any trouble, and they probably will, have them call me."

"I don't know how to thank you, sir."

"Don't thank me. The Navy should have commissioned you a year ago." Then he called at the open door, "Get Worth whatever paper he needs to buy duds." Then he turned back to Nick. "Just be back here first thing in the morning the day after tomorrow ready to go. And don't go near Bedell's boat yard, *Indomitable*, or Boatswain Jenks until we get you commissioned. He eats college boy second class yeomen for breakfast."

Nick thought of something. "Am I allowed to have a private vehicle, sir?"

"Why the hell not?"

"I don't know. Ask the Navy. My car's in New Haven; can I have tomorrow off to go get it if I have to wait around anyway? That's if you don't have anything you want me to do."

The Exec pushed two paper-covered books and a thick file to Nick. "Read these on the train." The first was a dog-eared copy of *The Coast Guard Officer's Handbook*. The other book was the manual for the Halicrafter's two-way radio that was being installed on the boat. The file contained the information on the men who had already arrived in Stratford and the three that were on their way. Then Nelson told the chief, "Give Mr. Worth a pass to New Haven so he can get his car. He'll need it to get around while he gets his boat ready for sea."

It was the first time he had been called mister since he entered the service. Everything was going by like images from a fast-moving train and his mind kept catching bits of detail that he wasn't sure he understood or knew how to fit into a coherent picture. Maybe things would become clearer when he got to the boat. Everything always became clearer when one got to the boat. Sailboats, especially schooners, were extremely complicated machines, yet there was nothing obtuse or ambiguous about them. Maybe that's why they had a way of clarifying things.

"Thanks again, sir."

"When you're out there on a night like this, see if you still want to thank me."

The next morning Nick went across to the Navy base to order his uniforms and then caught the Shore Line train to New Haven. From the station he took the trolley car to the East Shore area where his parents' home was located on a street off Townsend Avenue. New Haven was one of the last cities in the country to still have its part of the street railway system operating. It had once stretched from Boston to Baltimore. He had not been home since he joined the Navy after his mother died and he graduated from college, so he rang the doorbell rather than just enter.

The housekeeper answered the door bell. When she saw him she threw her arms around him, hugged him, then stepped back and said, "Oh Nicholas, it's so good to see you."

"Hello, Mrs. Gray. Is my father home?"

"No. He's in town at the university doing whatever he does there."

"Good."

"I thought you'd say that." She motioned him into the entrance foyer and closed the door. "My lord, but it's cold. Whatever will we do if that dreadful man with the bushy eyebrows cuts off the coal supply?"

"How is Mr. Gray?" Her husband had never recovered from being gassed in what was now being called the Last War rather than the Great War.

"He has his good days and his bad. When he's feeling well we walk down to the shore for lunch. There's a nice little place that serves the best soft-shell crabs. But when the weather is like this, he doesn't have many good days. The cold air really affects him. But why have you come home? You look so good in your uniform."

"I need to get a few things from my room, and I want to get my car. Do you think it will start?"

"Oh, yes. Your father starts it every month when he goes to get your gasoline ration stamps."

"I should have guessed. I don't suppose he rides the trolley to Yale."

"Lord, no. He takes the Chrysler every day. He says that every time he gets on the trolley someone gives him a cold." Then she smiled a sarcastic little smile. "You know how delicate his health and his sensibilities are."

"I'm surprised you're still here, Mrs. Gray."

"After your mother passed away—a truly fine lady, Nicholas, don't you ever forget her—I thought about leaving, but where would we go?"

"All the defense plants are hiring." As soon as he said it he realized how dumb it was. Mrs. Gray, with her apron, her hair in a bun, and her invalid husband who, like his mother, needed constant loving care, was definitely not going to become Rosie the Riveter.

"No. This is a good place for me and Mr. Gray. He likes to be able to walk down to the harbor occasionally, and your father and this house are not hard work. After all, I've been doing it for almost twenty years. Can I make you something to eat?"

"I have to get going. It's a long drive back to New London, and I hope my father didn't use up all my gas."

"There's plenty of gas in the garage. Your father has been getting it any place he can and hoarding it. Take all you want. Mr. Gray and I have been afraid the place would blow up and take us with it. The keys are on the board in the kitchen."

Nick went up to his room and pulled his old sea bag out of the closet. The oilskins in it, after being rolled up for years, were stuck solidly together and would probably leak like a screen door if he pulled them apart. He didn't need them anyway. The Navy had given him a pretty good set. The sea boots appeared to be serviceable though. An extra pair could always come in handy. He went to his desk and got his own parallel rule and dividers, *Morning Glory's* chronometer in its mahogany box, and the sextant that had originally been his grandfather's, for luck as much as for anything else. The chronometer had long since stopped, but when he put the key into its eight-day movement and turned it a couple of times, it started right up. He'd have to rate it.

Then he thought of something and went back into the closet. The leather cases of two pairs of 7X50 Zeiss binoculars hung from a hook in the back. One pair had been his grandfather's and he had bought the other pair in Berlin in 1936 because he hadn't known that within a year he would inherit all the old man's navigation equipment. He gave the room one last look around, wondering if he would ever come back here again, and noticed the Zenith Transoceanic portable radio on the bed table. He'd take that too.

Mrs. Gray was right. Along the garage wall next to his Model A was a collection of metal cans and one-gallon glass jugs filled with gasoline. He used a funnel he found hanging on the wall to fill the gas tank, centered in front of the Ford's windshield, from the metal cans. Then he refilled the cans from the bottles, threw the bottles in the trash barrel behind the garage, and loaded the cans into the rumble seat along with the funnel and a varnished wooden box of tools that had been his grandfather's. He was sure his father had never lowered himself to even touch them.

He backed the car out of the garage, locked the doors, and took the key into the house. "You don't have to worry about the garage blowing up, Mrs. Gray. I took all the gasoline."

"Whatever will your father do?"

"Ride the trolley like everyone else. It can be his contribution to the war effort."

"He's going to be angry, Nicholas."

"He's been angry at me before, but if he tries to take it out on you, get in touch with me. This house was my mother's and it's mine now. If he gives you any trouble I will truly enjoy kicking him out into the street and turning him in for hoarding gasoline. You can tell him so."

"Oh, Nicholas. He is your father, after all. I wish there was some way you two could be reconciled. I'm sure you could find it in your heart to tolerate him if you tried."

"I don't have the time. There's a war on, you know. You stay well, Mrs. Gray, and if you need anything, anything at all, you can get in touch with me through the New London Coast Guard Base. They'll know how to reach me. I'll never forget how well you took care of my mother. You and Mr. Gray have a place here as long as you want." Then he thought of something. "Is my father paying you enough? Prices are skyrocketing."

"Oh, we don't need much and our room and board are taken care of."

"Okay, but don't hesitate if you need anything from me. Anything at all."

"I won't. You stay safe, Nicholas. War is a terrible thing. I had a letter from my sister in Miami Beach just this morning. She said they can see the fires and hear the explosions out on the ocean almost every night. They're trying to get the city fathers to turn off the lights so our ships won't be silhouetted, but it's the height of the tourist season so they don't want to do it."

The next day, with absolutely no ceremony, Nicholas Worth signed some papers, raised his right hand, repeated an oath, and became an ensign in the United States Coast Guard. He signed another paper that placed him in command of *CGR 3114* and that was that.

He parked the Ford outside the gate of the Navy base on the way to pick up his new uniforms and the same Marine was on duty. Nick showed him his new ID card in order to be allowed to enter. "So they made you an ensign. Why are you still wearing your sailor suit?"

"Sir. Why are you still wearing your sailor suit, sir?" Nick smiled when he said it, though.

The Marine snapped to attention as only a Marine can. "Of course, SIR." He too smiled. "Congratulations, SIR."

"Thanks. I have to go in and pick up my new uniforms so I can get out of this sailor suit."

"Could I be permitted to wish the ensign a successful career, SIR?"

"Of course, as long as you don't mention that it's in the Hooligan Navy." Then Nick held out his hand to be shaken. "Thanks, Marine. You're the first person to call me sir."

The marine shook his hand, then snapped back to attention and said, "It has truly been an honor, SIR."

FIVE

THE WIND WAS STILL OUT OF THE EAST, and although the rain had stopped, it was just as raw and felt like snow. With the canvas top of the Ford up and the windows closed, Nick was bundled in his new wool uniform and the Burberry duffle coat he had stopped at J. Press in New Haven to buy. The Model A's manifold heater was at its highest setting, but he was cold. Particularly his hands. The heater was poor, but the defroster was worthless. The only way he could keep his breath from making the windshield opaque was to hold one hand against it and peer between his fingers while steering with the other one. When that hand could stand contact with the freezing glass no longer, he would put it into its glove and steer with it while the other hand did defroster duty.

It was slow going. Every one of the hundreds of traffic lights on Route One between New London and Stratford seemed to turn red just as he got to it. Bedell's Ship Yard was on a tongue of land between a salt marsh and the Housatonic River. It was after three in the afternoon when he arrived and parked between a pearl gray 1939 Cadillac sedan and a battered old Chevy pickup truck. *CGR 3114* was tied to a dock beside the marine railway that led out of a big shed at the head of the tracks. Her mainmast was out of her and lying on horses on the dock. Two men were standing beside it yelling at each other.

One was about five feet six tall, three feet six wide, and was wearing a pea jacket and watch cap. His face was beet red, although Nick could not tell how much was the result of the cold wind and how much was the result of his obvious anger. He was sputtering, "If you think we're going out to the Banks in the winter with a candy-assed Marconi main, you're even stupider than I think you are!"

The other man was dressed in a business suit, a Chesterfield overcoat with velvet lapels and a gray fedora. He was holding onto the brim to keep the hat from blowing away into the river. He yelled back, "If you think I'm going to let you chop the top off a three-hundred-dollar mainmast in order to convert my boat into a stinking gaff-rigged fishing tub, you're the one who's stupid!"

They appeared to be about to come to blows, which Nick supposed would be very bad for the man in the fedora. The one he supposed was Roscoe Jenks looked like he could slug his way through the side of a ship. Nick intervened. "Okay. What's going on here? I'm Ensign Worth and I've just been assigned command of this vessel."

It didn't have the effect that Nick expected from his year at the Newport Navy Base. Jenks looked his new uniform up and down and asked, "When did you join the Coast Guard? Yesterday?"

Nick knew that this was a test and if he didn't pass it he was in deep trouble, so he replied, "It was actually this morning, but that doesn't matter. I'm still an officer and I can still have your sorry ass tossed in jail for the duration of the war. Now find something useful to do while I talk to Mister... Madison, is it?"

Jenks started to snarl something, thought better of it, and climbed onto the boat and into the cabin as Nick turned to Robert Madison, who said, "You heard that piece of waterfront shit. He wants to butcher my mast and if he does I'll have both you and him busted. Do you understand me, Sonny?" Madison appeared to be in his middle thirties. "My family is very tightly connected with the Roosevelt administration. If you fuck with me or my boat you'll be sorry."

Nick thought, *Jesus, what a pair.* But he said, "Nobody is going to cut down your mast, Mister Madison. I've sailed a lot of miles in a schooner with a jib-headed main and a gaff foresail, and no matter what Boatswain Jenks thinks, it's a fine offshore rig."

"Bullshit, Sonny. You look like you're still playing with boats in the bathtub. I don't think I want my boat going out under the command of some half-baked ninety-day wonder. I'm going to call that dumb lieutenant in New London and get you tossed off my boat right now."

Nick took a deep breath before asking conversationally, "Have you ever been on a Bermuda Race, Bob?"

"My name is not Bob. It's Robert, and to you it's Mister Madison, Sonny."

"I take it that's a no. How about that race from Block Island out around Nantucket to Mount Desert Rock and then back to Gloucester the year before last. A nor'easter blew like stink the whole way. Were you on that one, Mister Madison? I don't remember seeing you."

"No. I didn't make that one and doubt if you did either."

"I was on *Coquette*. We finished first in our class but couldn't save our time. Wound up fourth. You know, Mr. Madison, I don't think you've ever been out of Long Island Sound. So, as my grandfather used to say, I've wrung more salt water out of my socks than you've sailed over."

"That story may have fooled some pathetic Coast Guard recruiter, but it doesn't impress me at all. People whose life story would make them about ninety years old, if you believed it all, but look about nineteen and show up in what is obviously a brand new uniform don't impress me either."

Nick decided to make one more try at conciliating him. "Look, I'm not going to cut down the mainmast. While it's out I'm going to go over it, check everything out, and then it will go back into the boat tomorrow."

"You won't be around tomorrow, Sonny. I'll see to that."

Okay asshole, if that's the way you want to play it. "I have tried to placate you and reassure you, Bob, but that doesn't seem to work. So let me put it this way. If you call me sonny once more, I'm going to throw you off this dock and you won't be the first loud-mouthed bully to whom I've given a swimming lesson. Now walk off this dock or swim off, I don't care which, just so you get away from my vessel. *CGR 3114* is mine, not yours. Come back and see me when the war is over." He stood glaring down at Madison, who was about four inches shorter. Then he added, "Don't screw with me, Bob. There's a war on."

"You haven't heard the last of this." But he turned and strode off the dock still holding onto his hat.

Nick ignored the comment and climbed aboard. As he came down the ladder into the cabin, he asked Jenks, "Did you hear that?"

He grudgingly answered, "Yeah, but I only agreed with the part about throwing the bastard off the dock. You don't look old enough to have been offshore, and if you had been you'd know that gaff main and foresail's the only proper offshore schooner rig."

Nick said to the two seamen who were installing a radio and hanging on every word, "Why don't you guys go get some coffee or something. If you find some bring me and Boats back a cup."

When they had left he said to Jenks, "Okay. Listen carefully, because this is the last time we are ever going to discuss this. I sailed offshore on a schooner just like this one from the time I was eight, so don't try that salty old fisherman crap with me."

"Yeah. Gentlemen candy-ass racers. Go out and then run for cover the minute the wind pipes up. I know your type. I saw them chicken out and come running back into the Great Salt Pond in that race they ran from Block Island to Gloucester in 1940 because they were afraid the big bad U-boats wouldn't let them go to Bermuda. I was on a forty-five-footer at Block and saw them come dragging back with their tails between their legs."

"I was on that race and nobody chickened out. The first leg was right into a nor'easter out to Nantucket Light Ship, and some of the smaller boats, I think it was four of them, couldn't make any headway into the breaking seas from Nantucket Shoals so they ran off and withdrew. They weren't dumb enough to try to anchor in the open sea like you salty-assed fishermen. So the boats that ran for cover didn't get overwhelmed by breaking seas or rammed by other schooners that dragged their anchors. That's how a lot of the Gloucester fleet disappeared in '38, when they anchored on the Banks, wasn't it?"

"That storm in '38 was a bitch."

"But most of the vessels that ran off under bare poles survived, didn't they? If you and I go out there together, and I emphasize the word *if*, forget gaff mains and anchoring. We're going to do things the way we candy-ass racers do, or you aren't going. Am I making myself perfectly clear, Jenks? And if you don't go, I will do my very best to see that you spend the rest of the war as a turd counter on Poop Lake in Wisconsin some place."

Jenks scowled in silence for a moment, then said, "I saw hard-assed young officers like you in the Marine Corps in France. They didn't last long."

"That was in the trenches, not in a fifty-four-foot boat. If I don't last long, neither will you. Now tell me what your worst problems are and don't tell me that we need to take a saw to the mainmast and get a huge anchor and a half mile of chain, or you're done on *CGR 3114* right now." Then he thought of something else. "One other thing so we understand each other perfectly and can end this conversation for good. Whenever anyone else is in earshot you call me either Sir or Mr. Worth and I'll call you Boats. I understand that is a term of some respect in the Coast Guard. Try to deserve it. Do we have a deal?"

Jenks looked around the varnished mahogany cabin that was strewn with pieces of the half-installed Halicrafters radio, engine parts, and tools. He finally said, "Yeah. Yeah, okay.

"Good. Now tell me what your worst problem is."

"The sails. That bastard gave us the oldest, shittiest set of sails you ever saw and claims those are all he has. Everything else on the boat is top shelf but these things were probably her original set back in twenty-eight. There's no storm sails either."

"Show me."

The bagged sails were in a pile in the corner of the boat shed and when Nick tried to drag the foresail out of its bag, it tore. Jenks was right. Mildew is the fatal enemy of cotton canvas sails and this set was black with it.

"You see, Mr. Worth, these things haven't been on the boat in years."

"Okay, Boats. The sails are my first job. How's the engine. We won't need it much for propulsion, but it's going to have to generate the juice to light up all those vacuum tubes in the radio."

"It's a six-cylinder Gray and those things are indestructible. Besides, Madison obviously had someone who knew what he was doing take care of it. Not like his fucking sails."

"I told you, I'll take care of the sails." He was wondering if he could get the sails from *Morning Glory,* or if Ratsey and Latham in Stamford could make a set, but either of those alternatives would take weeks. No. By hook or by crook he would get the sails he was sure Madison had hidden. "Can we put the mast back in the boat tomorrow? I want to go over it with you first."

"The main backstay is being cut and spliced around insulators so the top section can be the radio antenna. But I don't like the whole rig being held in the boat by a pair of glass balls."

"What about the running backstays?"

"There aren't any. Just the one backstay that goes from the bumpkin on the transom to the top of the mast. There's tangs on the mast and pad eyes on the deck for running backstays but I think that asshole Madison got rid of them because they were too much trouble to slacken and tighten every time he tacked."

"Can you scrounge up some cable and tackles? I don't like the idea of the whole rig being held up by glass balls either. You take care of the mast and I'll take care of the sails."

He walked up the dock to the yard office, introduced himself to the yard foreman, and used the phone to ask Information for Madison's number in Redding. He knew the bastard probably wasn't home yet, but maybe he could reach someone who was more reasonable. Besides, if he talked to Madison directly he was sure Madison would hang up on him. He got the number, then told another operator, "Redding 3727, please."

He heard the phone ring a couple of times and then a woman's voice answered. "Hello?"

"Is Mr. Madison at home? This is Ensign Worth at Bedell's shipyard in Stratford."

"I thought that's where he was. I'm his sister."

"He left here a while ago."

"Should I have him call you?"

He knew Madison would never call him back. "Tell him I need the proper suit of sails. All of them. Storm sails included. The ones he supplied are totally rotten and he knows it. Tell him I'll call him in the morning about how we are going to get them here." Then he thought of something. "Do you know where they are, ma'am? The sails, I mean."

"There's a bunch of boat stuff in the attic."

"Give him the message, please, and tell him I'm serious. Tell him if he doesn't bring the sails, Boatswain Jenks and I will come and get them by any means necessary."

"It sounds like my brother and you are not getting along."

"Just give him the message, please, ma'am."

After he hung up he looked around the office. Besides the shoddy furniture one would expect, there was a two-burner kerosene heater that made the place almost livable. All of *Indomitable*'s bunk cushions were piled in the corner along with three sea bags. Their owner's names were stenciled on them: Jenks, Longo, and Borg.

Longo and Borg were the engine mechanic and the radioman. He'd have to find out who was who.

He thanked the yard boss and walked down to the dock where Jenks and Longo, the mechanic, were measuring the mast for the running backstays. The other specialist, who must have been Borg the radioman, was watching one of the yard's riggers splice the top section of the backstay around one of the black insulators the power company used for the guy wires on its poles.

Nick introduced himself to the two specialists, then asked, "Where have you guys been sleeping and eating?"

Jenks answered, "The yard boss's been letting us use the floor in his office. It's not bad with the bunk cushions. There's no chance of the stove in the boat getting the cabin warm with the main hatch open all the time. Somebody is always going in or out. We've been grabbing breakfast and lunch in the galley on the boat. Mostly cold sandwiches. At night we get supper up around the corner at Ryan's. The guy who owns it has been giving us a real break on the price."

"Where are you supposed to eat and sleep?"

"The Army has a squadron of Bell Aero Cobra interceptors over at the airport and we're supposed to eat and sleep over there. If we did that, we'd spend all our time either going back and forth or waiting for the Army to send a bus to pick us up."

"Makes sense. I'll get a couple of bunk cushions and join you. I've got a car, so we can go over to the airport to eat."

"Ryan's food is better than Army chow, Mr. Worth, and we can eat whenever we can get there. The chow hall has set hours."

"Okay. Ryan's it is. I'll try to get you reimbursed."

"How did you make out on the sails? Any progress?"

"One way or another I'll get Madison to cough them up."

"Well, good luck. The bastard is a big-shot Wall Street lawyer. Those guys can jerk you around forever."

"Not with a war on."

The next morning the wind dropped a bit but it started to snow at dawn, small flakes of powder. It was still snowing at ten o'clock when they were ready to put *Fourteen Boat*'s mainmast back into her. All the standing and running rigging was carefully laid out so nothing could snag, the yard crane that was mounted on an old firetruck chassis was ready to lift it, and Jenks was getting ready to climb to the top of the foremast to connect the triatic stay that connected the tops of the masts. Nick thought that one of the younger men should do it, but when Jenks insisted, he decided to let him. If he fell on his head it would solve the Jenks problem once and for all. The congenial atmosphere they had established at dinner in the bar the night before had evaporated when Madison didn't show up with the sails and no one answered the phone at the house in Redding.

When Nick came back from the office after calling the second time, Jenks had asked, "Well, is that asshole on his way with our sails or not?"

"I don't know where he is. There's still no answer."

"I knew you wouldn't be able to do shit."

"Let's get the mast into her and then I'll go track him down."

"The thought of you coming after him must have him pissing in his pants."

"Jenks, shut up and let's get the mast into the boat."

The crane was just starting to take up the slack in the lifting cable when a 1940 Pontiac convertible drove up to the end of the dock and the driver started to blow the horn. Its top was down despite the wind-driven snow. Nick thought, *Shit. What now?* He motioned the crane operator to stop and walked up to the car. The driver, the car's interior, and the sail bags stacked high in the back and front passenger seats were covered with snow.

AUGUST 2008

Nick's granddaughter drove off of I-91 at the first Vermont exit as he repeated that long-ago greeting from the person driving the convertible. "Hi, I'm Amy Madison. You're Ensign Worth and these are your sails, two sets."

It took the girl by surprise. "Was that Grandma? Amy, the lady I'm named for?"

"Yup."

"So that's how you met her? I always thought you met her in college." She teased the old man. "Was she a dish like you said she was, Grandpa?"

"She had a ski cap pulled right down to her eyebrows, a full-length camels hair overcoat, slacks, and the whole outfit was covered by a huge woolen scarf wrapped around her about six times. She could have looked like Frau Bucher in *The Young Frankenstein* for all I could tell at that point."

At the mention of Frau Bucher, Amy made the required horse neighing sound, then asked, "Her brother had her bring you the sails? That was pretty chicken of him."

"No, he didn't send her or the sails. When she gave him my message he only said where I should go and what I should do to myself when I got there, and went in to New York. I guess he thought I wouldn't have nerve enough to come after him in his own ballpark. Bringing the sails was her own idea. She said she had to come to Stratford anyway."

Amy pulled up in front of a gas pump and asked if her grandfather wanted to get something to eat at the fast food joint next to the gas station. "Sure. One of those chicken breast sandwiches and a chocolate shake would hit the spot."

"Grandpa, nobody knows what's in those shakes except for sugar and cholesterol. They're probably made from the by-products of some paint manufacturing process."

"But they're awfully good."

"I don't think they're a good idea for someone your age."

"At my age they're a great idea. Don't you realize if I don't have one and drop dead this afternoon, all the way to the floor I'll regret not having it."

"No milkshake. I don't want you to drop dead when you're with me. I'm supposed to take care of you."

"Do you have any idea how much you sound like your grandmother sometimes?"

"Oh, okay, you can have a milkshake if you tell me about the day you met her. I thought you met her when you were in college at Dartmouth."

"She went to Wellesley and was one of perhaps a half dozen college girls in New England I didn't seek out and pursue during my not-altogether-successful college career."

After the gas tank was filled, they parked and walked into the restaurant where he immediately headed for the men's room. When they had their food and were seated at a table she asked, "Do you want to stop in Hanover and look around on the way back?"

"Naah. I don't have any loyalty or curiosity for the place. Besides, everyone I knew there is long dead."

"So you have no old grad feelings toward your alma mater?"

"I went there to become a doctor like my grandfather, and because it was a halfway Ivy League school that was far away from my Yalie father. A non-Ivy League school would have been beneath consideration. I had what we called a double major, beer and girls, with a minor in premed chemistry on the side."

"Dartmouth wasn't co-ed then, was it? How could girls be a problem?"

"That's exactly why girls were a problem. There were no girls. The place was a testosterone-soaked nut house. There's an old school song that goes, 'Dartmouth's in town again, run girls run.' It was completely accurate. Between that and the rest of the goings on at the Deke house, I was lucky to graduate at all. I didn't get into med school. Now, can we drop this subject?"

"So you don't want to visit the scene of your misspent youth?"

"No, and not just for that reason. Now the place is a hotbed of what they call political correctness. I saw their kind of political correctness in Germany in 1936. Certain words and certain viewpoints are outlawed and anyone who tries to discuss them is shouted down and assaulted by the local Brown Shirts. I hate fascists. My crew and I didn't do what we did, and endure what we endured, so this country could be taken over by a bunch of goddamned fascist draft dodgers from the sixties."

In order to get his mind off of what was obviously a very sore subject, Amy said, "Go on about Grandma and the *Fourteen Boat*. I really want to know how it was. Those days were so different from today."

"No, they weren't. The same wars with the same sorts of people. It's just that they're not being fought nearly as well today as they were then, so they last a hell of a lot longer."

They finished eating in silence, then she asked, "Are you ready to go, Grandpa?"

"Just let me hit the men's room first.

JANUARY 1942

"WHY DON'T YOU DRIVE INTO THE BOAT SHED, Miss Madison? I'll open the back doors for you and we'll unload the car in there." As he opened the shed doors he heard the crane motor start to labor. "I'll be with you in a bit. It sounds like the mast is going into the boat without me." He hurried through the shed and down to the dock.

She stood in the front door watching them sway the mast into the boat. When it was in place and Jenks and the rigger were setting up the rigging, Nick walked up the railway with Longo and Borg, whom he told to unload the car. She greeted them by saying, "There's two sets: the one that was on the boat when my brother bought it and a new one he had made last year."

"Does he know you brought them?" Nick asked.

"I don't care what he knows. My brother is a twerp. He's fourteen years older than I am and thinks that makes him my boss. He thinks he's everyone's boss."

"You said you had to come to Stratford anyway?"

"I start work at Chance Vought on Monday. They're going to build fighter planes for the Navy and I'm going to be a secretary."

"Did you go to Katy Gibbs?"

"Gracious, no. But I have an English degree from Wellesley so I can spell. I already knew how to type. I just finished a shorthand course and I've got pretty good legs so I'm completely qualified to be a secretary, although I've never had a job before." Nick could hear the two sailors trying to stifle laughter as she continued, "There's a war on, you know. Everyone has to do something. Even if my brother doesn't think so."

They finished emptying the car and were sweeping the snow out as best they could with their gloved hands and an old piece of plywood as she said, "Put those old sails in the car. I want to give them to my brother the next time I go home. Stack them in the back seat and scrunch them down so I can put up the top. It's really cold with it down. I hate the cold."

Longo asked, "Should we put them in the trunk, miss?"

"No room. My clothes and stuff are in the trunk. I'm moving into a boarding house on Elm Street, Marion's, because I'd never get the gas stamps to commute between here and Redding."

As they stacked the rotten old sails in the back seat, Nick thought, *This is the most interesting woman I've met in six years. They sure don't come along very often.* So he asked, "Miss Madison, I have to get down to the boat now, and I'll probably work late, but would you have dinner with me when I get through tonight?"

"I thought you'd never ask. Anyone who is an enemy of both the Axis Powers and my brother is a friend of mine."

The next four days were a blur in his memory. At nine-thirty that night he walked the six blocks to Marion's boarding house for young ladies. He and Amy had a scratch meal at Ryan's although the kitchen was long closed and then they walked back to the boarding house through the newly fallen snow. The following morning and the next three mornings they met at the little breakfast and lunch place across from Ryan's at five-thirty for pancakes, so he could be at work on the boat by dawn. In the evenings they had dinner together. By the fourth morning, when *Fourteen Boat,* as they now thought of her, was almost ready to sail, they had reached an unspoken agreement of sorts that they were interested in each other. Those things went quickly in the winter of '42. He was going to leave his Ford in Marion's backyard so she could use it. It got much better gas mileage than the eight-cylinder Pontiac her parents had given her for graduation.

The other three seamen were supposed to arrive from the Cape May Training Station but they didn't show. When Nick called the chief in New London about it, he said, "We didn't expect you to be ready for sea this quick. They don't get out of training until… Hold on." He put down the phone and Nick could hear him pawing through the papers on his desk. "They gave Slade a quick cooking course, and then a first-aid course right after boot camp. Mainly teaching him how to warm canned stew without setting fire to the boat and how to immobilize broken bones. I hope they taught him how to deal with people who've been swimming in an oil slick. We're getting a lot of those. He finishes today. The other two are scheduled to be done on Friday."

"You're giving me three guys right out of boot camp?"

"The cook/medic is completely green, but the other two are gentlemen yachtsmen who volunteered to serve offshore in the Hooligan Navy. We're getting a lot of them now that the word is getting around. Some of the other boats will be manned almost exclusively with them."

"What kind of experience do those two have?"

"One of them has been working around boatyards since he was a little kid. He's twenty-one and he's had some sailing experience, working on delivery crews mostly."

"Why wasn't he drafted, or was this a dodge to avoid it?"

"He got his right hand all mashed up. No one else would take him."

"What about the other one?"

"From Larchmont and money. You might know him: name's Langdon. He supposedly has flat feet. The Army isn't taking anyone with flat feet."

Nick thought about it. "Nope, never heard of him. I don't know anybody in Larchmont."

"Very experienced small boat sailor. Raced Star Boats mostly. He might see this as a way to beat the draft, if the army starts to take guys with flat feet, but I don't know. He might see it as his patriotic duty like the rest of the volunteers. He's a couple of years older than the other one: Langdon's his name, Prescott Langdon. Sounds like a gentleman yachtsman, doesn't it? Anyway, we sent them both to an orientation thing somebody cooked up at Cape May. Not quite boot camp. Only three weeks because they already know how to tie a bowline. We're rating them as Seamen. We don't know how to rate some of the old guys on the other boats. The ones we're putting in command of boats, some of which are their own, we're rating as boatswain's mates."

"Then how come I'm an ensign?"

"Don't ask me, Mister Worth. Everything is changing from day to day as we try to get you guys out there. The U-boats are really kicking our ass. That's your whole crew, and it's a pretty good one, I guess. Almost all of them know what to call the pointy end. The other one, the cook-medic, Slade, claims to be eighteen and is from

Oklahoma, so God only knows what he knows about sailboats. We have to do the best we can with what they give us, Mister Worth. There's a war on, you know.

"Chief, I'm about ready to sail. It would help if I knew where I'm supposed to go."

"We sent you orders in care of the yard the other day. I guess you didn't get them yet. Thank God the Post Office isn't running the war. You'll be home-ported in Greenport but they want you to come here first so we can inspect the vessel. There's some stuff you have to draw before you go on patrol and the trip down the Sound can be a shakedown cruise. Can the four of you sail the boat alone?"

"Sure. The tide starts to ebb at ten tomorrow morning and we'll leave then and ride it as far as we can down the Sound."

"I'll get your other guys shipped here."

"We'll see you late tomorrow night if all goes well."

"Shit, Mister Worth, haven't you been in the Hooligan Navy long enough to know that nothing ever goes well?"

SIX

FEBRUARY 1942

THE LOW FINALLY PASSED and the weather cleared the night before they sailed. With the last-minute preparations Nick only had time late that night to drive the Model A to Marion's, kiss Amy goodbye, and hurry back to the boat. A cold northwest wind followed the low as it always does, but when Nick opened the hatch a wave of heat told him the kerosene heater had made the boat almost comfortable.

The hatch, as on many of John Alden's designs, was offset to starboard and the ladder from the cockpit descended into an aft cabin. The motor box that also served as a chart table occupied the aft end of the eight-foot-long room with a bunk on either side of it. Jenks had had Longo move the engine controls below and mount them on the side of the engine box so the holes in the side of the cockpit, where they had been mounted, could be sealed. Nick was glad of the change because *Morning Glory's* had always leaked in a blow. The rubber boots that were supposed to seal them while still allowing them to be moved, never sealed completely. Wind-driven rain and spray always found their way onto the bunk below.

He and Jenks would use the berths in the aft cabin because they were closest to the cockpit. The mainmast came down through the deck at the forward end of the cabin and the deck was braced just forward of it by the aft bulkheads of the galley on one side and of the head on the other.

The rest of the crew would sleep in the four bunks in the main cabin. There was a folding table on the centerline. Because there were five crewmen, the one who drew the short straw would be assigned the folding berth in the fore cabin. It hung over the small workbench Jenks had installed, and was opposite the storage lockers and sail bins that filled the port side. Nick didn't think anyone would be able to sleep there in a seaway so it would be a matter of hot bunking in the main cabin. Just like the racing crews in *Morning Glory*, if the boat was reaching or going to weather and there was any sea running, the watch off duty would sleep—or try to, anyway—in the bunks on the high side of the main cabin.

When he came below, Nick was thinking about how uncomfortable, crowded, and smelly the cabin would be, particularly with all of the extra gear and the three weeks' food that would be needed if they were to stay on station for fifteen days and have a cushion for emergencies.

Jenks was lying in his bunk smoking a cigarette. He asked, "Did you bid your teary farewell to the lovely Miss Madison, Mr. Worth?"

Instead of replying to the snotty question, he said, "Put out that cigarette. It's within six feet of the gas tank, for Christ's sake." The forty-five gallon tank was under the cockpit sole, just aft of the bulkhead behind Jenks' feet.

The boatswain grudgingly put the butt out in the quahog shell ashtray he had balanced on his chest. "Can I take that to mean that you and Miss Madison did not exactly cling to each other as "The White Cliffs of Dover" played in the background?"

"Leave Amy out of this. From now on there will be no smoking in the cabin. If you have to do it, you can do it on deck or not at all."

Jenks' reaction was what he expected. He put his ashtray on the motor box/chart table, swung his legs out of bed, and sat up as he said, "Bull shit, SIR. Everybody but you smokes. The whole fucking war is running on cigarettes and coffee. The Services all hand out cigarettes for free. We've got a right to smoke any damn place on the boat we want, SIR."

"Okay. You can smoke in the cabin if that's a right given you by the U.S. Government. But you have to pull a soaking wet sail bag over your head and fasten it tightly around your waist when you do. We only moved aboard yesterday and already the cabin stinks. I can't do anything about smelly socks and armpits in a space that's not much bigger than the inside of a Buick Roadmaster, but we don't have to endure cigarette smoke on top of it."

"Was it your Daddy or your Mommy who told you not to smoke, SIR?"

"No, it was my grandfather, a very fine physician. And stop shouting sir at me. No smoking below. It's a hell of a fire hazard with all the gasoline, kerosene, and other flammable stuff we have aboard. Have you ever been in a fire at sea, Jenks?"

"No, and I've been smoking since I was twelve on more boats than you've ever seen, SIR. I suppose you're going to tell me that you have been in a fire at sea, SIR."

"Nope. And I don't intend to be either. No smoking below. I'll tell the crew but you're going to enforce it by example. If you won't, when we get to New London I'll get a boatswain who will."

Jenks was still pissed when they got ready to leave the next morning at slack water when the tide had crested but not yet begun to run out of the river. He took his time getting the spring lines and fenders off the boat and stowing them in the forepeak, then he lit up and strolled aft blowing smoke rings in Nick's general direction. He had to be told to get the main, foresail, and staysail ready to hoist. While he and the other crewmen did it, Nick looked over the stern at the outgoing current that was just beginning to run and knew that this was another test. They had missed slack water. A soon as they got the ties off the main and foresail he called, "Longo, get the engine running. Boats, you and Borg stand by to cast off." He'd have to get steerageway on the boat quick before the Housatonic's five- to six-knot current took charge and piled him onto the next dock downstream.

Borg and Longo hurried to their stations, but Jenks strolled aft into the cockpit, lighting another cigarette, as Longo went below. Nick looked down the hatch and watched the motor mechanic's mate lift the top of the engine box and sniff for gasoline fumes before he hit the starter button. *Good. Someone's on the ball this morning.* The engine started on the first crank. "Let's go, Boats. Move it."

Jenks took one last puff, threw his cigarette overboard, and took all but the last turn of the after dock line off the cleat. Borg was on the bow ready to let go forward. Over his shoulder Jenks said, "She'll back to port no matter what you do with the wheel, SIR."

"As will every other right-hand turning, single-screw vessel in the world. Put it in reverse, Longo, and give me quarter throttle." Nick was glad they had been tied to the downstream side of the dock; the current was pushing them away from it. "Let go aft and be careful with that line, Boats. I don't want it in the prop." Jenks' only response was a dirty look. Nick raised his voice as *Fourteen Boat* started to move. "Let go forward. Give me half throttle and a little more, Longo." Nick's grandfather had always said that if you maneuvered around docks fast enough, the wind and tide became negligible. He was holding the wheel dead amidships because he knew that if the rudder got at all sideways, the water pressure generated by the backing boat would tear it out of his hands. He thought, *It's a big engine swinging a big prop, it's going to be a drag under sail but it's awful nice right now.*

When they were clear of the other docks and into the channel, Nick said, "Put it in neutral, Longo." He was glad that Longo had sense enough to cut the throttle first. He should have given him an "all back slow" or some such naval-sounding command. He'd have to look up and memorize the proper engine and rudder commands and get Longo to learn and repeat them. Then he smiled to himself as he thought, *That's what the big people do.* She slowed, and he spun the wheel to port. As the schooner swung her bow into the outgoing current he ordered, "Put her in forward and give me half throttle." *That should be enough to hold her against the current and the northwest wind.*

It wasn't. Now that they were out in the river, the wind coming down over the Route One Bridge and the snow-covered salt flats below it had some teeth to it. "Give me a couple more notches of throttle, Longo. Well, Boats, are you going to get some sail on her or stand there admiring my seamanship while we cruise up the river to Shelton? The mainsail—that's the back one—goes up first."

"You want it reefed?"

"Naah. Let's see what it's like outside first."

Jenks and Borg hauled up the main and when Nick sheeted it in, the boat surged forward and the engine pitch changed. *Should I have Longo shut down the engine and go forward to help with the foresail?* As if to answer, the shifty wind coming off the land swung ahead of them and the main started to flog.

It was a two-man job to sweat up the peak and throat halyards of the foresail's gaff, but Borg was big and young and Jenks had the strength of a gorilla so it was no problem. When it was up Nick yelled "Neutral" and then, "Going about" as he put the wheel over and *Fourteen Boat* came around and headed downriver under sail. Nick eased the main sheet, Jenks did the same to the fore, and the boat, with the wind now over her quarter, heeled down, and as his grandfather would have said, lifted her skirts and ran. "Done with the engine, Longo."

They put up the staysail and Nick turned the varnished mahogany wheel over to Jenks—it was the only thing on the boat they could not bring themselves to paint gray—and went below to write up the log. He had just started when Borg called down to him. "You'd better come up, Mister Worth. You'll want to see this."

The Chance Vought plant had originally been built by Igor Sikorsky to build flying boats; it had a concrete ramp into the river from which to launch them. They were abreast of the ramp now and standing at its head was a madly waving figure in a camel's hair coat, ski cap, and a huge scarf. He lifted his hat and bowed deeply and when he looked around Longo and Borg were doing the same thing while Jenks, who was steering, studied the sails. The figure then turned around and walked away. She knew not to watch them out of sight. It was bad luck to watch a ship sail out of sight.

AUGUST 2008

"**That was Grandma, wasn't it?**" They were just driving up the ramp back onto I-91.

"Yup. I didn't know it then but the guys had sort of adopted her as the ship's mascot, or good luck charm. That afternoon Borg, who had volunteered to cook until the combination cook and medic they had assigned joined the ship, produced a big chocolate cake with 'CGR 3114, The Scourge of the Seven Seas' written on it in frosting. She had smuggled it to him somehow. Your grandmother was the very best thing that happened to anyone in 1942. It was a lousy year for just about everyone else on earth."

He mused in silence for a while, then said, "That winter and spring the Japs took the Philippines, Singapore, Burma, the Dutch East Indies, and were threatening Australia. The Germans were blitzing England's cities—they just about leveled Coventry. They had overrun France and Poland and had invaded Russia. And they had begun to implement their final solution to what they called the Jewish question in Germany, France, Poland, Scandinavia, and Czechoslovakia."

"Grandpa, calling the Japanese by that name has definite racial connotations. I wish you wouldn't do it."

"Is that what they taught you in college? Does your father know he's spending all that money to have you politically indoctrinated? Maybe he ought to send you to Katy Gibbs, or set you up in a plumbing supply business. Have you considered maybe getting a degree in civil engineering? Something useful. We have an overstock of politically correct journalism majors already. I'm going to talk to him."

She became indignant. "You mentioned all the horrors of 1942, but forgot to mention the Internment of the Japanese. That was possible because they were dehumanized by calling them Japs in the tone you always use. That internment is a stain on American history just like slavery."

"I don't want to argue about slavery. Besides, I think we probably agree about that. But did you know that ten thousand Germans were interned too? And a bunch of Italians. I forget how many. Besides, the treatment of the internees was a tea party compared to the way slaves were treated, and are still treated in some parts of the world. Parts of the world your profs never discuss because it might upset the slave holders there. And even that is Boy Scout Camp compared to the way the Japs treated their prisoners. Japs is about the kindest thing I can call the bastards."

She tried to shift the conversation away from the Japanese. "No, I didn't know that they interned Germans and Italians, too."

"Maybe you should ask why you weren't told that Germans and Italians were interned too. Maybe they didn't fit someone's continuing story about American racism. All this yelling about how evil the Japanese internment was—putting aside the political agendas behind a lot of it—is a classic example of what I told you one should never do: judge the actions of people in history by what we know now, not what they knew them. Let me try to explain what it was like to be alive in the first six months of 1942 and what we knew then. The Japanese, as you insist I call them, had been behaving like beasts for ten years. They had committed horrible atrocities in China: the Rape of Nanking, for instance. They had launched a sneak attack on Pearl Harbor without a declaration of war and killed three thousand Americans. They were brutalizing and murdering American prisoners of war in the Philippines. The Bataan Death March had taken place. A few people had escaped into the hills and radioed the news of it. To say that the American people were pissed off at the Japs with good reason would be the greatest understatement in history."

"Oh, Grandpa, don't you see, that was the Japanese Japanese.

Not the ones living peacefully on the West Coast."

"Ironically, we knew some facts then that have been conveniently forgotten now. In every country that the Germans and Japs invaded, they were aided by their ethnic minorities living there. The Sudeten Germans who undermined Czechoslovakia, the Japanese living in Manchuria who had acted as a fifth column for their invasion of China, the Japanese in Hawaii who had spied on the fleet just before Pearl Harbor and sent back a diagram of where the ships were berthed, the Austrian and Polish Germans who helped the Krauts take over their countries. The young Germans and Austrians who the Norwegians had taken into their homes in the thirties when things were tough in the Fatherlands who acted as scouts for the invasion in 1940. One other thing we were aware of then, that's been completely forgotten now: we knew we could lose that war and that we were well on the way to doing it. To you and your profs it's now obvious we won, but at the time we had no way of knowing we were destined to win. We just could not take any chances we did not have to take. Because our backs were against the wall, we had to do everything anyone could think of to defend ourselves."

"Even if what you say is true, it was still a clear violation of the Constitution."

"Every single one of them was released in good shape as soon as the war ended. Besides, Lincoln suspended habeas corpus in the civil war and what's his name… Teddy Roosevelt appointed him to the Supreme Court. He was a colonel in the civil war… Was from Massachusetts… His father was a famous essayist. Hart, Hastings, something like that."

"Charles Evans Hughes?"

"No, damn it. Not Hughes but something like it. Anyway, he said that the Constitution is not a suicide pact. Holmes, Oliver Wendell Holmes. Why was that so hard to remember? Before I couldn't remember Amy's brother's first name. It was Robert, and he always insisted on being called Robert. Like you're not supposed to call James Bond Jimmy. He got mad if you called him Bob so Amy and I always called him Bob." He paused, then asked, "What were we talking about?"

"Hughes, Holmes, the Constitution, and Grandma's brother Bob."

It took him a moment to get back on track. "Oh, yeah. Would you believe that jerk ran all over the East Coast trying to get some judge to sign an order giving him the schooner back. He said that it was an illegal taking under the Fourth and Fifth amendments; he was dead right but no judge would sign his order. We did a lot of things in '42 for no better reason than we thought they might be necessary to defend ourselves."

She didn't like arguing with her grandfather. Maybe he had trouble remembering proper names or what day or sometimes what month it was, but he was a compulsive reader and seemed to remember just about everything he had ever read. If she got into a disagreement with him she always wound up feeling like a grade school kid. So she said, "Like sending people in sailboats out in the Atlantic to look for U-boats."

"Exactly."

She again decided to change the subject. "How did the trip down the Sound go, Grandpa? I've sailed on the Sound a lot, but never in winter except for frostbiting in Milford harbor."

"Then you know that when the air's cold it has a lot more molecules, so it pushes the boat harder."

"So it was a fast trip. How did you get along with Boatswain Jenks?"

"Not all that well."

FEBRUARY 1942

THEY STAYED ON THE STARBOARD TACK until they were about five miles offshore because Nick hoped the wind would be steadier out there. "Okay, Boats, let's get ready to jibe her."

"Schooners don't jibe in a breeze like this."

"Maybe fishing schooners with big, awkward, overhanging gaff mains don't. Get ready to jive her. Harden the main and fores'l sheets."

Jenks said "Oh, shit." Then, "You heard him, Longo, get the fores'l in tight. Borg, you take care of swapping the running backstays."

Nick gave them a minute or two to get ready, then called, "Jibe ho," and spun the wheel.

It went amazingly well and when everything was trimmed and the boat was stepping along headed east with Charles Island coming up on the port beam, Nick said, "I thinks it's dropping a bit, Boats. Maybe she could carry the jib."

Jenks was still smoking and sulking. "This is plenty of sail. What's your hurry anyway?" Then he added, "SIR."

"This is a shakedown cruise so we're going to shake her down. Set the jib, Boats." Nick was getting damned sick of him. "Borg, help the boatswain with the jib."

The two of them went forward as Nick said to Longo, "Here, you steer. I have to write up the log."

The motor mechanic took the wheel, and when he began to get the feel of the boat, he said, "She schoons, doesn't she, Skipper?"

It was the first time anyone had called him Skipper. It made him wonder what the relationship was between Jenks and the other two crewmen. They seemed to work together satisfactorily, but now that he thought about it, he hadn't heard them exchange many extra words with the boatswain. "Yes, Joe, she definitely schoons. Where are you from?"

"Scranton, P.A."

"How'd you wind up in the Coast Guard?"

"My dad was the boss mechanic at the Cadillac agency in Scranton and he had a little sailboat, a Snipe, he kept on Lake Walenpaupeck just outside of town."

"I never heard of it."

"A pretty big lake. Not awful wide but about twenty miles long. Anyway, he and I and my kid sister used to sail on it all summer. Sometimes my mom would come along and we'd have a picnic on one of the islands. Then the crash came and by 1933 nobody in Scranton wanted any Cadillacs anymore, so the dealership closed. By then most of the factories had either closed or cut way back. My old man scratched out a living any way he could. Fixing people's cars in our backyard and hoping to get paid. Fixing farmer's tractors and stuff. Picking fruit and vegetables on farms. We all did that. Did you ever pick strawberries, Mister Worth?"

"No, never." He was impressed that Longo was snaking the boat up toward the wind when it went light and down away from it in the puffs.

"Well, don't if you can find any way to avoid it. You work on your knees in the dirt and come home with your hands and knees all scratched up, the back of your neck and arms with the worst sunburn you ever saw, and three cents a peck. If you're a kid in short pants, or a little girl in a skirt, the backs of your knees are sunburned too. Believe me, having the backs of your knees sunburned is no picnic. It hurts every time you take a step for about a week. Then the next crop is ready and you start all over. I had a paper route, too. Thirty-six customers spread over about three miles, and you had to deliver every day, no matter what the weather was, or risk losing them. A nickel a paper a week. If I had a good week for tips, I'd clear about two bucks. I have vague memories of trudging along with a big gray bag over my shoulder every day after school. But the thing I remember most clearly was those damned strawberries, although it was only about six weeks a year."

"How far did you get in school?"

"I graduated high school in thirty-nine. My dad was a bear for getting us an education. He said I shouldn't wind up a grubby-handed mechanic like him, but look at me. But when I graduated, there was no way we could swing college. My sister was still in high school and I have a kid brother who's in fifth grade now. So I decided the best thing I could do was go in the service. I've always been a nut for boats, I've read everything I could find about them, so the Coast Guard seemed to be the place for me." Then he laughed. "That Snipe made me love sailboats, but until this assignment came along, I was working in an engine repair shop in Bayonne, New Jersey. The only boats I got to ride on were 40-foot patrol boats and old six-bit boats left over from prohibition with engine problems. This is the first time I've been sailing since Lake Walenpaupeck and it's great. I've looked at thousands of boats like this in every yachting magazine and book I could find, but I never dreamed I'd ever be roaring up Long Island Sound in an Alden Schooner."

"It's down. Going east is down in New England. And I have to warn you, Joe, it isn't always going to be flat water, offshore breezes, and clear skies."

"That's all right, Skipper. Whatever happens, this trip is well worth it."

AUGUST 2008

"It sounds like Machinist's Mate Longo was a good man, Grandpa."

"That he was, Toots, a very good man. He would have gone to college on the G.I. Bill after the war and built a fine life for himself and his family. If he had lived."

FEBRUARY 1942

They were down off the mouth of the Connecticut River by three o'clock when the tide started to turn at Long Sand Shoal off the river's mouth. By then the breeze had dropped off considerably and they were ghosting along at a couple of knots or so. Nick took a series of bearings on the shore and decided that they were still making headway over the ground against the tide, but not by much. He called down the hatch to where Jenks had been hiding all day, "It's time for the fisherman's topsail, Boats. That ought to make you happy."

Jenks came up into the cockpit and said, "Why don't we just start the goddamned engine?"

"Because this is a shakedown cruise and the boat isn't all I want to shake down. I want to see if you know how to set the fisherman." Turning to Borg, who was in the galley cleaning up from their late lunch of canned soup and chocolate cake, he said, "You help him, Borg. You too, Longo." Nick took over the wheel, which he hadn't had the heart to take away from Longo until now.

Jenks mumbled, "I hate the fucking things but I know how to set 'em," and went below to get the sail.

When the big, four-cornered sail set high up between the masts was up and pulling, Jenks came aft lighting another cigarette and said, "Are you happy now, SIR?"

Nick said to Borg and Longo, "Why don't you two take a smoke break on the foredeck while Boats and I have a talk." When they were alone Nick said, "Jenks, do you know what silent insubordination is? I found it in the *Coast Guard Officer's Handbook* the other day. It's a court-martial offense and your behavior is a perfect example of it."

"Yeah, I know what it is and I also know it's impossible to prove. I have not failed to carry out a single order, and do it well."

"You probably won't get convicted even though it's listed under offenses to the discipline and good order of the service. But when I get through charging you, the next ship you'll get will be a rowboat on Lake Poop. Look Boats, we've got a good boat and the makings of a fine crew, so why don't we bury the hatchet and do what's best for everybody."

"Can I speak frankly, SIR?"

"As long as you stop shouting SIR in my face. If you keep that up, so help me, I'll get rid of you any way I can."

"Okay, sir. Is that better?" Nick nodded yes, so he went on, "We didn't need you. I've been busting my ass getting this boat ready for sea despite everything that asshole Madison could do. Then, when we're about ready to go, you show up and take over. That's not right."

"You do need me, Jenks. I've sailed a lot more miles in a schooner like this one than you have, and I'm a qualified navigator. You're not, from what they tell me."

"I would've figured it out and Borg is good with numbers. He'd a helped me."

"Listen to yourself. Don't you hear what a grab-ass operation that would have been? You chased the navigator they sent you off the boat."

"That guy was a complete drip who didn't know one end of the boat from the other and would probably have been puking his guts out by the time we got out of sight of land. Completely useless. If we left the navigation to him we'd a had to leave a trail of bread crumbs to get back."

"I promise I won't puke my guts out, I'll find our way back, and that's the pointy end, that one up in front."

Jenks suppressed a smile, and said, "Can we smoke in the cabin, sir?"

"Sure, as long as you follow the wet sail bag rule. Otherwise no dice. We can't take a chance on fire in a wooden ship way offshore. Think about how this boat will bounce around in a seaway and how easy it would be to drop a butt into a bunk cushion or a pile of sails or one of Longo's oily rags in the slop bucket."

"Once we're offshore everything will be so clammy wet that we'll be lucky to get a cigarette to burn. You just don't like the smell. You gotta be the only person in this whole war who hates the smell of good tobacco."

"There's that, too.

"The whole crew wants to be able to have a cigarette below when they're off watch."

"Oh, then we'll have to do this democratically and vote on it. Only I have one more vote than all the rest of you together. I don't want people on deck waving around lights at night either. There's a war on, Boats. Haven't you heard?"

AUGUST 2008

"**DID THINGS GET BETTER** between you and Jenks after that, Grandpa?"

"A little. He was like old Mister Gray; he had his good days and his bad."

"What happened to him. Did you finally have to get rid of him?"

"No. He died too."

SEVEN

FEBRUARY 1942

JUST AFTER DARK they saw the flashing light on Great Gull Island off the starboard bow. It supposedly had a range of eighteen miles and Nick was surprised it hadn't been turned off. It had probably been left on because of all the traffic in and out of the New London Navy Base and because it was fourteen miles inside of Montauk Point. He supposed they might have cut back on its range, though.

By then the wind had just about died, so they dropped the sails and started the engine. When they rounded the breakwater at the mouth of the Thames River the tide was running out so fast that even with the engine at eighty percent throttle, it was slow going. There was no point in opening the throttle further; all it did was pull the boat's stern down without pushing her any faster. It was 2216 when they tied up to the dock at the Coast Guard Base and Nick logged their arrival.

A guard wearing leggings and a holstered pistol came down from the head of the dock and told Nick, "Good evening, sir. I called the duty officer and told him you've arrived. You might as well catch some zees. Breakfast starts at 0530 and the Old Man comes in about that time so you want to be up and about by then." The idea of a good night's sleep had great appeal. They had all been working eighteen-hour days and Nick had spent much of his sack time planning the next day's work. Once they got to sea, the chance for a quiet six or seven hours in a motionless bunk would be zero.

The guard had been right; when Nick walked into the officer's side of the mess hall at 0520, a very old captain was already there, waiting in line for them to begin serving. He had to be seventy if he was a day. Nick strode up to him trying to decide if he should formally report or just introduce himself. The question became moot when the captain held out his hand and said, "You must be Mr. Worth from *Thirty-one Fourteen Boat*. You had a good trip down the Sound?"

"Yes, sir. Took us just about ten hours breakwater to breakwater."

"That's good time. You ran the engine most of the way?"

"No sir. We left Stratford with a pretty good nor'wester that didn't die until just the other side of Niantic. We motored from there. When we were off Duck Island we set the fisherman. I don't think it had ever been out of the bag before. It helped to move her along."

They started through the line, pushing their aluminum trays along the counter rails. The captain took a small scoop of scrambled eggs and a couple of slices of toast. Nick took a stack of pancakes and it made him think of those breakfasts with Amy. As soon as he got a chance he'd have to call her.

When they were seated at a table by the window that was reserved for the captain, he asked, "No problems with the boat then, and you finally got a decent suit of sails."

"Two sets."

"How'd you get that guy who owned the boat to cough them up? He was driving Lieutenant Nelson nuts."

"Well, he didn't cough them up. His sister did. He wasn't happy when he found out."

"As long as you got them. What else do you need?"

"My radioman has a few spares that he wants. Extra tubes and such. He says the two things vacuum tubes don't like are salt air and being bounced around. Other than that it's just the things a boat never has enough of: spare blocks, shackles, cordage and such, plus whatever else you want me to draw here."

"How about the crew?"

"The ones I've met are okay, sir."

"All of them?"

"There are three more joining today. I don't know about them yet."

"I meant the ones you've already met." The captain looked at him for a second, and when Nick didn't add anything said, "Okay. It's your boat. When do you think you'll be ready for sea?"

"As soon as the stuff I have to draw here is aboard. That assumes you don't find anything wrong that I've missed, sir."

"I don't mind telling you that we need every boat we can find out there, to pick up survivors if nothing else. Between Nantucket and Atlantic City we've lost seven merchant ships in the last five days alone."

"If all goes well, I'll sail with the tide tonight. It turns at eleven hundred."

"That would be good. Every minute counts to someone on a raft or in a lifeboat in the Atlantic this time of year." He had already finished his breakfast and as he stood, Nick started to stand too, but he motioned him to sit back down and said, "Finish your breakfast, Mister Worth. I want to check in at the office and then the chief and I will come down and look at the boat."

AUGUST 2008

"**Why didn't you get rid of Jenks** when it was offered, Grandpa?"

"The devil you know is always better than the one you don't know. And he was a very competent sailor. I might have gotten some guy who had never set foot on a sailboat except to count the fire extinguishers and life jackets and whose attitude toward ninety-day wonders was as bad or worse than Jenks'."

"How did the captain's inspection go?"

"Oh, fine. He and the chief had both wrung so much salt water out of their socks that they knew the boat was okay in about two minutes. The captain's main duty was finding seaworthy boats for the picket line. It was officially called the Corsair fleet. Some meathead in Congress had thought up the name. I never heard anyone refer to it as anything but the Hooligan Navy, though. It was like Yankee Doodle. It was originally meant as a term of ridicule, but the people it was supposed to ridicule adopted it with a sort of backwards pride."

"It sounds like the captain was okay."

"Oh, yeah. This was his third war. He had served as a young ensign in Cuba during the Spanish American war, been a hell-for-leather cutter commander fighting U-boats in the First World War, and retired about 1930. The day after Pearl Harbor he volunteered for any service he could perform. He was an experienced offshore sailboat sailor and even offered to come back as an enlisted crewman. They had found the right job for him."

"So you were all set as soon as your crewmen showed up?"

"They showed up that afternoon. The fun really started later that morning when I sat down with Lieutenant Nelson to discuss the ship's armament."

"Armament?"

FEBRUARY 1942

"THE CAPTAIN IS PLEASED WITH YOUR BOAT, MR. WORTH. So is the chief, and he's a harsher critic. You'll be based at Greenport and draw galley stores there before you go to sea. Your radioman can get his spares there too. All you have to do here is draw your weapons."

"Weapons?"

"The Congress, in its latest directive, has decreed that the Corsair Fleet, as they call our beloved Hooligan Navy, shall each be armed with a .50 caliber machine gun and four 300 pound depth charges. One of your guys will be taught how to set them."

"Four 300-pound depth charges? Whose bright idea was that, sir?"

"Probably some congressman from Arkansas."

"Three hundred pounds of what?"

"TNT."

"Just me, my crew, and twelve hundred pounds of TNT on a fifty-four-foot boat. What's the blast radius of one of those things?"

Nelson smiled. "Anything within about a hundred yards of a U-boat is considered a direct hit. Water is really good at transmitting shock waves, you know."

Nick did a quick calculation. "How long after you drop one of those things overboard does it go off?"

With half a smile still on his face, Nelson said, "Depends on the depth setting. Anywhere from twenty seconds to a minute. If it goes off at all. Then again, it could go off prematurely. They're all left over from the last war so I don't think anyone knows how well they'll work after all these years."

"Lieutenant, at six knots it takes me thirty seconds to go a hundred yards, and if the blast from one of those things can sink a steel sub at a hundred yards, what will the shockwave do to a wooden boat?"

"I take it you don't want them, even though the Congress of the United States has decreed that you shall have them. And I'll bet you're already planning to drop them overboard with the safeties still set as soon as you get into deep water. We've already had three boats jettison them because it was, quote, necessary to lighten ship in foul weather, unquote."

"All that weight high up and way aft could really hurt a boat's sea-keeping ability in foul weather, sir."

Nelson turned serious. "You don't have to take them. The commandant has decided that smaller vessels, anything under eighty feet, can carry, quote, other suitable weapons for attacking submerged U-boats, unquote, until such time as smaller depth charges are procured."

"What are these other suitable weapons, sir?"

"Hand grenades. They'll go boom and hopefully keep the

U-boat down until help arrives. You'll get a half dozen fragmentation and a half dozen white phosphorous. If you hear an airplane or blimp coming, throw some Willie Peter grenades overboard where you think the U-boat might be and get the hell out of the way. That will tell them where to drop their bombs. That stuff burns fiercely under water, so make damn sure nobody gets any of it on them. There's no putting it out."

"What about the machine gun?"

"Substituting grenades for the depth charges will be bad enough if someone in Congress finds out. Besides, you may need the machine gun, Mister Worth. If you find an empty drifting lifeboat, we want you to sink it, otherwise the Air Corps will report it again and again. You may have to set off a drifting mine too. One was found in the Ambrose Channel last week. The U-boats are dropping them. We're wondering if some of the ships we thought were torpedoed may have hit mines. We've had a load of sinkings off Atlantic City that could have been mines."

"We could set off a mine with a rifle."

"If you were Daniel Boone. With the boat going up and down and the mine doing the same you'd have to get close to do it with a rifle. You don't want to get close to a mine you're going to set off, Mr. Worth."

"No, I guess not."

"Another thing: if a U-boat gets away and some Congressman blames it on your not being able to sink it with hand grenades and a rifle, there'll be hell to pay. I don't know if the Navy will give you a .50 caliber, though. If they do, you can put it down in the bilge for extra ballast. Those things weigh close to a hundred pounds. You'll draw it over at the Navy Base, along with a .45 pistol."

"What's that for?"

"If you go into some harbor where there's no military base you'll have to post a gangway guard." Then he brightened. "It could also come in handy if you have to shoot Jenks."

Nick, Jenks, and Borg took the launch over to the Navy Base and went to the armory. It was a beautiful day to be out on the water. A thaw had set in, pushing the temperature into the low sixties and melting the snow. There was a light southwest wind blowing that still had some chill to it, but there was a feel that even if spring was probably months away, it would come eventually.

There was an old Marine master sergeant behind the counter at the armory and when he saw Jenks, he said, "I know you."

"You should. You were my squad leader in the Fifth Marines in 1918."

"Jenks. Is that right? I never forget a name or a face."

"That's right. Jenks."

"Where do you work?" He eyed Jenks' Coast Guard uniform. "Don't tell me you're across the creek in the Hooligan Navy. What happened? The Corps wouldn't have you back?"

"They said I was too old. How did you get back in?"

"Stayed in, going for thirty. Is he still a hopeless wiseass, Ensign?"

Nick smiled. "Hopeless."

"What can I do for you?"

"We're on *CGR 3114* and we're here to pick up our weapons." Nick pushed the paperwork signed by Captain Morris across the counter. "A .45, an M2 machine gun, suitable ammunition, and some hand grenades."

Jenks said, "You didn't tell me we were getting Old Ma Deuce, Mister Worth. That thing will shake the boat to pieces if we ever have to fire it."

"If we're lucky, we'll never have to fire it. Look, the Congress in its wisdom decreed that we should have a heavy machine gun and four three-hundred-pound depth charges. Just be thankful somebody found a way to avoid making us take the depth charges."

"You're not getting an M2 either." The sergeant was adamant.

"Look, Ensign, the M2 is about the best antiaircraft weapon we have right now. It's what they mount in aircraft, too. I'm scrounging every one I can find to give to those submarines Electric Boat is building just as fast as they can. Every M2 I have is assigned to one of those new boats. Where you're going, the other side of Montauk, you're not going to be attacked by Stuka dive bombers or Jap Zeroes. But where those subs are going there's a hell of a good chance of it. I'm not giving you an M2 even if Senator Claghorn himself says you should have one."

"In their latest directive the Congress ordered that what they call the Corsair Fleet shall be armed with a machine gun and depth charges. Thank God the Hooligan Navy is ignoring that whacky idea about the depth charges. I don't think we can avoid the machine gun, though. If some Congressional committee of the uninformed finds out we're being sent out to fight the mighty U-boat with only a .45 and a box of grenades, there'll really be hell to pay. Besides, if we have to sink an empty lifeboat or set off a drifting mine we'll need something.

Jenks thought of something. "Look, Gunny, don't you have something lighter? An M-1919 .30 caliber you don't need, maybe? What about a BAR?

Nick interjected, "A BAR?"

"Browning Automatic Rifle, .30 caliber." Jenks explained. "Only weighs nineteen pounds. Twenty-round magazine. Best light machine gun ever made. It's so good that they wouldn't give it to us in 1918. Made us use a French piece of shit because they were afraid the Krauts would capture one and copy the design. That was probably the same Washington asshole who came up with the M2 and depth charge idea."

The Gunny chimed in. "The Shosho. It had a big opening on the side of the magazine, so you could tell how many rounds you had left. You usually had them all left because the mag and action was so full of mud that it wouldn't shoot at all." Then he said, "I could give you a BAR, but your requisition is for an M-2."

Nick thought about it before saying, "If you don't have any M-2s available, I'll reluctantly accept one of these BARs instead. Give us the pistol and the grenades now and Boatswain Jenks will come back with a requisition for the light machine gun this afternoon. I guess that will comply with the Congress' wishes. We must be flexible. There's a war on, you know."

"You'll have to come back yourself, Ensign. I can't issue any kind of machine gun unless an officer signs for it."

Nick thought of something. "Jenks, suppose we have to shoot this thing. Do you know how to operate a BAR? Clean it and all? Or do I have to get you a familiarization course of some kind."

"Yeah, I know how it works. Gunny, give me a half-dozen magazines and some spare firing pins. The firing pin is the only weakness a BAR has."

The sergeant said, "I'll give him this, Ensign. Jenks here is good with weapons. It wasn't lack of weapons skill that kept him from being allowed to reenlist in the Corps."

AUGUST 2008

"**WHY WASN'T JENKS ALLOWED** to reenlist in the Marines, Grandpa? Did you ever find out?"

"There was nothing in his service record. In the twenties they were cutting way back on the military, but he had been decorated in the First War and should have been allowed to stay. I never asked him, but I suppose it was his generally lousy attitude and smart mouth that made him unsuited to peacetime service. The sergeant remembered it after all those years."

"So *CGR 3114* was now an armed ship of war."

"The scourge of the seven seas, just like your grandmother's cake said. We lightly oiled the guns, and locked them in the cabinet under my bunk along with the ammunition, the pistol belt, the holster, and the grenades. They gave us a box of .45 ammo and a steel box of .30 caliber ball ammunition for the BAR. We were really well armed to hold up a bank but would be in real trouble if a sea battle broke out.

It was okay. I didn't expect to take them out again until the war was over."

"Did you? Take them out I mean."

"Oh, yeah. That we did."

FEBRUARY 1942

WHEN NICK CAME BACK ABOARD that afternoon lugging the machine gun, Jenks was sitting in the cockpit cleaning the pistol. "Fucking Cosmoline is a bitch." He had the parts laid out on an old towel on the cockpit seat next to a saucepan of a black liquid that smelled like gasoline.

"Is that gasoline?"

"It's the only way to get this grease off. They dipped everything they could find in it after the last war and it's had twenty years to congeal. The gas works better if it's hot, but I figured you'd be pissed if you came back and caught me boiling a pot of gasoline on the galley stove. I know how scared you are of fire in a wooden ship and all."

Nick pointed at the saucepan. "Are you done with it?"

"Yup."

"Then get rid of it, and don't dump it over the side. How are you going to clean this thing?" He pointed to the BAR that was wrapped in brown paper and also covered with the preservative grease. "And don't tell me you're going to cook it in a washtub of gasoline."

"I'll think of something. Whatever it is, I'll do it far from your delicate nose and eyes."

"Just don't burn the base down or blow it up. Did the new guys arrive?"

"Yup. They came down to dump their gear, I think they couldn't wait to see this mighty warship. I sent them up to the chief to get their paperwork straightened out. You didn't get any bargain with that bunch, Mister Worth."

"Why not?"

"The cook looks like he's about fourteen and he's got such a heavy shit-kicker accent you can barely understand him. Until he got to Cape May I don't think he'd ever seen salt water, or more than about ten gallons of any kind of water in one place. Just what we're going to need, a seasick cook."

"Give him a chance. What about the other two? They're both supposed to be experienced sailors."

"One of them might be, but he's only got one hand. How much use is he going to be? The other one looks like he might be a fairy."

"That was quick judgment. Why?"

"You can always tell. All nicey-nicey, and just bursting to show the other two how much he knows about boats. Let's give him the focs'le bunk. I don't want him sleeping in the main cabin with the other guys. That could be trouble."

"How long were they here before you sent them up to deal with the paperwork?"

"Just long enough to dump their sea bags below."

"And you already know that one of them is going to be seasick, another is useless, and the third one is queer. You know, Jenks, you never stop amazing me. I'm going to go up and talk to them one at a time. As each of them comes down, get his gear stowed and show him around the boat. The tide starts to run out at eleven tonight, so that's when I want to leave."

"What's the rush? It starts to run out at noon tomorrow, too."

"That will cost us another day before we can get on station. There's a war on, you know. Get the new guys settled, get that gun cleaned, and do anything else you need to do. Oh, and throw away that saucepan and scrounge up a new one. I don't want to eat anything that's been cooked in it, even if you do. And Boats, give the new guys a chance. Keep an open mind. You've got enough enemies as it is, so try not to make any more."

AUGUST 2008

"How were the new guys, Grandpa?"

"Well, the cook did look about fourteen alright. He had joined the Coast Guard by mail."

"Huh?"

"He was from a little town in Oklahoma where his mother ran a diner. His dad had gone to California during the dust bowl and was never heard from again. There was a diner in town that had gone bust and been abandoned and his mother had taken it over at just the right time. The local Army base was about to be expanded. Anyway, he went to both the Army and the Navy recruiters in Midwest City, but they took one look at him and told him to come back in about five years. So he wrote to the Coast Guard Station in Corpus Christi and told them he was an Eagle Scout and an experienced short-order cook and could they use him? They sent him the paperwork to join and that his local doctor needed to give him a physical. He actually was eighteen, but nobody would believe it. His voice hadn't even broken yet, but he was a tough little bird like most of those kids that grew up in the dust bowl."

"So he was all right. What about the one-armed seaman and the other one?"

"Henry Snow was older, twenty-three, and he had both arms. He was only missing three fingers from his right hand, although what was left of the rest of the hand had been pretty badly mangled."

FEBRUARY 1942

"Seaman Snow reporting, sir. " He stood at attention in the unfurnished anteroom in front of the chief's office.

"At ease, Seaman. I'm Ensign Worth. Your paperwork is taken care of?"

"Yes, sir."

"I just want to get to know you before you go down to the boat. It's a bit cramped to hold a private conversation. You're from Milford?"

"Yes, sir." He was still standing stiffly.

"We got the boat ready at Bedell's just across the river in Stratford."

"I know it well, sir. I did some jobs there: painting, caulking, and such."

"Do you know anything about engines, Snow?"

"Some. My uncle owns the boatyard where I mostly worked. My father was killed in the last war, sir. My uncle looked out for my mother and me. Your boat has a six-cylinder Gray, sir. I've worked on them doing just routine stuff. Plugs, filters, oil changes, winterizing them in the fall. You know. Those are good engines. They don't need much else."

"How'd you find out?"

"Find out what, sir?"

"What kind of engine we have."

"I lifted the engine box cover when I went below to dump my sea bag."

"We've got a mechanic's mate deuce who's pretty good. I think I want you to backstop him. I want everyone to have a back-up in case someone gets sick or something." There was no avoiding it so it had best be put to bed right now. "What happened to your hand?"

"My own stupidity, sir. I got a job helping a customer bring a boat he had just bought back from Maine. It was the ugliest-looking thing you ever saw. A gaff-rigged sloop with powder horn sheer. You know, that's where the sheer line goes up instead of down from the bow then curves down again about a third of the way back. It's supposed to be better because the sheer line follows the shape of the bow wave. Only it makes a boat look like somebody dropped it. Anyway, the guy who built it had a lot of strange ideas. The peak and throat halyards of the mains'l were rusty plow iron wire. They were raised by this weird British-made winch. Anyway, sir, by the time we were in the middle of the Gulf of Maine that damned winch had let go on us twice and let the gaff fall down with a rush. We were lucky it didn't bean somebody.

"Anyway, we had just shaken out a reef and I was about go aft when I had a bright idea. I decided to push on the pawl that stopped the drums from turning to make sure it was seated. Well, the thing let go and a loop of that wire halyard wrapped itself around my middle three fingers and started to lift me right off the deck. I probably should have let it do it, but instead I grabbed the crank handle of the winch with my other hand. Then something had to give. It was the fingers, of course." Then he added, "That was two years ago and I haven't been offshore since. Or even on a boat. I've been doing what I could around my uncle's yard. I felt I should tell you that, sir."

Nick tried to suppress the willies the story gave him and asked, "What can you do that requires two hands? I wouldn't ask if I didn't need to know."

He was glad to see that the seaman thought about it before answering. "Some things but not everything." He held up his mangled and scarred hand. "You see, I can't get my thumb to touch my palm or my little finger so I can't pick up or grip anything small. I've taught myself to write and do a lot of things with my left hand, and I can haul on a rope by wrapping it around my wrist. My arm works fine."

"Look, Snow, I think you'll be okay. Get down to the boat and get your gear stowed."

"Thank you, sir."

As Snow left, Nick stuck his head into the chief's office and motioned to Seaman Langdon. "Let's talk."

Langdon stepped through the door and as Nick closed it he held out his hand and said, "Hi. I'm Prescott Langdon but everybody calls me Scotty. You must be Nick Worth."

Nick, on reflex, shook the offered hand but recovered by saying, "That's Ensign Worth or Mister Worth, Seaman."

"Oh sure, when anyone's around I'll play the game, but we belong to the same group and know the same people and it's an exclusive little group, isn't it?" Nick decided to let him talk. "Not like the rest of the crew: fishermen, mechanics, and a twelve-year-old farm boy. My mother would call them, NOKD: not our kind, dear."

"Why'd you volunteer for this duty?"

"The Army wouldn't take me. I've got flat feet. The women started to look at me like I was a draft dodger and it was getting harder to get them to have anything to do with me. Besides, who wouldn't prefer to go sailing rather than lie in the mud someplace and be shot at. I'm damned glad I've got flat feet, I tell you."

Nick wondered if this talk about women was a cover. "There's a rumor that you prefer men to girls? Is that true, Seaman?"

If Nick had belted him with a two-by-four he could not have removed his smart aleck smirk more completely. "What… Who… I… ? Finally he got enough control to say, "That's nuts. Who told you a crazy thing like that? It's a lie and I can get half the girls in Larchmont to verify that it's a lie. Why would someone say something like that? It has to be because they don't like me or are jealous of me."

"It could be the supercilious way you look down on everyone who's not from Larchmont. Do you think that could be it?"

"That's not true. I treat everyone alike."

"Everyone that's not NOKD, that is. Stand at attention." Langdon slowly straightened as Nick continued, "What did you do before joining?"

"I held a position in my father's firm."

"My father's firm, SIR. And what does your father do, Seaman?"

"He's an investor."

"What?"

"An investor, sir."

"And you helped him invest?"

"That's right." Nick glared at him until he added, "Sir."

"But mostly you sailed, seduced the young ladies of Larchmont, and lived off your father. Is that right?"

"No, sir. I have my own trust fund."

Nick shook his head, thought about it for a minute, then said, "Okay Seaman, here's the deal. I'm really tempted to kick you off the boat. If I don't want you no one else will take you so they'll probably find some really shitty job for you. Do you understand, Seaman?"

"Yes, sir."

"Good. You're learning."

"My grandfather taught me that any man who does not have a job or is not actively looking for work is a bum, no matter how much money is in his trust fund. So you were a bum before you volunteered for the Hooligan Navy. Is that right, Seaman?"

"Yes, sir. I guess that's right."

"Another thing you'd better understand. We are going out into the North Atlantic in winter to confront the German Navy, which is, at the moment, the finest submarine navy in the world. We are going to do this in a sailboat that's fifty-four feet on deck and is armed with a box of hand grenades, a light machine gun, and a two-way radio. If you think that's a better deal than the Army, quite frankly, Seaman, you're an idiot."

Nick paused to let that sink in. "Tell me about your sailing experience."

"A lot of small boat racing." It again took a glare to get a "sir" out of him. "Snipes when I was kid, and Two-tens and Stars since then. I've also crewed in the Vineyard and Block Island races a couple of times, sir."

"Any schooner experience?"

"Only my dad's yawl, sir." He tried to lighten the conversation. "My only schooner experience was watching that big transom of *Nina*'s sail away from us."

"Okay, Seaman, I'll give you a chance. But there are only seven of us on the boat, so things of necessity will be relaxed, but they will not be slack. Do you know the difference between relaxed and slack?"

"Yes, sir."

"Learn to get along with your shipmates and respect them. Do you have anything you want to add? Now's your chance."

"Sir, I don't know who started that vicious rumor about my sexuality. But it's not true."

"I know that, but don't ever forget that it's a court martial offense. Dismissed."

AUGUST 2008

"Is that true, Grandpa, being gay was a court martial offense?"

"Yup, and it wasn't called gay then. Someone who was gay was happy and cheerful. That's not something today's gay activists are noted for, is it? They're always deadly and brutally serious, aren't they?"

"Years of persecution have made them that way."

"Have you ever noticed that once the persecuted stop being persecuted for what they are, they rush right out and persecute anyone who isn't the way they are. Human nature never changes."

"Of course it does. There's a lot more respect for the sanctity of human life now than there was back then."

"I don't think there is any more respect for human life now than there ever was in most of the world. A lot of what is now called respect is just a convenient excuse for being too cowardly to confront evil. In this country there is far less respect for what you call the sanctity of human life than there was then. A lot less."

"How can you say that? We've made great strides. No more capital punishment in a lot of states. No more bombing cities the way your generation did."

"My generation used methods that are now unacceptable, granted. But so did Sherman when he marched across the South and said that if a crow wanted to fly from Atlanta to Savannah he'd have to carry his own supplies. But one thing you're missing, Toots. My war and Sherman's had one important thing in common: they were short. They both lasted less than four years. Waged with horrendous brutality, yes, but over in less than forty-eight months. And wars fought Sherman's way lead to definite conclusions. Now we wage half-hearted spectator sport wars that drag on for decades and never lead to anything useful. McNamara's Wars. "

"Did the Civil War and your war lead to anything useful?"

"I think the abolition of slavery and ending two of the most murderous regimes in history were useful."

"I wouldn't want my country to ever wage what you call Sherman's War again."

"Then it should never wage war at all. Probably the very worst sin a politician can commit is to wage half-assed war. It is truly despicable to send men out to risk everything they have, encumbered with all sorts of rules of engagement and strictures that are not designed to protect anyone except the cowardly politicians who sent them. If they don't have the guts to wage Sherman's War then they should not be allowed to wage war at all. If that had been the rule, Vietnam would never have happened, and this war on terror would have been over by now."

"That can never happen. We care about collateral damage. We are so much more concerned with the sanctity of human life than your generation ever was. "

"Could we stop at this rest area, Toots?"

She was glad to end the conversation. It was another one of those she didn't like to have with her grandfather.

But after they had used the restrooms and were once more on the highway, he said, "I don't think your generation understands the dignity of human life nearly as well as mine did. Forget the gangs and the serial killing and all that. Those things have always been a part of American life. I'm talking about the culture. The movies are much more brutal now and much more explicit in the way they treat violence, particularly against women. And some of the other stuff... I was watching the trial of that creepy little guy out in California with a history of threatening women with guns, the one who killed the actress."

"It took them two trials but they finally convicted him. That shows that the justice system works: all his rights were protected."

"That may be, but that's not what bothered me. They showed the jury the autopsy photos, but the TV station wouldn't show them."

"Good. What's wrong with that?"

"They put them on the Internet and a couple of hundred thousand sickos looked at them."

"Did you look at them, Grandpa?"

"God no, and I hope you're pulling my leg by asking, Toots. We had sickos in my day and probably just as many. But they were repressed and had to keep their psychoses hidden. Now we not only let them flaunt their psychoses, but we bombard them with things like those autopsy photos to feed their psychoses."

"Those photos are a matter of public record. They had to be released."

"My generation found ways to keep that sort of stuff from being shown to the public. Yours isn't able to. Forget the alleged rights of the public and the creep who killed her. That poor woman had a right to have some dignity left to her. Being a murder victim didn't deprive her of that right. That creep and those who released those photos so other creeps could look at them took away her last bit of dignity. My generation understood that, yours doesn't. Have you ever seen someone who has been shot in the head?"

"No, grandpa, I haven't, thank God. Have you?"

"Yes, I have and I cannot tell you, Amy, how glad I am that you never have.

EIGHT

BY SEVEN O'CLOCK, when the crew came back from supper, *Fourteen Boat* was almost ready to sail. There were, of course, last-minute jobs. It had taken Jenks several hours to get the Cosmoline grease off the BAR and out of its innards. Then, with Langdon hauling, he had gone to the top of the foremast in a boatswain's chair to put a longer shackle on the jib halyard block because the lead was not quite fair and could cause the halyard to chafe.

Longo and his new helper had given the engine one last going over and then started it and checked that both of its generators—one for the starting battery and one for the bank of batteries that supplied the lights and the radio—were putting out the required voltage and current. They had the engine box open, so Nick spread his charts and worked at the table in the main cabin.

He had been issued a code book and a mimeographed list of the code designations of the grids into which the area between Atlantic City and Nantucket had been divided. These were fifteen miles on a side and went out over a hundred miles to the edge of the continental shelf, where the water went from fifty to three hundred fathoms in just a couple of miles. He went through the radio code book with Borg and made up a list of those groups he wanted the signalman to memorize, so if it was necessary to send them, he would be able to do it immediately without hunting through the book for them. My position is... Enemy in sight. Enemy course and speed are ... Enemy is on surface. Enemy is submerged.

While they did this, Slade was washing all of the dishes, pots, and pans in the galley and arranging things the way he wanted them. "I want you to know those code groups by heart too, Cookie. Borg will show you how to operate the radio once you get settled in."

"I'm just about done here, Mr. Worth."

Borg said, "Let's go in the fore cabin and learn these together then."

When they had left, Nick spread a chart of the East Coast from Atlantic City to Nantucket on the table. He plotted and labeled the grids so that if he had to report something he would be able to do it without having to first plot the grid location from its latitude and longitude.

The day had stayed warm, although it was cooling quickly now that the sun was down, and the water was about as cold as it could get at the end of winter. Nick expected it to be a hazy if not a foggy night, so his next job was plotting the courses they would follow out of the Thames, across the Sound, through Plum Gut, and along the North Fork of Long Island to Greenport.

The base courses were easy, just a matter of using his parallel rule and the compass rose printed on the chart. But correcting those base courses for the speed and direction of the current at the times he expected them to be at the various locations along the route was a good deal trickier. The tidal currents at this end of the Sound ran at up to five knots and because they flowed through three different passages their directions and speeds were confused at best. At some points on the trip the current would be pushing them, at other places they'd have it on the nose, and at others it would be abeam.

This work had to be done now. It was required by what his grandfather had said was the first rule of piloting in enclosed waters: always stay ahead of the boat. An Englishman he had once sailed with had stated it another way. "Make sure you always know where you are so you can stay away from the crispy parts around the edges." Nick did not want to be plowing along in a foggy night while he tried to figure out where the tidal currents had taken them in relation to the crispy parts. One way to locate the nearest land was to run up on it. It would also be a good way to undermine the faith of his crew in his piloting and navigation skills. But if he could guide *Fourteen Boat* across one of the most difficult tidal areas on the East Coast on a dark night with absolutely no fuss….

As he corrected each course for the expected speed and direction of the current, he wrote the answer with his fountain pen onto a piece of white adhesive tape. These he stuck, in order, loosely onto his parallel rule. He would stick them, in turn, to the binnacle each time they made a course change so there would be no mistaking what course the helmsman should follow.

Nick had just finished calculating the course diagonally across the Race to Plum Gut when he noticed Longo standing quietly beside him. "You want to talk to me?"

"Sir, it was my fault. I found a new set of spark plugs and two new fuel filters in the tool locker when we were in Stratford and assumed they would fit."

"Back up. What are you talking about?"

He kept talking in a rush. He had obviously been planning this speech as he waited for Nick to finish what he was doing. "The plugs are the correct ones, sir, but the fittings on the new filters don't match the ones on the fuel line. Those spare filters are useless unless we can find some fittings to adapt them. A plugged-up fuel filter is about the surest way there is to stop a Gray. I'm sure glad Hank noticed it when I showed him the locker where the tools and spare parts are. Mr. Worth, it was a dumb mistake and it's my fault. Hank's on his way up to the engine shop right now to see if they've either got the right filters or some fittings so we can adapt these." He obviously expected some punishment, up to and including being kicked off the boat.

"How long ago did you find this out?"

"Just now, sir. Hank just noticed it, thank God. I was too damned dumb to check it before. They were new and still in the boxes so I didn't even look. A really dumb mistake, sir. Hank knows what he's doing. If you want to get rid of me, I understand."

Nick thought about it, then said, "Nope, it was a mistake but it wasn't a dumb mistake. The minute you found out about it you took steps to correct it and came and admitted it to me so I could help you fix it if you need help. Dumb mistakes are when someone screws something up and then doesn't admit it hoping no one will notice—or worse yet, lies about it. Do you need anything from me?"

"Not yet, sir. It depends on what we can find in the engine shop. We had one piece of luck. The guy who runs the engine shop is the duty petty officer tonight."

"Why don't you go help Snow look. Let me know how you make out. I really want to leave on the tide at eleven."

Nick was just rolling up his charts when he heard Longo and Snow come aboard. He went into the aft cabin to meet them. "How'd you make out?"

"Not as good as we'd hoped, Mr. Worth. The filter that's on the engine is for some other engine. An old Kermath, maybe. They don't have any and have never stocked them. They've got a half dozen of the correct filters in stock, but they're the same as the two spares we have. The setup that's on our engine is a mongrel and there aren't any fittings to adapt these filters to it."

"Do we absolutely need spare filters aboard tonight?"

Snow answered, "Once the boat starts to really bounce around in a seaway... It's an old gas tank, Mister Worth: steel, tinned inside. Once the tin breaks down and the steel starts to rust..."

A picture of the schooner caught in a five-knot tidal current with no wind and a dead engine flashed through Nick's mind. "What do you want to do? Wait until tomorrow? Will we be able to find a spare mongrel filter then? I really wanted to get out of here and through the Gut with a fair tide tonight."

"Hank and I talked it over with the chief that runs the engine shop. We all agree that the best thing would be to cut the fuel line and change the whole set-up over to the proper fittings. If we have to replace the whole fuel line, we can. He's got plenty of tubing. If we do that we can get all the spares we want and we'll have a new filter installed and a couple of extras if we need them. We brought the tools, new fittings, a coil of tubing and an extra filter. We'd like to fix it once and for all, if it's okay with you, Skipper."

"You want to do it now? How long will it take?"

"Maybe an hour, a little longer."

"Get at it."

They were meticulously cleaning up the small amount of gasoline that had spilled when they removed the old filter and were airing the bilges when Nick walked up to a pay phone and called Marion's. She answered and said, "Oh, you're Ensign Worth. Amy told me you might call some time. She gave me her work number in case she wasn't here. All I have to do is remember where I put it. Oh, here it is." She gave him the number of the company and Amy's extension. Although he knew it was probably useless to try her work number at nine o'clock at night, he did it anyway. No one answered her extension.

He walked back down the dock telling himself he was an idiot. They had only known each other about a week. She had probably forgotten him by now.

When Nick got back to the boat, Jenks greeted him with, "Did you reach the lovely Miss Madison, or has she already found herself some 4-F who will fill her empty evenings for her?"

Jenks seemed to have an uncanny ability to sense what would hurt a person most at any given moment. Nick started to seriously consider shooting the boatswain. "Are we ready for sea?"

"Just about. They're putting the engine box back together now. But the fog is starting to roll in. Don't you think it might be better to wait until morning, sir?"

Nick had been considering doing just that as he walked down the dock and saw the lights on the other shore growing more indistinct. But he couldn't resist striking back at the bastard. "Afraid to go to sea in the dark, Boats?"

"Hell, no. But I don't want to wind up hanging on Race Rock."

"We aren't going anywhere near Race Rock. Of course, if you're really scared you could take the Orient Point Ferry and meet us in Greenport. I don't know if that will help your image of a tough old sea dog, though."

"If you've got the balls to go out on a night like this, so have I."

"You know what they say, Boats, you have to go out, but you don't have to come back." Nick thought, *You're letting this son of a bitch and your disappointment at not reaching Amy provoke you.* Then he thought, *What the hell, there's a war on.*

"How did you make out with Langdon, Boats?"

"He knows how to pull on a halyard and he didn't drop me, but I still have my doubts about him."

"Keep those doubts to yourself. If you breathe one word of them, you're off the boat and on your way to Lake Poop. Get the sails ready to hoist and the lines singled up. I'll tell the duty officer that we're leaving."

"I don't think we're going to do much sailing tonight. There's not much of a breeze."

"And what there is, is puffy and all over the place. This may turn out to be a motorboat ride. We should have plenty of gas."

"Plenty, sir. I dumped the stuff I cleaned the BAR with in the tank because you told me not to dump it overboard. I'm sure glad we have all those filters, sir."

Nick shook his head. "Boats, you'd better be kidding or you'll wind up clinging to Race Rock as you watch us sail away."

Jenks turned serious. "I still don't like the idea of leaving in this. These are a lot trickier waters than the entrance to Gloucester Harbor."

"Get the lines singled up, Boats, and get the crew to where you want them for leaving port. It might be a good idea to put a lookout on the bow."

"Should I give him a bag of potatoes, sir?"

"A bag of potatoes?"

"An old Maine trick. In a fog you have a guy on the bow throwing potatoes out in front of the boat. If he doesn't hear a splash you turn around and get the hell out of there."

It went amazingly well. From the time New London Ledge Light disappeared into the haze over the starboard quarter until they turned to port to pass through Plum Gut they saw absolutely nothing but blackness. Jenks insisted on doing the steering himself. When Nick, having run down his time, pulled one piece of tape off the binnacle and replaced it with another and told him to turn, the boatswain started to show his nervousness. They were running at about six knots, still on the engine. With a five-knot tide pushing them, it felt as if they were going about ninety miles an hour. Finally Jenks told Langdon to steer and pushed past Nick to go below. When the red light over the chart table came on, Nick looked down the hatch and saw him staring at the chart.

He looked up and saw Nick watching him. "There's a gong buoy on Great Eastern Rock in the middle of Plum Gut. If we're where you think we are, we should have seen it or heard it by now."

"I know right where it is, Boats. Don't worry about it."

"Yeah. Well, where the hell is that buoy then?"

"It's just the other side of the head stay and we should see it or hear it in..." Nick looked at his watch, "in, oh, about three minutes or so."

AUGUST 2008

"WAS IT, GRANDPA?"

"Yup. It showed up right on time, and I'll tell you Toots, no one in the entire history of the sea was more relieved than I was when Hank Snow called back that he could hear a gong. We ran the rest of the time down on that leg and then turned to starboard for Greenport. Jenks never questioned my navigation again. He didn't understand how I had done it so he developed an almost religious faith in my skill. He was still a wiseass, but navigation was one subject we never had to discuss again."

"Was it really all that mysterious or difficult, Grandpa?"

"Today it wouldn't be. But back then we didn't have GPS or Loran or radar. Big ships were running aground all the time. A week later a freighter ran up on Long Sand Shoal. We had a compass, a watch, a chart, and tide tables. It was pretty mysterious to the uninitiated that anyone could find his way around on a dark, foggy night. Anyway, the only person who was more amazed than Jenks, when that buoy showed up, was me, and like every lucky navigator in history, I didn't show it at all. We dropped the hook in the outer harbor behind the Greenport breakwater and stayed there until morning. I didn't feel like pushing my luck any further. At dawn we motored into the inner harbor, the Sterling Basin, where the Coast Guard Station was."

FEBRUARY 1942

NICK REPORTED TO LT. COMMANDER NEWTON as soon as they were tied up. "You came over from New London last night in the soup?"

"Yes, sir. It was an uneventful trip."

"But a dumb one."

"Yes, sir, I suppose you could call it that." Nick could not quite suppress a smile when he said it.

"Tell me, Worth, who were you trying to impress? Me, your

crew, or yourself? The last thing I need is a goddamned show-off."

Nick's first reaction was anger at being called on the carpet for a superb piece of navigation. But then he noticed just how tired Newton looked. Although he was a relatively young man, his face was gray and the skin of his cheeks and under his eyes sagged. The man was obviously past mere exhaustion. "It was an uneventful trip, sir. I didn't expect any problems and we didn't have any."

"Look, Worth, no one doubts your piloting skills. But did you consider that a sub out of New London might have run you down and hardly noticed? The water is thick with them. Every time somebody spots one we have to go running around looking for it to make sure it's not a U-boat. You obviously had all the piloting problems solved. But did you consider the chance of collision?"

"We were showing proper running lights, sir, and keeping a sharp lookout."

"Terrific. Did you know that there's a war on and others might not be showing proper running lights or might not notice yours in the fog? Particularly the scared freighters that are sneaking into the Sound to avoid the U-boats?"

"No, sir, I didn't consider that." It was then that Nick realized that Newton was right and so had Jenks been. His brilliant piece of navigation was a dumb adolescent stunt. He fell back on what he had learned in OCS. "No excuse, sir. And yes, I guess I was trying to impress everyone, myself included. It was inexcusable."

"Okay, Worth. At this point in the war we're all learning. I just hope we learn enough before we lose it. Use your head and think of all the possibilities the next time. That's the tough part: considering all the possibilities without scaring yourself so silly that you can't do anything. And when you're on patrol, please don't show proper running lights." Then he changed the subject, to Nick's great relief. For a minute he had thought he was the one who was going to be kicked off the boat. "You've got a medic?"

"I don't think I'd call him a medic. He had a five-day course that seemed to be at about the same level as the Boy Scout's first aid merit badge."

"Bandaging wounds will come in handy, but he shouldn't have to set any bones. Any survivors that need serious medical help are brought to New London. Better facilities. The bad cases can be taken to Grace-New Haven Hospital on special trains from there. Sit down, Worth."

"Thank you, sir."

"Mostly your job will be finding and rescuing survivors. Our few cutters and destroyers have better things to do. Besides, the Krauts have been known to hang around a sinking and then torpedo any ship that stops to pick up survivors. The Brits warned us about this and now we're seeing it for ourselves. The hope is they won't think you're worth a torpedo, and won't want to surface and shoot you because you've got a radio. At least that's the theory. You'll let us know if we're wrong, won't you?" He gave a wan, exhausted smile.

"Just as soon as I get a chance, sir."

"Other than the burned victims, those who went into the water are the worst cases. The Krauts are concentrating on tankers and the water is always full of oil. Of course with the water temperature in the low fifties, if they stay in the water they don't last long. It's the ones who go in the water and then get into a lifeboat or onto a Carley raft that are in the worst shape. Being soaked in that oil is truly a terrible way to die. The only thing worse are the burned ones. We have a doctor here who served in the last war, and he'll give you and your whole crew, not just the medic, a talk on how to treat those poor bastards who are suffering from oil poisoning."

"Yes, sir."

"He'll also give you the medical supplies you need and explain them. At least, what supplies we have. When you pick up survivors, we'll try to get a power craft to you to run them into New London fast, but every situation as to location and what's available is different. We have to play it by ear."

"What about the dead, sir?"

"Pick them up, too, and sink any lifeboats and bring the Carley floats back if you can. Those things are full of cork so you can't sink them, and if you leave them drifting around they just cause more false alarms. How much water tankage do you have?"

"Forty-five gallons, same as fuel."

"We've found that a seven-man crew can get by on about three gallons a day. At least in the winter. We'll give you three extra five-gallon cans; where you store them is your problem. That will give you two weeks cruising with a cushion and some extra water for treating survivors. You'll go out for ten days on station to begin with. We'll also give you an extra five gallons of gas. That's in case your main tank springs a leak or gets contaminated. I would recommend against storing that below. How about kerosene for the cabin heater and stove?"

"A twelve-gallon tank under a bunk."

"You'll have to make do with that. It's enough to cook with and occasionally heat up the cabin if it gets so cold and clammy you can't stand it anymore."

"Food, sir?"

"You have an ice box?"

"It takes about a fifty-pound block."

"Well, get what you can find for fresh stuff, although there isn't much to be had this time of year. For the rest, it will be mostly cans. The quartermaster has a seventeen-day package you'll be issued." Then he smiled a very tired smile. "Your boat should be right down on her lines by the time you're loaded, Mr. Worth."

"The doctor?"

"You and your crew have an appointment with kindly old Doc Brace at one this afternoon, if nothing comes up."

AUGUST 2008

"**WAS A QUICK,** one afternoon lecture from a doctor of any use, Grandpa? Nowadays you'd get at least a month's training before they'd let you treat anyone."

"Yeah, but most of that would be on how to protect yourself from tort lawyers. Doc Brace was a distinguished-looking man with a full head of gray-black hair who looked every bit as exhausted as Commander Newton did. By the time the meeting was over I understood that the exhaustion was not just from the long hours, it was from having to live with the unrelenting pressure of their responsibilities and with what they saw. Even when they found time to sleep, they probably couldn't. That was the first time that I realized, really realized, Amy, that there was a war on and what that meant.

"When we were settled in a room in the base infirmary Brace introduced himself and said, 'Okay, you all learned to give artificial respiration in boot camp, so I'm not going to go through that again.'"

"Artificial respiration? Is that what they called CPR back then, Grandpa?"

"Nope. We didn't have CPR. In artificial respiration you lay the person on his stomach, place your hands just below his bottom ribs, and then repeatedly push at a normal breathing rate."

"Did it work?"

"Not nearly as well as CPR, but then I don't know if I'd want to give CPR to someone who is about to barf up crude oil."

"Grandpa, that's disgusting."

"War is disgusting. Particularly war that burns people and puts them in an oil slick. The oil was the worst problem."

"Swallowing it must have been horrible."

"We were issued restaurant-size cans of evaporated milk. If you're swimming in an oil slick you don't swallow much of it and the lining of the digestive track is pretty tough. What killed most of them was the fumes. Heavy crude was bad enough, but lighter distillates were even worse. The fumes attacked the throat and lungs and there was no escaping them. Distillate fumes are as bad as poison gas. Most of those poor guys could not stop coughing until they died. Even those who survived were debilitated for life, just like what the mustard gas did to Mr. Gray."

"Wasn't there any way you could treat it?"

"They gave us a big jug of surgical green soap and we washed off their heads and chests, but we couldn't wash it out of their eyes with that soap. All we could do was rinse them as best we could. Some of them were blinded for life."

"So you did rescue survivors."

"Oh, yeah. The Hooligan Navy, even those of us that never saw a U-boat, rescued a lot of survivors, thousands. But it was no picnic."

"Did you ever see a U-boat, Grandpa?"

"Oh, yeah."

NINE

"**AMY, IT'S YOUR YOUNG MAN.**" No one had ever called him that before, either. It was eight-thirty that evening.

"Hi, Nick, I just got in."

"Out dancing?"

"Hardly. Working. I'm in the personnel department and we're hiring like crazy. The Navy is mad to get this new fighter plane we're going to make. It's called the Corsair."

"Named after the Corsair Fleet?"

"No, then it would be called the Hooligan. You know, that wouldn't be a bad name for a fighter plane either. How are you, Nick? I'm sorry I missed your call last night. I must have been on my way home when you called. How's the boat and the crew?"

"They want me to thank you for the cake. We devoured it on the way down the Sound. I've really lucked out on the crew. They're pretty green, but smart and willing. I just hope I'm good enough for this. Sometimes I think I'm in way over my head."

"Everybody thinks they're way in over their head, Nick. I know I do. A month ago I was a useless debutante, now I'm helping to staff a plant that will make airplanes that are essential to the war effort." There was a silence on the phone long enough so she asked, "Are you still there?"

"Yeah, I'm still here. Amy, I am capable of doing really dumb things. I've always suspected that, but repressed it. Now I can't hide it anymore, either from myself or from other people."

"As long as you admit it, you'll do fine. I know it."

"I've got a boat, six guys, and an important job for the first time in my life, and I don't have my grandfather or anyone else to back me up." Again he was silent, so she let him take his time. "Amy, you're the only person I can talk to. My whole life I've been dead sure of myself, sure that what I wanted to do made sense, even when it didn't. Last night I did something really important and really stupid, and didn't even realize how stupid it was until someone told me this morning. I was proud of it until my new boss explained to me just how stupid it was."

"What did you do, for God's sake?"

"I brought the boat from New London to Greenport in the middle of a foggy night because I knew I could do it. We could have been run down by one of the subs that are always going in and out of New London. Or by a freighter running down the Sound to duck the U-boats. But I was so fixated on solving the navigation problems that I didn't even consider that possibility."

"What did Roscoe Jenks do?"

"He warned me not to do it, but I ignored him because he's such a sarcastic SOB. Besides, he can barely read a chart and I'm the greatest navigator since Prince Henry. What could he know?"

"Did he warn you about the danger of collision?"

"No, but when he started to warn me I did such a good job of belittling him that he just shut up. I told him if he was afraid to sail across the Sound in the dark, maybe he should take the ferry. I was just so absolutely sure of myself. Amy, I'm the skipper; the old and most precise name for this job was master and commander. I always thought that sounded great and it's what I always wanted to be, even if it is only a fifty-four-foot schooner. Now I'm afraid there's no way I can do this job. I feel like some little kid wearing an adult's clothes and hoping no one will notice. I don't have my grandfather looking out for me and telling me what to watch out for."

"Maybe you do. Did you ever think of that? Maybe he's inside your head someplace, Nick. All you have to do is shut up and listen to him. Think about it." She paused to let that sink in. "Where are you? Can you tell me?"

"It's hardly a military secret. Greenport. We'll be home-ported here."

"Great. I could come and see you sometime. The ferry from Bridgeport to Port Jefferson is still running."

The operator interrupted and he had to deposit another quarter for another three minutes. "Maybe sometime. We'll probably be out a lot, and you're working a lot."

"I'll check on the train and ferry schedules. I've been hoarding what little gas I'm allotted by walking back and forth to work. If you're in port when I can get some time off, I'll come see you one way or another. Where can I write to you in the meantime?"

AUGUST 2008

"**DID SHE, GRANDPA?** Come see you and write to you every day? Tender yet passionate letters like in one of those old black and white World War Two movies?"

"Hell, no. She was too busy, and so was I, to do much more than write letters that sounded like they came from summer camp: I am good, how are you? Mostly we talked on the phone when we were in port, which wasn't often. We were out on patrol as much as possible."

"That's disappointing. I was hoping you had saved the letters, carefully tied with a ribbon, and one day I could read all the fiery details of my grandparents' mad love affair."

They both laughed, and he replied, "I'm sorry to disappoint you, Toots. We were too busy being members of the greatest generation. You, my dear, are obviously a member of the oversexed generation."

"Did she come and see you in Greenport?"

"Still digging for the sordid details, are you? She came to New London for a couple of days that summer, but a lot happened before that."

"Oh, what?"

"A lot."

FEBRUARY 1942

COMMANDER NEWTON'S YEOMAN came down the dock, climbed around the supplies piled there and in the cockpit, and said to Nick, who was supervising the loading, "The boss wants to see you when you get a chance, Mister Worth." This was the military equivalent of, "Get your ass in here right now," in the civilian world.

"You wanted to see me, sir?"

He waved Nick into a chair. "How's it going?"

"We're getting there. That's a lot of stuff they gave us."

"More than a Bermuda Race, huh? Did you draw any navigation gear in New London? We can't give you a chronometer. Not enough to go around. Do you have a good watch? We'll give you a time tick by radio four times a day. The list in the back of the codebook tells you how many minutes and seconds to add or subtract from it to get the correct time."

"I have my own chronometer, sir, but I'll use the time ticks to check its rate. I brought my own sextant, too."

"Good. We have barely enough to go around. What about binoculars. Did they have any to give you in New London? We're asking civilians to turn theirs in."

"They tried to give me a pair of 10 by 30 birdwatcher's glasses, but I brought my own 7 by 50s. I've got two pairs. Zeiss. Really good ones."

"That's another technology where the Krauts are way ahead of us. Keep them. We're trying to give the offshore boats two pairs because you have no radar or sound equipment. We're supposed to start getting some hydrophones soon. We'll install them on the bigger yachts first."

He paused and rubbed his already reddened eyes with the heels of his hands. "Your only way of finding anything at sea is the eyes of your crew. I cannot emphasize enough the importance of keeping a sharp all-around lookout, particularly at night. The U-boats prefer to operate on the surface at night. They're a lot faster than when submerged; they don't have to worry about their batteries and they're almost as invisible. Just the small silhouette of the conning tower.

"They've also taken to using their deck guns more in order to save torpedoes. It's a long way back to France for more, unless they can hook up with a supply ship. We'd really like to catch one of those."

"Sir, I'd like to run something past you because I don't want to make any more dumb mistakes. This is a whole different ball game for me."

"Okay, shoot."

"I'm planning on using three, two-man watches, sir, with the cook standing out of the watch and me pulling one. Besides the cooking he'll pull radio watch when my radioman is standing deck watch. He's from Oklahoma and green as grass. Until he gets some seagoing experience I thought that would be the best way to handle it. I'll vary the length of the watches depending on weather conditions and have the helmsman and the lookout swap every thirty minutes so neither gets bored or sloppy."

"Sounds okay. What about sail changes?"

"We'll try to do them at the change of watch whenever possible. Otherwise, Jenks and I will help."

"Is that the system you used when racing?"

"Naah. Everybody did everything they could to make the boat go fast and grabbed what sleep they could when they could. Being able to stay on station for two weeks is a different ball game."

"That system may work. If it doesn't, then change it. You

understand the radio drill?"

"Maintain a twenty-four-hour watch and call in our best estimated position, course, and speed twice a day. The book gives the times and frequencies so the Germans won't be able to get our position by radio direction finding."

"Yeah, although if they aren't any better at it than we are, it won't do them much good. Look at this." He handed Nick a typed sheet. "These are the precise latitudes and longitudes of subs the Navy has located by RDF right down to a tenth of a degree."

Nick studied the page. "I see what you mean. Each of them says that the sub is suspected to be within either a hundred or two hundred-mile radius of that precise position. There's one that might be within a fifty-mile radius, though." He did a quick mental calculation. "That's only about two thousand square miles. That really narrows it down compared to the others."

"Keep a very sharp lookout, Mr. Worth. You do have one advantage in this game of blind man's bluff. When you're under sail, the Krauts can't hear you. When you're charging your radio batteries they'll be able to hear your engine, though. I'd suggest charging them at midday when they'd be able to see you anyway."

Newton got up and motioned Nick to join him at the drafting table in the corner. Pinned to it was a chart of the eastern seaboard with the locations of sinkings, oil slicks, and survivors as well as U-boat sightings. It was covered with marks and labels. "Back in January, when this first started, most of the attacks were out toward the edge of the continental shelf because that's were the ships were. As you can see, they got lots of ships. So we ordered them in closer to shore and the U-boats followed them. That also made the hot spots more concentrated. Here, from Hatteras to Cape Lookout, and here along the Jersey coast and the approaches to New York. That does not mean that other areas are immune. I'm sending you here, to grid KL612. It's about a hundred and thirty miles southwest of Montauk and sixty miles east-northeast of Atlantic City in the approaches to

New York. If you pick up any survivors, where you land them will depend on where you are. When will you be ready for sea?"

"Probably tomorrow morning."

"Not in the dark of night?"

"At first light, sir."

AUGUST 2008

"So, Grandpa, how was your first patrol area?"

"We never got there."

"Huh? What happened?"

FEBRUARY 1942

THEY CLEARED MONTAUK around noon with the last of the ebb pushing them, and turned southwest with a light easterly breeze driving them under a heavily overcast sky. There was a long ground swell from the east, so the schooner, despite being heeled down by all plain sail, rolled as she reached the top of each swell, then started down the next. It reminded Nick of a line from a Kipling poem: "*It's up and over with a wiggle between, and the steward falls into the soup tureen.*"

Just as Jenks had predicted, Slade was as sick as Nick had ever seen any person, except his father, be seasick before. He lay in the cockpit, at first vomiting over the lee side, and then dry heaving. Langdon and Snow ignored him as best they could as they did exactly what Nick had told them to do. He had bought a kitchen timer, and every half hour when it went off, they would swap positions between steering and keeping a sharp lookout all around. When they changed over, the man who had been steering noted the compass course he had been steering and the reading on the mechanical log mounted on the after deck. It was actuated by a towed impeller.

He sent a report when they turned Montauk. With no chance of getting a sun sight, Nick could only give his DR position in the report he was scheduled to send at 1722 that afternoon. He wondered what to do about Slade. He was afraid the man would injure himself by the recurring violent dry heaves that wracked his body. He went below to get him some water and some dry crackers that he had heard somewhere were good for seasickness. When he came on deck, Jenks was leaning over Slade saying, "Careful now, Cookie. If you feel something that tastes like a hairy donut coming up, swallow quick. It's your asshole."

Jenks then looked around as if he expected either laughter or applause. Once more Nick considered shooting him. "That's a really big help, Boats. Here, Cookie, eat these, and drink some water. Then keep looking at the horizon."

Slade lifted his head, took one bite of a cracker and a sip of water, and asked, "Will that help?"

"It's supposed to."

"I have to make lunch."

The idea of lunch set him to heaving again so Nick said, "I'll put something together. No, I've got a better idea. Boats will do it as penance for his last comment. There's bread and peanut butter. Try not to overcook it."

As he went below, Jenks said, "Didn't I tell you? Isn't this just what I said would happen?"

The shore of Long Island was just a barely distinguishable gray bump on the horizon when Nick plotted their 1700 DR position, double-checked it and gave it to Borg to encode and send on the required frequency at the required time. By then he had bundled Slade below and tucked him into his bunk because his teeth had started to chatter. Maybe if he got to sleep he'd be all right when he woke up.

Nick had never heard of anyone actually dying of seasickness, but there was a first time for everything and Slade looked like a good candidate. If he wasn't better in another day or two Nick knew he would be faced with a difficult decision.

That evening the wind veered into the southeast so they were on a close reach by midnight when Nick, after again plotting their DR position, climbed into his bunk, hoping to get a couple of hours of sleep. He had just nodded off, still thinking about what to do with his seasick cook, when Borg shook him. "Skipper, I just got an *Operational Immediate* with our call sign."

Nick dragged himself to consciousness. "Huh? What? Operational immediate? Us?"

"Skipper, are you awake? Should I read it to you?"

"Yeah, yeah. What's it say?" He swung his legs out of the bunk and sat up.

"Operational immediate. Aircraft reported oil slick at 1820 hrs. EWT, 22 February 42. Bearing 115 True, distance seventy-two miles from Ambrose Buoy. Investigate." It's signed with Commander Newton's code group for the present date and time."

By then Nick was bending over the chart table. "115 True?"

"115 True, seventy-two miles from the Ambrose Buoy."

"That's twenty-two miles southeast of us." He moved his parallel rule to the compass rose, then wrote *143 Mag* on a piece of white adhesive tape, stepped into his sea boots, and went up the ladder into the cockpit. Over his shoulder he said, "Send 'will comply'."

Langdon and Snow were on watch. "Bring her up onto the wind, Snow. Try for 143 degrees magnetic, but I don't think she'll sail nearly that high." Nick started to haul in the main sheet and Langdon did the same with the foresail as Jenks appeared in the hatch and went forward to tighten the staysail.

The boat's motion changed radically. Instead of lazily working her way up and over the ground swell and the waves that were running with it, she now heeled down and began to fight her way up each swell and through the wind-driven waves on top of them. Nick checked the compass. She was sailing a little bit better than due south, but not much.

Jenks came into the cockpit. He was wearing his oilskins and Nick wished he had taken the time to put on his own. Spray was now being blown aft in sheets. "If she has to fight her way through this shit, Skipper, she's gonna need more sail to do it."

"Yup. Set the jib."

Longo had also come on deck without being called. He, too, was wearing oilskins. Jenks said to him, "Come on, Joe. You can help me fall off the widow-maker." The jib was hoisted from the end of the bowsprit that was periodically plowing through the head of a breaking wave.

Other than the white of the bow wave and the occasional breaking sea, it was as black as if they were sailing inside a cloud of oil. When the jib was set, Longo and Jenks came aft. Nick sent the other two below and then ducked below himself to get dressed for battle. When he came back on deck in his oilskins, Jenks, who was steering, said. "She'll go about 175. If I pinch her any higher than that, she can't get through the slop and slows right down."

Nick looked at the log on the stern rail. "I wouldn't trust that. The impeller keeps coming out of the water. I'd guess we're doing better than six, but it always seems like you're going like a bat out of hell when you're going to weather in the dark."

Nick went below to the chart table and when he returned said, "We'll hold onto this until 0400, then go about. That slick, if it was where it was supposed to be at 1800 last night, should be moving north in this wind and I don't want to overshoot it. We ought to be about where it should be around dawn. Is that precise enough for you, Boats?"

"Whatever you say, Mr. Worth."

AUGUST 2008

"**WERE YOU RIGHT, GRANDPA?** Did you find the oil slick?"

"That and a lot more. The wind kept rising and it started to rain. At two o'clock we had the jib off her again and a little while after that we put a reef in the main. It was a wet, wild, wonderful ride. We tacked on schedule and an hour or so later smelled oil. That's when the fun—and with it my youth—ended."

She decided not to question that last statement. If he wanted to clarify it he would.

He sat in silence with his eyes closed for a while and then kept them closed when he said, "You know, Toots, like you said before, everybody thinks of World War Two in black and white because of those old movies. But most of my part of it, as I remember it now, really was in black and white. Dirty gray ships and boats. Gray sky, gray sea, canvas sails weathered gray, and everything else either the white of breaking seas or the black of oil."

TEN

FEBRUARY 1942

AS PLANNED, THEY TACKED AT 0400. An hour later the faintest gray light of dawn was just starting to illuminate the slick as they sailed into it. The wind-blown chop on top of the ground swell stopped as if someone had turned off a switch. The wind remained steady at twenty to twenty-five knots, but the oil smothered the chop completely. The white-topped gray of the breaking waves disappeared and the surface of the sea became a slowly rising and falling shiny black syrup. Slade came on deck as Borg asked, "You hear that? It sounded like someone coughing."

Slade answered him, "Survivors."

They all heard it now: several people coughing off the port bow. Then in the gathering light they saw two Carley floats tied together. They were black with oil and filled with people who were also black with oil. Longo asked, "You want the engine, Skipper?"

Nick thought about it for just a second before saying, "No. Let's do this quietly under sail in case someone's listening. Boats, get everything off her but the foresail. Langdon, you and Snow help him." He took the helm. "Longo, Borg, don't take your eyes off those rafts for one second; I don't want to lose sight of them now." Slade seemed to be over his seasickness. "Cookie, get the first aid stuff laid out on the foredeck. That's the best place, I guess. At least there's no spray coming aboard now."

As the sail handlers moved forward he spun the wheel and

said, "Coming up," and brought the boat up into the wind. An ancient phrase came to mind and he used it without embarrassment. "Handsomely, now."

When the main and staysail were furled, he spun the wheel again and headed for a point just alee of the rafts. As Langford tied down the main and Snow did the same to the staysail, Jenks said, "We may have to hoist somebody aboard." He rigged a sling onto the main halyard.

Slade pushed an arm full of blankets and rags through the hatch into the cockpit, then handed up the first aid kit, the green soap, and a couple of buckets of water. "We have to get that oil off them, at least off their heads and necks."

Nick replied, "I'm glad to see you're feeling better."

"The fumes and the shock are what will kill them. We have to get the oil off them, and get them warm and out of this drizzle." He was all business and seemed to have forgotten his own earlier sickness.

Nick was doing calculations in his head: the boat's speed and leeway in the stiff breeze, the wind's speed and direction, the direction of the rafts' drift. The survivors had finally seen them and two of them separated themselves from the black coughing mass and started to wave. "We'll take them aboard on the starboard side, Boats. Get a line on those rafts first thing."

Jenks had already moved amidships on the starboard side. He held up a coil of half-inch line and said, "Yes, sir, Mister Worth, sir. I'm glad you told me that, sir. You just get them alongside."

The survivors were waving and yelling frantically now, afraid that the schooner was going to sail right past them. When he reached the point he had selected, Nick brought the boat up into the wind and watched her speed trail off as she approached the Carley floats. She was almost stopped when Langdon used a boat hook to grab and lift the rope that hung in loops around the edge of the leading raft. Jenks, lying on the deck, reached down and passed his line through it and secured it to a deck cleat. Then the hard part began.

Nick kept the boat hove to as the first two survivors, those who had waved, were helped aboard and forward to Slade's aid station on the foredeck. He handed each of them a rag soaked with soapy water with which to clean their faces, hair, hands, and arms. When they had the worst of the oil off, he gave each of them a blanket and sent them aft to the cockpit to go below. One of them went below but the other quietly sat down in the cockpit like he was waiting for a bus or something. Nick asked, "You're the captain?"

"Yes, but you're busy. I'll wait until you have a moment free."

By then two more men had been lifted from the floats and led forward. One of them was able to sponge himself weakly, but the other collapsed with a coughing fit and Slade had to clean him off. He did it with an amazing gentleness while talking to the poor man in a soothing voice. The last three in the rafts were neither coughing nor moving. Snow climbed down and checked them. "This one is still breathing, barely, but the other two are dead." He hitched the halyard sling around the man's body under his arms and supported him as Jenks hoisted him and Longo swung him aboard, freed him from the sling, and then carried him forward. Snow, who was still in the float, asked, "What do you want to do with the dead, Skipper?"

"Get them aboard too. We're supposed to bring in everyone we find, dead or alive. Then get the floats aboard too. Tie the first one to the cabin top, put the dead guys in it, then tie the other raft on top of it. I think there'll be room under the fore boom. I hope there'll be room." There was not quite enough room for the boom to swing across the boat until Jenks, with two of the others helping, hoisted the throat and peak halyards a bit higher than normal.

The captain, who had been sitting quietly in the cockpit between occasional fits of coughing with a sodden blanket wrapped around him, now lifted his head. As Nick let the boat pay off, the man held out his hand. "Captain McKay." He pronounced it *McKey*. "Captain, I can't express my gratitude."

Nick shook the still-filthy hand. "Ensign Worth. Part of the job.

What ship, Captain?"

"*Cayuna.* 6200-ton tanker. Panamanian registry on charter to English Petroleum. We were on passage from Galveston to St. Johns to join a convoy to the U.K."

It was full daylight now, gray drizzly daylight, and Nick still had a dozen things to think of at once. "Excuse me, Captain." The rafts and the dead were secured on the cabin top now. "Boats, can you get up to the gaff jaws? There may be more survivors."

"You mean climb the parrels that hold the foresail to the mast? Of course I can. What do you think I am, a yachtsman?"

Nick ignored Jenks' reflexive needle. "Take a pair of glasses with you. Borg, get your message pad."

McKay said, "I don't think there are any more survivors. We got hit by two torpedoes, bang, bang, and she broke in half. The only people who got off were those of us in the deckhouse and on the bridge. The rear half sank right out from under us in less than two minutes. I don't think anyone in the engine room or in the crew cabins got out."

"When were you hit?"

"About three yesterday afternoon. We heard a plane just before sunset but didn't think they saw us."

"They didn't. They reported the slick, though." The last of the living survivors were being helped below. "Have them sit on the cabin sole." Two dead men and two Carley floats on the cabin top wouldn't help the schooner's stability. The best place for five extra men was amidships and as low as possible. "Why don't you go below and get warm, Captain?"

AUGUST 2008

"DID YOU FIND ANY MORE SURVIVORS, Grandpa?"

"No. Just two more bodies floating in life jackets. We took them aboard too. When we found the first survivors we radioed in and were told to continue searching until noon. A plane came out to help and circled the area but they didn't find anyone else either.

"Just before noon I ducked below to work out my best guess as to our dead reckoning position. The chart, the hatch, the ladder, the cabin sole, and just about everything else were soiled with oil from the survivors and the crew as they climbed below. All I could think about was that the whole damned boat was going to be an oil-soaked mess and how we'd ever get it clean again. I couldn't seem to get my mind to focus on what I was trying to do and had to force it to recall what courses we had steered since the last DR plot."

"You mentioned EWT. What was that?"

"Eastern War Time. It was double daylight savings time. I've never been able to understand the purpose. There weren't any more daylight hours. But I suppose someone in Washington thought it was a good idea. At least it helped to remind everyone, every day, that there was a war on."

FEBRUARY 1942

HE STARED BLANKLY AT THE CHRONOMETER in its box on the shelf over his bunk and was having trouble deciding what it showed when it dawned on him that he had been awake since before they left Greenport yesterday—or was it the day before yesterday? He knew that most of the mistakes made by competent navigators were made when they were exhausted. He worked out a rough position, checked it four times, and corrected it twice before he was reasonably sure it was right. He checked the chronometer again and realized that a job he would normally do in a minute or two had taken twenty.

As he was doing it, Snow came out of the main cabin and handed him a message slip and a glass of cream-colored liquid. "Here you go, Skipper. A late breakfast."

"What is it?"

"Eggnog. Non-alcoholic eggnog. Slade made a couple of gallons of it to feed to the survivors. He said it would help to push the oil through their pipes. It's pretty good. They're all asleep and there's plenty left."

"How's Slade doing?"

"He's sick again. Once he had washed and fed them and done everything he could for them, he cleaned himself up as best he could and climbed into his bunk. A couple of minutes later he started to retch again."

Nick read the message. "Return toward New London. *Eagle Boat 19* will meet you to take survivors aboard." He dictated a will-comply message with his updated DR position for Borg to send to Greenport. As he was doing it he remembered that he hadn't entered anything in the log.

Jenks had just come down from the mast, where he had been while they searched, and Nick told him, "We're supposed to head for New London and an Eagle Boat will meet us. Get sail on the boat and get her headed northwest while I work out a more precise course."

Jenks took the wheel, headed the boat up toward the wind and yelled, "Come on guys, let's get the main on her." When it was up he let her pay off and then ordered the staysail hoisted as Nick came up and stuck a piece of adhesive tape to the binnacle.

AUGUST 2008

"WHAT WAS AN EAGLE BOAT, GRANDPA?"

The old man smiled as he explained, "The Tin Lizzy of the sea. They were built by Henry Ford in Detroit near the end of the first war, and were supposed to be better than the wooden sub-chasers the navy was then using to hunt U-boats. They were about 200 feet long and sort of a slab-sided box with one pointy end nailed on. They looked exactly like a ship designed by some guy from Michigan who had designed the Model T. The navy didn't want the damn things, so guess who they gave them to.

"Did they manage to find you and meet you?"

"The wind was over the quarter, Toots, and when we left the oil slick that was starting to break up at the edges, we again entered the white-capped seas. The waves were running in the same direction as the swell and it was the schooner's fastest point of sail. The speedo said we were doing over nine knots as she climbed the backs of the rollers, and sometimes eleven when sliding down them if the swell and the chop happened to coincide and reinforce each other.

"The true wind was blowing about twenty-five, but with the speed of the boat subtracted from it, because we were running away from it, to us it was just a perfect fifteen- to twenty-knot Force Five sailing breeze. The Eagle Boat had it on the nose, so to them it was twenty-five knots plus the twelve knots or so they were trying to make as they plugged into the seas. To them it was a Force 8 gale.

"It had started to clear up when we left the slick so I was able to get a series of running sun sights and send a position, course, and speed message every four hours but we didn't see any Eagle Boat or any other ships until almost noon the next day when the coast of Long Island was just starting to solidify along the horizon. Then we saw a slab-sided dirty gray ship fighting its way toward us with obvious difficulty."

"Did you transfer the survivors?"

"No. The Eagle Boat captain and I shouted back and forth and decided it was too rough. He had a hard time keeping up with us. When Ford built them they were supposed to be able to do sixteen knots. By the spring of 1942, between their fouled bottoms and worn-out machinery, about twelve was the very best they could do in flat water. Anyway, we went into New London instead of Greenport. They're both about the same distance from Montauk and we rode a fair tide all the way."

FEBRUARY 1942

AMBULANCES WERE WAITING FOR THEM. So was the huge job of cleaning up the boat. The oil had found its way everywhere, from the gaff of the foresail where Jenks had dragged it when he went aloft, to the bilges. They used the surgeon's green soap and a mountain of rags to clean it up. Nick didn't know what was worse, the smell of the oil or of the green soap that now permeated the boat.

Slade, being the smallest, drew the claustrophobic job of going under the cabin sole and cleaning the oil out of the bilges. He had done it well and without complaint and was cleaning the galley when Nick called him aside. "Let's take a walk up the dock, Peter."

When they were out of earshot of those working on deck, Nick said, "Look, Cookie, you did a fine job taking care of those poor people. No one could have done better. And you provided us with good meals on the trip back. The eggnog was terrific."

"My mother used to make it for the guys coming off the oil rigs if they had swallowed any of the stuff."

"That's right. You grew up around the Oklahoma oil rigs, didn't you? Anyway, no one can fault the job you did, but I've never seen anybody who was so seasick for so long. You were still barfing periodically when we were back in Long Island Sound even if you never let it interfere with your job. If you want me to try to find you a shore job, I will."

"Mr. Worth, are you kicking me off the boat?"

"No, of course not."

"Look. Other than the first couple of days I was able to control it and not let it stop me from doing what I had to do. When Borg is off duty, he lies there listening to the big bands on your big *Zenith* radio over his bunk. Snow reads the engine overhaul manual. Jenks prowls the boat looking for anything that's not right and someone to insult. What they do when they're not on watch is their business. Well, if I want to lie in my bunk, being miserable and occasionally throwing up, that's my business. One thing I found out on this trip is that I'm pretty good at my job and I want to keep doing it." Then he smiled. "There's a war on, you know.

AUGUST 2008

"**It took three or four days** to clean up the boat and provision it, if I remember correctly."

"Did you see Grandma?"

"Nope, we were both too busy. We talked on the phone every day, though. Her brother was trying to get her to quit her job and come to New York to act as his hostess. He was angling for some important government job regulating Wall Street, and entertaining bigwigs was part of his campaign. Besides, he thought that working in a factory was demeaning, not only to her, but to him and the whole family."

"She didn't quit, though?"

"God, no. But there was a lot of family pressure. Her mother thought that entertaining bureaucrats was far more important than helping to build fighter planes."

"So you went right back to sea. Did they send you to the same patrol area? The one you never got to before?"

"Nope. By then the center of U-boat action had moved a bit south. From the mouth of the Chesapeake to Cape Fear and from Hatteras to Cape Lookout were real hot spots."

"Did they send you that far south?"

"No, they sent us way offshore. The great circle route from the U-boats' home ports on the Bay of Biscay in France to Cape Hatteras comes right down the Canadian and U.S. coast past Cape Sable and Cape Cod. We went out a hundred miles to the edge of the continental shelf and sailed back and forth over a thirty-mile track at right angles to the expected U-boat path. They hoped we would spot one running on the surface—they ran on the surface as much as possible when on passage—and call in blimps and aircraft. We never saw anything."

"Was it boring?"

"Going from A to B in a sailboat is seldom boring, Toots, especially offshore." He thought about it in silence for a while and then said, "Once, when a bunch of us, all very experienced sailors, were sitting in the yacht club bar telling lies about offshore voyages and races, one of us said something that we all knew but no one usually admits, even to himself. He said, 'Those trips and races are wonderful to think about and plan beforehand, and great to talk about afterwards; it's just that while you're actually doing them that they are so utterly miserable.' Everyone around the table agreed with him."

"Was the weather bad?"

"Not that bad for the Atlantic, as I remember it. Considering that the time of the equinoctial storms was approaching. But it was still hard work and wet and cold most of the time. No matter how I fooled with the watch system, nobody ever got enough good sleep. Dozing in a damp bunk that smells like surgeon's green soap, while the boat bounces around in a seaway, is not conducive to good sleep. We were all tired all the time and often irritable. But the crew had shaken down by then and got along pretty well. We even learned to tolerate Jenks."

"How long were you out?"

"Usually about fifteen days on station and a couple of days or so each way going and coming."

"And then you went back to Greenport?"

"Yup. Just long enough to provision and get two decent nights' sleep. Then we went back out to the same area."

"Did you see any U-boats this time?"

"No, but there were survivors and other signs of one."

MARCH 1942

IT WAS THEIR THIRD DAY ON STATION. Nick was reducing and writing up a noon sun sight when he heard a low-flying aircraft approaching. He climbed into the cockpit as the twin-engine patrol plane turned to circle them. It was a Douglas B-18 Bolo. The copilot's window was open and as it passed them an arm came out of the window and gestured in the direction from which it had come. It turned and made a second pass repeating the same gesture.

Nick turned to Langdon, who was steering, and said, "Follow that airplane."

The boat had been on a close reach under full main, foresail, and staysail. As he let it pay off he said, "Bearing off," and Nick and Snow trimmed the sails. The plane went over the horizon, then came back to circle them once more, only this time it waggled its wings and Nick dipped the ship's colors to show that he understood.

The plane kept flying back and forth between the schooner and whatever it was leading them to for an hour or so and then with a final wing-waggle flew off toward shore. A few minutes later Jenks, who was once more standing on the foresail gaff jaws, called down, "It's a lifeboat, low in the water and right ahead."

AUGUST 2008
"WERE THERE MORE SURVIVORS, GRANDPA?"

"Not in the lifeboat. There were fifteen corpses in the lifeboat. All shot to death. The Krauts had machine-gunned the boat. The reason it was floating so low was that only the air tanks under the bow and stern thwarts hadn't been punctured."

"That's awful. Why would anyone murder people in a lifeboat who couldn't hurt them?"

"A couple of miles away we found six survivors lying on a Carley float and five more in the water hanging onto it. They had stayed alive by taking turns getting out of the water. They told us what had happened.

"They were from a freighter that had been torpedoed right at dawn by a surfaced U-boat that was to the west of them, the dark side. The U.S. Navy had started to put gun crews on freighters so they could defend themselves against surfaced U-boats. The ship got hit amidships and as it rolled over, the sun gave enough light so they could see the sub and the gun crew got off one round that hit the side of the conning tower and ricocheted off without exploding.

Then the gun crew piled into the only lifeboat they had managed to launch, along with the crewmen who had been aft. The ship was on fire amidships so the people who were forward jumped into the water, figuring the lifeboat would pick them up.

Nine of the people in the lifeboat were in the nondescript clothes merchant seamen wear, but five of them were in U.S. Navy dungarees and pea jackets. Shooting back had obviously angered the Krauts, even though the shot was a dud and had done no discernable damage. The master race didn't approve of people shooting back. Everybody was supposed to line up and be marched off to the gas chambers in a properly disciplined manner."

"After all these years, you still haven't completely forgiven the Germans, have you, Grandpa?"

"Churchill said that the German is either at your feet or at your throat. That generation of Germans swallowed that master race crap and then tried to shove it down everybody else's throat. Anyone who wouldn't swallow it they killed. Or tried to. We never found out if the Krauts hadn't seen the people in the water and the float or if they had seen them and left them alive so they would warn everyone else not to shoot back. If that was their idea, it sure didn't work."

"Did you take the survivors into New London?"

"Yup. We went into New London and then around to Noank on the Mystic River to get the boat hauled."

MARCH 1942

LIEUTENANT NELSON WAS STILL IN A WHEELCHAIR, but now there was a pair of crutches leaning against the corner of his desk. "Come in, Nick. I hear that you've been vindicating my judgment."

"I hope so, sir. We got in last night."

"What's your crew doing?"

"I let them sleep late. They were all pretty bushed."

"Being offshore in a small, short-handed boat will do that. So will finding murdered survivors. "

"I suppose you want us to go back to Greenport and get back out on patrol."

"Not right away. We're going to increase your chances of finding something. We've taken over a boatyard in Noank and they're going to haul your boat and install a couple of hydrophones. We've also gotten some 120-pound depth charges. Instead of ash cans, they look like beer kegs. Your steering gear is in a box centered against the aft bulkhead of the cockpit, isn't it? You might be able to carry one on either side of the box. That will get the weight farther forward and lower down than mounting them on the afterdeck."

"How are we supposed to launch them, sir?"

"Two men, or one really frightened man, should be able to pick one up and dump it over the side. We'll give you four of them to finally comply with the congressional mandate. Where you carry the other two is up to you.

"We want your whole crew to report to the sub school this afternoon to take a hearing acuity test. Those who pass will be given a hurry-up course in operating the hydrophones. That's not as easy as it might seem. There's a lot of noise in the ocean and telling a U-boat from a whale or a school of fish is a lot harder than you might think."

"What happens if none of my crew passes the test?"

"Then we'll have to do some shuffling."

"I'd hate to break up my crew, sir. They've shaken down nicely."

"Even Jenks and your seasick cook?"

"We've all learned how to live with Jenks, and Slade is still queasy sometimes, but it never interferes with his job."

"Well, let's see how the tests go. Those that don't pass the test can help you go around to the yard in Noank. If you need more help we'll give you someone. Maybe the chief. He'd love to go for a boat ride."

AUGUST 2008

"How many passed, Grandpa?"

"Borg, which wasn't surprising. He had aced the test before. That's why they made him a signalman in the first place."

"I thought the military only gave tests so they can be sure to assign people to jobs they can't do."

"More myths peddled by your draft-dodging professors. Snow and Slade passed, too. They went to school at the sub base the next morning while the rest of us, with the chief as a passenger, took the boat around and watched as they shored her up on the marine railway and hauled her out. Jenks was all over them making sure the yard guys, who were all older men who had done it a thousand times, did it right.

"While they washed the bottom and got the last of that damned oil off the topsides, the chief and I looked at the prop. It was a three-bladed one and we were both pretty sure we could swap it for a bigger two-bladed one we could hide behind the dead wood when we were under sail and pick up maybe a half a knot. That would make up for the added drag of the hydrophone housings. The yard had one that had obviously seen some hard use but we decided to go with it. We only used the thing for maneuvering in harbor anyway.

"The chief and I walked up to the yard office, where he phoned the base for a car to come pick him up while the yard boss and I looked through their collection of propellers in a back room. After he hung up, the chief came and told me that the car was on its way and I might want to ride back with him. I had had a call from a Mrs. Gray. Something about my father. The yeoman who had taken the call said that the lady sounded very upset. The chief said that Jenks and Longo could handle any problems that came up with the boat if I had to go home.

"When we got back to the Coast Guard base I called the house twice, but couldn't get an answer."

"What did you do, Grandpa?"

"I went to New Haven and dealt with my father. I was actually lucky, although I didn't realize it at the time. God only knows how many family problems festered for years while guys were in places where they couldn't do anything except worry about them, and I don't mean just Dear John letters."

MARCH 1942

IT WAS SEVEN O'CLOCK IN THE EVENING when he got off the train in New Haven. He showed his ID card and the two-day pass that Lt. Nelson had issued him to the M.P. who asked to see them, then phoned the Personnel Department at Chance-Vought. "Personnel. Miss Madison speaking."

"Is this the Miss Madison who didn't go to Katy Gibbs but has pretty good legs instead?"

"Nick. Where are you?"

"In the New Haven railroad station on a two-day pass. There's a problem of some sort at home."

"Look, I was just about to leave here. Where can I meet you?"

"At the house."

"What house? Marion's?"

"That's right, you've never been there. My parents' house. It's off Townsend Avenue on the east side of New Haven harbor. Just stay on Route One all the way through the city until you come to it. If you find yourself in Branford you went too far." He gave her the address. "I'll take the trolley over."

"I'll be an hour, probably more, I would guess. I have to walk over to Marion's to get the Pontiac. I've been keeping it full of gas in case you could get off."

When he got to the house he didn't go in but went around to the garage and climbed the stairs to the apartment above. He knocked and Mrs. Gray opened the door. The small living room was stacked with boxes. "What's going on, Mrs. Gray?"

"Your father fired us, Nicholas. He said you had agreed."

"This the first time I've heard of it. Why did he say he was doing it?"

"He's got a new girlfriend, and she doesn't like me. I must say, the dislike is mutual and was at first sight. If you could imagine a woman more different than your mother, that would be her. It's just as well. Mr. Gray is finding those stairs more and more difficult to climb, and I find it harder and harder to conceal my contempt for your father over the way he treated your mother that last year and the way he's behaving now."

"Don't bother to pack. No, just stop packing. You may have to move over into the main house. Is my father home? All the lights are on."

"They're having a dinner party to announce their engagement. He hired a caterer."

"Where's Mr. Gray?"

"Lying down. The tension over moving is not easy for him to handle. I'm really worried about him. When he gets tense he has trouble breathing."

"Give him my best and tell him he has absolutely nothing to worry about."

Nick went downstairs and rather than barge in and strangle his father as he wanted to do, he walked down to the harbor and stood looking out to sea for a few minutes. Then he went back to the house—his house.

ELEVEN

"I **SUPPOSE YOU LET THE GRAYS** live rent-free over the garage and gave them an allowance? That would be a reasonable compromise."

"It was 1942, Toots, and reasonable compromises had fallen into complete disfavor worldwide."

MARCH 1942

HE LET HIMSELF IN and as he hung up his coat in the entranceway he listened to the conversation going on at the dinner table. One of the guests was saying, "Here we've been in the war almost four months and we still haven't opened up a second front by landing in France. It's no wonder that Comrade Stalin is upset with us and the British. Their unwillingness to act is what you would expect, given Churchill's dislike of the Soviet Union, but Roosevelt should do better than listen to that warmongering has-been. The Russians are suffering terrible losses and we're doing nothing to help them."

The twelve people around the table all nodded in agreement. Earnest Worth summed up the consensus by saying, "I could not agree more, Professor." Nick recalled that his father and his cohorts often addressed each other as either doctor or professor. They always did it in a semi-mocking tone, but he was sure they did it to help prop up each other's tenuous sense of self-importance.

Nick walked into the dining room and without introducing himself, addressed the man in a Harris tweed sport coat and bow tie who had spoken. He appeared to be about thirty. The woman sitting next to him was about ten years younger and had been adoringly hanging on his every word. "Maybe if Comrade Stalin hadn't stabbed the Allies in the back in 1939 when he signed a pact with Hitler in order to steal half of Poland, the Germans wouldn't have swept across France in 1940 and Comrade Stalin would have his beloved second front already. Hell, if Comrade Stalin hadn't done that we might not be at war at all. And father, why is a devoted friend of Goering, Goebbels, and the Fuehrer siding with this pinko fellow traveler? Just last year you and Lindbergh and your other buddies in America First were saying that Hitler was not our problem. Now you want us to rush up the beaches to save Stalin's ass from the big bad Nazis. Of course, none of you guys is about to do the rushing yourselves, are you? I seem to have the only uniform in the room."

The tweed sport coat and bow tie became indignant. "I'm deferred because I have a critical occupation."

"What's that, scoffing at the efforts of better men, or maybe diddling coeds?" He nodded at the girl sitting next to him. "I didn't know either was important to the war effort."

His father replied, "Doctor Hanson is a professor of political science and an advisor to several government entities. What are you doing here, Nick?"

"I came to congratulate you and the blushing bride. I cannot believe you didn't invite your only son to your engagement party. Rather rude, I would say."

"I thought you were at sea."

"And so I was, until day before yesterday. And is this the blushing bride?" He gestured to the obviously confused woman sitting at the foot of the table in his mother's place. "You're not Frau Betzhold, are you?" She did in fact resemble Ruth Betzhold. "You didn't swim ashore from one of the U-boats I've been hunting, did you?"

"Nick, that's quite enough. Cheryl and you too, Doctor Hanson, will have to forgive Nick. He's obviously had a bit too much to drink as he unwinds from his seagoing duties. He's a Coast Guard officer. Nick, I think we should go in the kitchen and talk. The caterer has some coffee left, I'm sure. You obviously need a great deal of coffee."

He got up and stalked out of the room, but Nick didn't follow him as he obviously expected. He turned to his father's fiancée instead and held out his hand. "Hi, I'm the ne'er-do-well son and I'm dead sober. Haven't had a drink in weeks. There's a war on, you know. I'm always like this around my father and his friends. They bring out the worst in me. Has he told you how his close friends, the Nazis, kicked me out of Germany in '36, to his great embarrassment?"

She took his hand in both of hers and, with a forced smile, said, "You may find this hard to believe but I'm really happy to finally meet you. I look forward to getting to know you, Nick."

"I doubt if that's in the cards." With that he pulled his hand away and went into the kitchen.

His father started on him as soon as he came through the door. "How dare you ..."

"At times like these must you always sound like bad movie dialogue?"

"You insulted Doctor Hanson and you were genuinely cruel to Cheryl and you don't even know her."

"I know about her. Mrs. Gray doesn't like her and that's good enough for me. And if you want to play How Dare You, how dare you bring her and your bunch of draft dodgers and borderline traitors into *my* house and fire *my* housekeeper?"

"We don't need Mrs. Gray anymore, and no matter who I decided upon to be the next Mrs. Earnest Worth, Mrs. Gray's loyalty to your mother would keep her from approving. Why don't you have a cup of coffee and we'll go in and you can join the party. My guests are very distinguished professors and their wives and just because you don't agree with their politics—or mine, for that matter—is no reason you can't respect them."

"I've never been able to figure out what your politics are, Father, except whatever seems to be the latest fad in the faculty club. As far as respecting them goes—" The front doorbell chimes interrupted him. "As long as this seems to be the night for introducing fiancées, I think that's mine, although she doesn't know it yet. But maybe she does. She's pretty sharp." The bell chimed again, so Nick leaned through the swinging door to the dining room and said, "That's the front doorbell in case you've never heard one before. Will one of you geniuses please answer it?" Then he turned back to his father. "Let's talk about the Grays."

"I've given her two weeks' notice and rest assured I'll give her a nice bonus. You might want to chip in as well. But there is no way Mrs. Gray and Cheryl can live under the same roof or even on the same property."

"Okay. That's easily fixed." He walked over to the calendar Mrs. Gray had hanging in the corner next to the back door, counted the days remaining in March, then flipped the page up to the next month. "Let me see… We're going to be in New London for another ten days or so, then on patrol for about seventeen." He counted out the days remaining in March and then the rest of them in April. "We should be back about the twentieth of next month. When I come back, I don't want to find you still living here. That's a lot more notice than you gave the Grays, but I'm not going to give you a nice bonus. You'd only blow it on cheap women."

"You can't just throw me out. Who do you think you are? I've been living in this house ever since your mother and I were married."

"Yup, and my grandfather, who never trusted you, incidentally, put it in my mother's name. He always suspected that you were screwing anything in skirts. But when you didn't treat Frau Betzhold with your usual discretion and I told him about it, he got Mom to change her will and, as you know, she left everything to me. I hope the Frau was as good as she looked, because she was undoubtedly the most expensive piece of ass you ever had. The twentieth of April. Not one day later."

"I'll need far more time than that. I have a very busy schedule and besides finding someplace to live, I have to arrange for movers and all."

"There's not that much to move. Most of the furniture is mine, too. Get Cheryl to help you. It's a lot more time than you gave the Grays. Throwing those old people out was truly despicable, Father. Throwing you out is a long overdue act of justice. April twentieth."

He turned and saw Amy standing in the doorway, her fist tight against her lips. "Nick, are you sure you want to do this?" She seemed to be on the verge of tears.

"Absolutely. Let's get out of here so my dear father can get on with his packing."

AUGUST 2008

"I LET THE GRAYS move into the main house as caretakers and converted the downstairs study into a bedroom so Mr. Gray wouldn't have to go up and down the stairs anymore. Then I rented the garage apartment to a couple who had come up from down south to work at Winchester. But that was later."

"What did Grandma think of all that?"

"She tried to talk me out of it. She couldn't understand why I was being so brutal to my own father. I suppose if I hadn't walked in on that idiotic second front conversation, and if Cheryl hadn't looked so much like Ruth Betzhold, I would have done it differently. But the contrast between those self-satisfied twits and the people I had been associating with and fishing out of the sea was so great... Then there was the other thing..."

He paused, "If I had it to do today I probably would have done it differently. Then again, I hope I wouldn't. My father and his friends were a large and festering carbuncle on the backside of freedom for anyone but themselves. There are still a lot of them around..."

He lapsed into a long silence and this time she was fairly sure the old man was asleep. He wasn't. He was remembering. Funny how he couldn't remember where he had put something he had had in his hand five minutes before but could remember every detail of that night all those years ago.

MARCH 1942

HE INTRODUCED AMY to Mrs. Gray and her thin, gray husband. He was sitting in a worn wing chair listening to the Eddie Cantor show on the radio. Cantor had discovered a new teenaged vocalist who was all the rage. Her name was Dinah Shore. Nick said, "Mrs. Gray, my father has decided that he and his bride would be much happier living somewhere else. He's moving out next month and I want you to move into the main house and take care of it. Do you have someone to help you move?"

"Oh yes, the men at the VFW have offered to move us and the ladies in the Forty and Eight, that's the ladies auxiliary, have been trying to find us someplace to live. Oh Nicholas, this is such a relief, I can't tell you." Mr. Gray tried to say something but only managed a hacking cough instead. It brought back unpleasant, oil-soaked memories to Nick and drove any second thoughts about whether he was doing the right thing from his head.

AUGUST 2008

"YOU WERE PRETTY TOUGH ON HIM, weren't you, Grandpa?" She was finding it hard to reconcile a man who could kick his own father out of a house where he had lived for twenty-five years with the quiet and gentlemanly grandfather she knew.

"Whatever I did to him was better than what he tried to do to the Grays and what he did to my mother."

"You mean being unfaithful in Germany?"

"Did I tell you about that?"

"A while ago when you were telling me about the Berlin Olympics."

"Oh yeah, I did, didn't I? Anyway, he was a cruel man—cruel is exactly the right word—and so totally self-centered that he had no idea, not the foggiest, of how cruel he was. Making them move would have killed Mr. Gray and probably destroyed Mrs. Gray as well.

"But it wasn't that he knew it and didn't care. It was worse than that. He was totally unaware of the effect on others of anything he did. He was only aware of what he wanted and the pleasant effect it would have for him. Other people really didn't exist for him as people; they were just ways for him to get whatever he wanted at the moment. Or obstacles to his getting it. He made the last years of my mother's life hell."

"How did your mother die, Grandpa?"

"She had a congenital defect in her heart valves. Nowadays they'd operate, fix them, and have her running marathons in a month. Back then all they could do was make her comfortable and happy. My father had no interest in making her, or anyone but himself, happy."

"What exactly did he do?"

He paused in thought before he told her. "He used to bring his bimbos home and take them into his study while my mother was still alive and upstairs slowly dying. I guess after my grandfather cut him out of the will, he thought he had nothing to lose."

"That's dreadful. How did you find out?"

"My sophomore year at Dartmouth I finished my finals early and came home. My mother was just slowly dwindling away and I used to spend a lot of time reading to her. She loved Somerset Maugham short stories and the poems of Edgar A. Guest."

"I never heard of him."

"He was quite popular at the time. If you want to get a feel for those times you should read some of his stuff. I'm sure you'll find him quite maudlin."

"Maudlin? Was he widely read?"

"Very widely read. He was very commercial in his day. Thousands of poems that were syndicated in newspapers all over the country. That's why reading him, if you can do it without snickering, will help to put you into those times. Those people had come through one horrendous war and the Great Depression and Guest knew how to appeal to them. He knew what was important to them and it wasn't getting the newest electronic gadget, or finding out what some drug-soaked celebrity was doing, or any of today's so important trivialities. He wrote about friendship and family and the passing of time. Gooey stuff that embarrasses this generation, so they belittle it."

She didn't quite know how to deal with that, although she suspected this guy Guest might be important to understanding those times. She made a mental note to read some of his stuff. She changed the subject. "How did you find out what your father was doing? Did he do it while you were in the house, or did Mrs. Gray tell you?"

"Neither, and although Mrs. Gray knew about it she never said a word. She, and I guess my mother too, just pretended it wasn't happening. After I found out, Mrs. Gray admitted that they both knew what was going on but never spoke about it. He claimed the women were students he was tutoring and they went along with the lie. I'm sure ignoring it didn't make it hurt my mother any less."

"How did you find out about it?"

"The Dekes at Yale were having an end-of-the-year party so I went into New Haven to attend. But when I got there the cops had already arrived. It seemed the party had started about noon, and by seven, when I got there, it had degenerated the way Deke parties had a way of doing sometimes. So I went home.

"My father's study was on the ground floor at the bottom of the stairs, and when I went by it I heard noises coming through the door that I won't describe to you. I knocked loudly and eventually he opened up and said she was a student from some girl's college that he was tutoring. But she was obviously no student of anything I'd want to discuss with you. My mother was upstairs dying at the time."

"Could you have been overly sensitive after what had happened in Germany?"

"I asked Mrs. Gray about it later, but I think my mother had sworn her to secrecy. She would only say that my father had tutored a number of students that year. When I asked her how many of them were male, she said 'Oh, a few of them were.' But she turned away when she said it. Mrs. Gray was a fine lady but a very poor liar. He could have taken them someplace else, but as I said, he was a cruel man."

"What did you do?"

"I quietly suggested that it might be better if he took his tutoring business elsewhere so it wouldn't disturb my mother. He immediately agreed and that was the end of it for the moment. I left it at that because I didn't want to cause my mother any more pain. But when I came home the night of his engagement party it had been festering in me for five years. The Grays were the last straw."

"What did you and Grandma do then?"

MARCH 1942

WHEN THEY WERE OUTSIDE, Amy handed him the car keys and said, "Here, you drive."

"Sure. Where do you want to go?"

"When do you have to be back?"

"I planned on taking the first Shoreline Express in the morning. I could catch it from Bridgeport just as easily as from New Haven."

"Then I guess you'd better take me back to Marion's, unless you have someplace better for us to go."

He pointed over his shoulder at the house. "It doesn't look like my dear father is about to break up his party and ask his guests to leave. If he did, and he took Cheryl home—assuming she has a home—we could go back inside. We could anyway, but I think I've had enough family confrontations for one night."

"Where are you going to spend the night?"

"I guess you could drop me in New Haven and I could get a room at the Taft. Or you could drop me at the Stratfield in Bridgeport. I could walk to the station in the morning and catch the train from either one. But there's something I'd like to talk to you about. I told my father you were my fiancée."

She turned sideways in the seat and asked, "Am I? Don't you think you should have discussed that with me first?"

"I also told him that although we hadn't yet discussed it, you probably already knew. That's what I want to talk to you about."

She slowly shook her head from side to side, then said, "This has to be the most backward and inside-out marriage proposal in history."

"Well, are you?"

"I can't very well deny it after you've told your father and God only knows how many others. I guess I'm stuck with you."

AUGUST 2008

"**DID YOU GO TO ONE OF THOSE HOTELS?** Come on Grandpa, fess up. I'm a big girl and I want to hear all the details."

"Sorry, Toots, there were no sordid details to satisfy your prurient interest. Back then good hotels demanded to see a wedding license before they'd let a young couple in and they had house detectives in case someone snuck up the back stairs."

"You mean house detectives that looked like W. C. Fields?"

"I don't know what they looked like. I never met one."

"Grandpa, it just occurs to me that you and Grandma had just met, really. What, about six weeks before? You had had dinner and breakfast four or five times?"

"We had talked on the phone for hours. Most of my pay went into phones. All I can say is the marriage lasted fifty-four years. Now young people shack up together for a couple of years, and when they finally get married they're lucky if it lasts fifty-four weeks. We didn't have time to horse around. There was a war on, you know. We went back to Marion's and sat on a sofa in her living room, holding hands and talking until about three when we both fell asleep. By then we had all of our plans made, tentative though they were. Marion woke us about six and we went to that little place and had breakfast. Then your grandmother dropped me at the Bridgeport railroad station and went to work. I went back to New London to get *Fourteen Boat* ready for sea."

Amy smiled. "I know. There was a war on."

MARCH 1942

WHEN NICK GOT TO THE BOATYARD in Noank, the schooner had a two-inch hole on either side of her bottom, amidships. A sailor from the sub base and Jenks were watching the yard's carpenter hand fit a wooden block to the starboard hole: one side curved to fit the hull and the other flat to fit the base of the sound head. As Nick approached, the carpenter pronounced himself satisfied, handed the block to the sailor and took his tools and a similar block to the port side. Borg and Longo had started painting the freshly scrubbed bottom from the bow and Langdon was aft, painting the rudder and the run. Jenks greeted Nick with, "Ah, and how is everything at the palatial home and with the delicious Miss Madison?"

"Every problem has been solved and thanks so much for asking, Boats." There was no way anyone, even Jenks, could irritate him today. "Where do we stand?"

"As you can see, we cleaned the bottom and the guys are priming it. It'll get a coat of anti-fouling paint just before it goes back in. Some new shit the navy came up with. We even got most of the oil stains off the waterline and topsides. I only hope this bottom paint is worth a shit."

Nick looked up at the hull. "How's the caulking? Did you go over it?"

"Of course not. The paint will cover it and when the boat's in the water you can't see it anyhow, so what difference does it make?"

"I take that to be your perverted way of saying you checked every inch of it and it's okay."

"One area on the port side along the garboard strake looked a little hokey so I had the yard recaulk it. Other than that she was as tight as a bride on her wedding night."

"Where're the other guys?"

"Aboard with the other swabby, rearranging the cabin to make room for the sound equipment."

Rearranging was a bit of an understatement. The Halicrafters radio sat on a shelf on the forward bulkhead of the main cabin where whoever was on radio watch could sit on the end of a bunk, half turned toward the radio. There had been just room on the shelf for Nick's Zenith Transoceanic portable radio. Now another shelf had been installed on the bulkhead over the opposite bunk and a sailor was installing the sound apparatus on it. Nick asked Borg, "Where's Slade?"

His high-pitched voice replied from under the cabin sole. "I'm down here snaking wires, Skipper."

"I hope those aren't power cables."

The sailor replied, "Nope. Those will come along the overhead. He's pulling through the wires to the sound heads."

"How much power does this stuff draw? How often will we have to run the engine?"

Borg answered, "A couple hours or so at midday if we go easy on the cabin lights at night. They're giving us an extra battery. You know, none of this stuff would draw any current to speak of if it weren't for the need to heat the filaments of the vacuum tubes. If someone could find a way to get rid of them, everything would be a whole lot easier."

The sailor said, "No way that will ever happen," and went on stripping the ends of the bundle of wires he was working on.

TWELVE

APRIL 1942

THEY MADE A ONE-DAY AND TWO-NIGHT STOP in Greenport to complete provisioning and for Nick to get a briefing and orders. At four the next morning they left to catch the ebb in the Race. As the sun came up so did a fine southwest sailing breeze. They shut down the engine and set the main, foresail, staysail, and jib and proceeded south of Fishers Island into Block Island Sound toward their rendez- vous with a submarine. They were provisioned for twenty-three days with about all the food, water, and fuel they could stuff into the boat, and were expecting to be out for about two and a half weeks. Their pa- trol area would be just beyond the edge of the continental shelf about 150 miles due east of Atlantic City. Again it was on the Great Circle route to Cape Hatteras from the U-boat bases on the Bay of Biscay.

The old S-boat was waiting for them on the surface with its escort, an even older World War One sub-chaser, slowly circling it about a half mile off. Ever since the Army Air Corps had bombed USS *Mackerel* in Block Island Sound the Navy had been careful to provide escorts for its subs.

Fortunately, the plane's crew had been no more accurate at bombing than at ship identification.

The submarine dove and circled at various depths while Borg, Snow, and Slade took turns trying to estimate its bearing. The equipment was not able to give any indication of the sub's depth. By noting the schooner's heading when the sound moved from one hydrophone to the other they were able to get a better bearing than they could from either of the supposedly directional microphones. But only the sketchiest idea of the range could be derived from the volume of the sound unless the sub was very close, or as happened on one pass, it passed right under them. It was all, as Jenks described it, "a grab-ass operation". But it was the best they had.

After a couple of hours of this, the sub surfaced, signaled "Good luck" by Addis lamp, and headed back to Newport with the sub-chaser tagging along. *Fourteen Boat* had been maneuvering under only her foresail and staysail. Now she hoisted her main and jib, and sailing as close as she could to the wind that had backed into the southeast, headed toward the open sea.

AUGUST 2008

"**HALF A DAY OF PRACTICING** with an actual submarine, Grandpa?" Traffic was now quite light and she had the cruise control set on sixty-five.

"And lucky to get that."

"I suppose the recordings they used at the school must have been pretty good."

"Actually, from what Borg told me, they were pretty bad. They were on celluloid and scratchy from having been played about a million times. Stereo and high fidelity didn't arrive until the Fifties. Like everybody, they were doing the best they could with what they had. Fortunately the submarines of those days were not nearly as quiet as modern ones. If they were on passage, not rigged for silent running, and were fairly close, you could hear the thrum, thrum, thrum of their props quite clearly. If they were any distance away, or running dead slow to be quiet, or beneath a temperature inversion layer, it was pretty hard to tell their sound from the other noises in the sea."

"Did you hear or see any U-boats?"

"Not on that cruise. Mostly we sailed around in the fog, with everything in the boat wet and clammy and only the vaguest idea of where we were. If I remember rightly we went almost two weeks without seeing the sun, the sky, or the horizon. Sometimes it would lift until we had maybe a mile of visibility, then it would clamp back down again until we were lucky just to see the bowsprit from the cockpit. All that time it blew steadily from the southeast. I think the fog was the result of the wind blowing over the Gulf Stream where it picked up a lot of moisture and then dumped it when it passed over the colder water north of the Stream. It rained intermittently. There was no chance of drying anything, so we all just stayed pretty much in the same damp clothes the whole time. Cold, wet, and clammy. Awful."

"Didn't you have any dry clothes sealed in plastic bags?"

"Dear, there were no plastic bags. Those didn't come along until years later. I suppose it's hard for you to even imagine a world without plastic bags. There was no Goretex either. Our foul-weather gear was the closest thing we had to plastic bags. It was completely impermeable unless, of course, it decided to leak like a sieve at the seams or a fold. Only when it was raining hard or there was a lot of spray coming aboard was it as wet outside as it usually was inside. It's a wonder we didn't all die of terminal mildew."

"Was it rough?"

"No, not that I remember. It was the North Atlantic so there was always a ground swell and a chop on top of it. But it never blew particularly hard. It really would have been pleasant sailing weather if it hadn't been so damned cold, wet, and clammy.

APRIL 1942

NICK HAD JUST FINISHED EATING yet another midday meal of *Dinty Moore's* canned beef stew, when Borg, who was on sound watch, lifted his left earphone and reached across to the radio. "That's our call sign, Skipper." Nick wondered how he had recognized it from the others while he was simultaneously listening for undersea sounds. The call sign was repeated, this time followed by a code group. Borg opened the code book that lay on the shelf next to the radio, looked up the frequency indicated by the group, tuned the radio to it, then pulled the earphone back in place and went back to listening for U-boats.

A few minutes later the voice read off a half-dozen code groups and repeated them. Borg copied them down the first time and then checked them the second time before picking up the microphone and saying, "Received," followed by their current call sign. Then he decoded the message while Nick looked over his shoulder. "Proceed south along the seventy-second meridian into the Gulf Stream to search for survivors of the *City of New York* torpedoed off Cape May on 20 March."

AUGUST 2008

"DID YOU KNOW where the seventy-second meridian was, Grandpa?"

"I knew precisely where the seventy-second meridian was; I just didn't know where we were. I had been at least ten days without a fix."

"Hadn't you been keeping the DR plot up?"

"Of course. I had been religiously logging and plotting our direction and distance run every four hours ever since the weather closed down. That only gave me my dead reckoning position. But that was not the same as an accurate estimated position that took into account such things as any current running and my best guess of the leeway *Fourteen Boat* was making. That varied depending on such things as how much she was heeled down and the size of the seas and from what angle they were hitting her. In daylight I could make an educated guess of the leeway angle by looking over the stern at the curve of the wake, if I could see it in the fog, but at night, unless the moon was particularly bright, I couldn't even make a halfway intelligent guess, let alone an educated one.

"My grandfather, your great-great-grandfather, once told me

that navigation is like the practice of medicine: an art, not a science. But that's no longer supposed to be true, at least for navigation, what with all the electronic stuff nowadays. Even with all the gadgets, though, people are still putting boats on the bricks. Last winter there was a French cruise ship in the Caribbean that was on its way from one island to another, so they just dialed the lat and long of their destination into the autopilot and went back to reading *Playboy*. Only problem was there was another island in the way. At three in the morning—crunch. So much for the science of navigation in the modern age."

"You must have finally found out where you were, Grandpa, or you wouldn't be here, having sailed off the edge of the earth."

"Wiseass. I figured we had to be east of the seventy-third meridian so we sailed south-southwest on a course I hoped would eventually intersect with it somewhere in the Gulf Stream. It was obvious when we hit the Stream because both the water and air temperature rose and the fog lifted. So I finally managed to get a sight."

"How far was your fix from your estimated position?"

"Only a little over five miles if I remember correctly. Not bad."

"Five miles, not bad?"

"On average about a half a mile a day. We used to cover maybe fifty miles a day when we were patrolling our grids. Less than a ten percent error. Today GPS will give a position within a few yards. That just shows how much better the equipment is now. But people who know their position within a few feet at all times can still pile cruise ships onto islands. We never bumped into anything geographical."

"Did you find the survivors?"

"No. Another yacht, I think it was one of the *Malabars*, found the lifeboat with twenty-four people in it. Mostly children being evacuated from England to avoid the bombings. They were all dead from exposure."

"My God."

"Yeah, my God. War is Hell." Then he mused, "That war, no,

the whole twentieth century, was hard on women and kids in a way that previous times seldom were. Even the Thirty Years War, that killed more Europeans than the Black Death, didn't intentionally target noncombatants for slaughter the way World War Two did. They might have been..." He hesitated. "I can't think of the damned word." Again he paused, then said, "...peripheral casualties. No, not peripheral. Incidental? No. There's a standard phrase for it. That shows how far we've fallen."

"Collateral damage."

"Collateral damage. That's it. Why the hell couldn't I think of that? Anyway, it wasn't just the Nazis intentionally murdering women and kids in the name of ethnic purity. Kindly old Uncle Joe Stalin, the hero of my father and his friends, intentionally murdered an estimated twelve million of his own people, mostly by starvation, when he collectivized Soviet agriculture. That's twice as many as died in the Holocaust."

"We bombed cities full of civilians."

"Your dumb-assed profs are still peddling their moral equivalency crap, huh? Toots, no American ever intentionally dropped a bomb on a little kid or starved one to death or pushed one into a gas chamber. The U.S. has fed more people around the world than all the other countries in history combined. And American troops are famous for giving Hershey Bars and their own rations to hungry kids. But the Left won't admit it, any more than they'll admit the immense evil of the Soviets.

"To be fair, I don't think the U-boat commander who sunk the *City of New York* knew it was full of kids. That makes him a lot less guilty than someone who knowingly herded them into a gas chamber or intentionally starved them to death. That huge difference in moral responsibility also applies to someone who drops bombs on a city to hinder the enemy's production capacity or in retaliation for bombs dropped on his own cities."

He took a deep breath, held it, then let it out in a sigh before he continued. "I'm trying to talk about moral equivalency, but not doing it very well. The kids are just as dead, aren't they? Moral and ethical differences don't make any difference to them. But they have to make a difference to us so we can prevent it from happening again and again."

"Didn't you just make my argument about war that you dismissed a while back?"

"What argument?"

"That war should be unacceptable to civilized people. They should just refuse to be sucked into it."

"You mean the old saw about what happens if they give a war and nobody comes?"

"I mean that the decent, civilized people of the world should find a way to come together and outlaw war."

"That's what the decent, civilized people did in the twenties and thirties and it led to the worst war in history."

"Just because it failed then, doesn't mean we shouldn't keep trying."

"And when we get done outlawing war we can start on the laws of nature. We could amend Newton's Laws of gravity; just think how that would reduce our energy needs."

"You're saying that war and the murder of children is an immutable law of nature. My God, Grandpa, that's the most cynical statement I've ever heard."

"No, that's not what I'm saying. I'm saying that war is an inevitable condition of mankind as long as it's the only alternative to tyranny, and trying to outlaw war while placating tyranny is bound to bloody failure."

"And how do you propose we should deal with tyranny?"

"You don't tolerate it and you don't negotiate with it, and you don't make excuses for it. You kill it any way you can, just as soon as you can. That's the great lesson my generation learned at tremendous cost, and that later generations are busy forgetting just as quickly as they can."

With that he closed his eyes and pretended to sleep while she drove north in silence toward the intersection of I-91 and I-89.

When she drove through the cloverleaf he said, "You asked if we ever heard a U-boat. It was on the next cruise that we might have encountered one."

She knew he was trying to change the subject and was grateful. "Might have? Tell me about it."

APRIL 1942

THEY WENT INTO GREENPORT and got three days to clean up and dry out the boat, provision, and catch a couple of good nights' sleep before being sent out again. Their patrol area was farther west this time and not quite as far offshore. There had been even more attacks along the Jersey shore and in the approaches to New York.

While in port, Nick was too busy to have time for much except a couple of calls to Amy, and one to Mrs. Gray. She reported that although there was no more talk of her leaving, his father showed no sign of leaving either. He wondered if his father was hoping he would just go out on patrol and not come back. There wasn't anything he could do about it. He had more important things to worry about. There was a war on, after all.

They rounded Montauk on a sparkling spring day when the sun actually felt warm on his back as he stood in the cockpit. The weather was definitely getting better. In the next ten days there were only two days and the night between them with fog and occasional rain.

On the eleventh day Nick woke up before dawn, looked out the hatch, and saw that the night was clear and the horizon would soon be visible. He was preparing to get a dawn sight when Longo, who was on watch with Langdon, called, "Skipper, I think I see something."

Nick jumped into the cockpit to see them both staring at the rapidly brightening eastern horizon. Langdon pointed. "There,

Skipper, aft of the port beam, right on the horizon. A solid lump." He handed Nick the binoculars. "Just follow along the horizon."

Nick saw it. Whatever it was, it wasn't a rogue sea. It kept disappearing and reappearing in the same place without changing its basically rectangular shape. The distance to his horizon as he stood in the cockpit was only four or five miles: eight to ten thousand yards. It had to be inside of that. He handed the glasses back to Longo as he thought about it. *Fourteen Boat* was reaching southeast across the brisk southwest wind and the ten- to twelve-foot seas it had kicked up. Whatever it was, it appeared to be getting more distinct as they watched it. The sun was not yet over the horizon but soon would be. Nick realized that he was missing the short period of nautical twilight when both the stars and the horizon were visible, but decided this might be more important than an updated fix. It wasn't a freighter. A freighter would be much larger at this distance.

He heard Jenks coming up the ladder and said, "Boats, hand me my hand bearing compass. It's on the shelf over my bunk next to the chronometer." With it, he took a bearing on the object and started the stopwatch that hung around his neck. Jenks stayed standing on the ladder in the hatch and Borg appeared behind him. Nick turned to him and asked, "Who's on the sound gear?"

"Hank."

"Tell him to search on the port side from aft of abeam to the forequarter."

Langdon said, "It could be a lifeboat."

And Jenks replied, "It could also be the top of the gaff mainsail of another sailing vessel just beyond the horizon. We used to see those on the Banks all the time."

It was rapidly getting lighter. The invisibility the dark westerly sky had given them would disappear any moment now; then the U-boat, if that's what the object was, had to see them. Maybe it had already seen them, and wasn't worried about some little sailboat.

Nick waited until the stopwatch said three minutes had passed since the previous bearing, then took another. He would have preferred to go below and work out the possibilities on the chart but he didn't have time for that. From the change in the angle of the bearing in the time between the sights, the object was obviously moving at a pretty good clip and would cross their bow before *Fourteen Boat* reached the intersection point.

A quote from Nelson popped into Nick's head. *"No captain can go far wrong who lays his ship alongside that of the enemy."*

"Okay, let's get the boat on the wind, get the reef out of the main, and get the jib on her." He wanted to be as close as possible to whatever it was when it crossed their bow. "Langdon, you keep watching that object and don't take your eyes off it for a second. Longo, help Boats with the main." He took the wheel and turned the boat onto the more southerly track.

Borg, who was still standing in the hatch, asked, "Should I send out a sighting report?"

After a second's hesitation Nick replied, "No, but get one ready. Call it a possible contact and use the DR position I just logged." If it was a U-boat and it heard their radio close by, God only knew what it would do. The main was two-blocked at that moment so he hauled in the sheet while he steered with his backside against the wheel and felt the boat heel down further and accelerate. When Jenks came back into the cockpit he told him, "Boats, get your depth charge key just in case." It was a T-handled wrench that took the charges off safe and set the explosion depth.

"The thing is gone, Mr. Worth." Langdon was desperately scanning the area with the glasses. "It could have dived. One second it was there and the next it was gone. "

Nick didn't know if it had dived because it had seen them, or if it was just the routine dawn dive after running on the surface all night, or if it was a U-boat at all. He really didn't know what it had been. He yelled down the hatch, "Do you guys hear anything?"

Borg appeared again in the hatch. "There could be a faint contact about twenty degrees on the port bow but there's a lot of noise in the water. The prop noise, if that's what it is, keeps fading in and out. I think we might be right on the edge of the Stream or an eddy. Or they might have dived under a temperature inversion layer that's masking the sound."

"No idea of the range."

"None, Skipper. Wish we could do better."

"Okay, send the sighting report. If it was a sub and they dove, they won't be able to hear it. Let me know the second Hank hears anything in the starboard hydrophone. Anything. I really want to be close when it crosses our bow."

Jenks came into the cockpit pushing the BAR in front of him and Nick asked, "What are you going to do with that?"

"Just in case." He left the light machine gun lying on the bridge deck at the front of the cockpit and held up the depth charge key. "What do you want me to do with this?"

"Get these two," he pointed at the depth charges on either side of the wheel box, "onto the afterdeck ready to push overboard, but don't take them off safe yet. What do you think? Set them on medium or deep?" They only had three settings.

Jenks freed the lashings on the starboard bomb, lifted its 120 pounds out of the cockpit as if it weighed nothing, and said to Longo, "Get up there and hang onto this thing and don't let it roll overboard." Then he did the same with the port one and said to Langdon, "If that thing falls overboard you better hang onto it and ride it down. What depth, Skipper?"

"Medium, I guess." He glanced at the device that measured their speed and recorded the distance run and noticed its actuator towed behind the boat. "We'd better get the log on board." There were just too many things to think of at once. Jenks held the depth charge as Longo pulled the log's cable aboard.

They were going about six and a half knots: a mile in a little less than ten minutes. About 190 yards a minute. "We'll drop them one minute apart and hope for the best—if we drop them at all. We can only do that if Borg and Snow give us some idea where to drop them."

At that moment Borg again appeared in the hatch. "Message sent and acknowledged, Skipper. The sound, when we hear it, is still to port but appears to be moving to cross our bow. But I have to tell you it's intermittent and indistinct, even though, when we can hear it, it sounds like a sub's propellers and seems to be getting louder." They heard Slade, who was obviously relaying messages, say something. Borg passed it on. "Hank's lost it. It's gone again." They were all silent for several minutes until Slade said something and Borg relayed it. "Hank says he hears it again and it's really loud right on the port bow. " A short pause this time. "He's stopped hearing it in the port hydrophone. There's an area of about ten degrees on either side of the bow, Skipper, where we couldn't hear that old S-boat in Block Island Sound when it was close."

"Drop the first one, Boats."

Jenks had already set the depth on medium, so he took it off safe and pushed it into the wake. Borg turned and yelled into the cabin, "Depth charge in the water. Turn off the sound equipment."

Nick swung the boat ten degrees to starboard and waited forty-five seconds before ordering the second one dropped. Just as Langdon pushed it overboard the first one exploded, making everyone and everything on the boat jump. As they stared at the column of water that leapt out of the sea, Langdon said, "Sweet Jesus. I've seen movies of those things going off, but the movies sure don't do them justice."

Jenks had already pushed Borg to one side and as he jumped down the hatch past him said, "Stop gawking and give me a hand with the other two, in case we need them."

AUGUST 2008

"**DID YOU, GRANDPA?** Need them, I mean."

"Naah. It took a while for the water to calm down but we never heard or saw anything again."

"No oil slick like in the movies?"

"Just a few dead fish. We crisscrossed the area all that day and another boat that was nearby, I think it was *Ziada,* came up the track that the U-boat, if it was a U-boat, would have been traveling. But they didn't see or hear anything either. A plane searched the area too, but we never found one blessed thing."

"*Ziada?*"

"Fifty-eight-foot yawl. Also a yacht instantly converted to a CGR vessel." He thought about it for a while and finally said, "You know, Toots, it might have been a lifeboat or some other floating debris, but we never found it. Or it could have been the topmast of another sailing vessel just over the horizon. But it might have been just a case of buck fever. We had been searching for U-boats for so many miserable days that maybe it was just some collective lunacy that let us talk ourselves into thinking we were onto something."

"But there might be a U-boat lying on the bottom of the sea."

"I doubt it. If we had hit anything there would have been something, oil or debris or something. No, at best that is just another mystery of the sea. But both Borg and Hank Snow were sure they had heard propeller noises."

"Was that the only time you found a U-boat—or thought you had?"

He sat with his eyes closed for a while before saying, "No. No, it wasn't."

THIRTEEN

COMMANDER NEWTON ASKED NICK as he walked into his office, "You didn't find hide nor hair of that U-boat, did you?"

"Sir, we were sure we were onto something, but now I just don't know."

"Don't worry about it. If it was a sub you at least gave him a fright that would keep him down for a while and deplete his battery. Think about it. Herman the German is cruising along in his U-boat, eating his sauerkraut and pig's feet for breakfast, thinking there isn't another vessel within miles, and suddenly someone drops a couple of depth charges on him. It's got to make him at least a little more paranoid and a bit less aggressive. Not a bad thing for us. If it wasn't a sub, you also shouldn't worry about it. The last thing I need is a skipper who waits until he is absolutely sure before he shoots. Of course that assumes he doesn't shoot at friendly vessels like the Army Air Corps does. You heard about *Mackerel?*

"Yeah. I guess that's another advantage of being a sailing vessel. Harder for the Air Corps to mistake us for a submarine. What do you want us to do next?"

Newton got up and walked over to the chart on the drafting table and Nick followed him. "Same general area but a different grid square about fifty miles southeast of where you were. We don't want the Krauts to start routing their boats around known positions of our picket boats. Oh, and while I think of it, an old rust-bucket hauling timber from Canada to the Newport News Shipyard is overdue. It's had a long history of engine breakdowns so it's probably halfway to England by now, drifting in the Stream. It'll turn up eventually I suppose."

"Unless..."

"Unless..."

AUGUST 2008

"**DID YOU GET TO SEE GRANDMA**, Grandpa?"

"No, but we talked on the phone early every morning. It had become a habit whenever we were in port. I also talked to Mrs. Gray and found out that instead of my father moving out, Cheryl had moved in, and he had given Mrs. Gray a new date to be gone: June first. I called him.

APRIL 1942

"**HELLO, FATHER**, and just what the hell are you doing in my house?"

"Oh Nick. Thank God it's you. I'm just so worried about you when you're out there in that little boat. When can we get together and straighten out this silly misunderstanding? I know that you were just in from one of your cruises that night and probably exhausted. Neither Professor Hanson nor I blame you. We understand and so does Cheryl. None of us was at our best that night, and I'm truly sorry about anything I might have said that offended you."

"I understand that Frau Betzhold has moved in with you."

"Cheryl is definitely not Ruth Betzhold, and I wish you wouldn't keep bringing up Ruth Betzhold. That was a long time ago and I am truly sorry about that whole trip to Germany. But you weren't too smart in your choice of women either, as I recall. Cheryl is a very fine lady and I'm sure you would come to like her and respect her if you would only give her a chance. We were married two weeks ago. Can't we just put all that behind us, sit down and reach some understanding like sensible adults? Let bygones be bygones."

"I understand you fired Mrs. Gray."

"She and Mister Gray will be much happier someplace else. I intend to give them a full month to find someplace else and three months' severance pay on top of it."

Nick was silent long enough so his father finally asked, "Nick, are you still there?"

"Yeah, I'm still here, but you'd better not be there much longer. Here's the deal. As soon as we hang up I'm going to call that lawyer that my grandfather used to fix it so you would not inherit one damned thing that belonged to him or Mom. I'm going to tell him to do whatever is necessary to get you out of my house just as soon as possible."

"I tried to treat you like a civilized human being, but I see that's hopeless. Let your lawyer take his best shot. With you out at sea all the time he won't have it easy because I'll have my friends in the law school tie everything up for years."

"Then I'll just have to throw you and your whore out in the street personally. I think I'll enjoy that. I'll be gone another three weeks or so and you'd better be gone when I get back."

Earnest Worth replied, "Of course there's always the chance you won't get back, isn't there?" and hung up.

AUGUST 2008

"YOU KNOW, AMY, that was the very last thing my father ever said to me. After the next cruise I was ashore for a while so I had time to sign the papers the lawyer had drawn up. When they were served on him he got out of the house right away. He had always been all bluff and bluster because under it all he was the worst kind of coward."

The subject obviously bothered him deeply, even after all these years, so she changed it. "A while ago you mentioned the yacht *Zaida*, Grandpa. Just how many other boats were there in the Corsair Fleet?"

"I don't know. Hundreds anyway, maybe thousands. Most of

them were powerboats, though. They didn't have the endurance or the sea-keeping ability of boats like *Tiger Lillie* or *Zaida*. They used the bigger powerboats for quick rescue runs, but if they went offshore they couldn't carry enough fuel to stay out much more than a day or two. The smaller ones, thirty- or forty-footers, were used for inshore patrols where they could run for cover when the weather looked bad. Did you know that Arthur Fiedler skippered one of them?"

"No. I didn't know that. Inshore patrols? Did the U-boats come in that close?"

"Sure. In June of '42 a sub landed a group of saboteurs on Amagansett Beach, near East Hampton, Long Island. Another one landed a group in Florida."

"And the inshore patrol boats spotted them?"

"Nope. It was an alert Coast Guardsman walking beach patrol."

"I never heard about that either. You're sure that actually happened?"

"It happened. The Coast Guardsman got help and they rounded them up."

"They made them prisoners of war?"

"Nope. They weren't in uniform and were planning attacks on civilian facilities: railroad stations, theaters, places where people gathered, that sort of thing. Sound familiar? So they gave them a fair trial and executed the ringleaders. The guys who had confessed and helped them round up the others were given long sentences but were released a few years after the war was over, as I recall. The whole thing was over in about a month and a half."

"They caught them, tried them, and executed them in a month and a half?"

"We had adults running things in those days, Toots."

MAY 1942

THEY HAD BEEN ON STATION for about a week, and the weather had generally been clear with moderate southwest winds and intermittent fog banks. They had been in a clear area at sunset and Nick had managed to get a solid three-star fix. After plotting their position, writing up the log, and sending off a position report, he decided to catch a couple of hours' sleep while he enjoyed the bliss an offshore navigator only knows when he is sure of his position.

He was sound asleep when Slade shook him awake. "Skipper, a message just came in. Harry is decoding it now."

Borg was sitting at the cabin table with the codebook and message pad. He slapped the lead-covered book closed, tore the sheet off a message pad, and handed it to Nick. It ordered them to proceed to a position about thirty miles to the east of their present location where an aircraft had seen what might be an oil slick and wreckage. The signalman asked, "Might be?"

"One of these wandering fog banks probably drifted over it before the plane could get close enough to confirm. Send a Roger Wilco."

AUGUST 2008

"ROGER WILCO, GRANDPA? I thought people only talked like that in campy old Z-movies."

"Received, understood, and will comply. It makes a lot more sense than calling everybody dude."

MAY 1942

HE WAS AT THE CHART TABLE writing the course—125 magnetic— on a piece of tape when there was a loud thud from the main cabin bilge. The boat shuddered almost to a stop as something scraped loudly along the bottom. Nick's first thought was that his sight reduction plot couldn't be so far wrong that they had run aground when he was sure that the nearest land was over a hundred miles away. They had been reaching across the southeast wind at about seven knots when it happened. He started up the steps to the cockpit as he called to Jenks and Langdon, who were on watch, "What the hell was that?"

Jenks was looking over the side, and replied, "A big fuckin' log. Look for yourself."

Nick had to agree, it was one big fucking log that bobbed up in their wake: easily thirty inches in diameter and forty feet long and floating just barely at the surface. Nick remembered the coaster from Canada with a cargo of timber that had disappeared in this area. "Boats, get up on the bow and see if you can spot any others." Of course at that moment they sailed into a dense bank of fog. "Let's slow her down." He yelled down the hatch, "Longo, Snow, get up here, we have to get the main and jib off her." He let go of the main sheet and let the sail luff, but he was too good a sailor to let it slat for long. "See anything, Boats?"

"Nothing." Then, "Yeah, come left, hard left." A minute later another log, even bigger than the first, floated past ten feet to starboard. "You can come back up, Langdon. We missed it."

As Longo and Snow went forward to drop the jib, Nick turned to the helmsman. "Keep coming up," he directed, then changed his mind. He yelled forward, "Leave the jib up and sheet everything in tight." The boat wouldn't point very high under just the foresail alone. He turned to Langdon and said, "We may be on the edge of this mess of timber. Let's get out of here. Sail as small as you can."

Jenks had Snow replace him out on the sprit looking for more timbers, then he went below and opened the hatch in the cabin sole. "Oh, shit. I thought she was starting to feel logy. Look at this, Mr. Worth."

Nick looked down the hatch and also said, "Oh, shit." There was already a foot of water in the normally dry bilge.

Then Borg said, "The port hydrophone is jammed and not working. Now I know why."

Nick said, "Get someone going on the pump, Boats."

The main bilge pump was a piston affair that emptied into the head. The idea had been to save a through-hull fitting. The thing was mounted in about the most inconvenient location possible, behind the toilet in the back corner of the tiny enclosed head. Slade, who had been listening, said, "I'm on it, Skipper," and went into the head and started pumping.

"No. Let me do that," Jenks said as he pulled him out of the way. "If we can get ahead of the leak you're going to have to get down in the bilge and see if you can stop it. Otherwise we're going to have to take up the sole. We'll probably have to do that anyway. Mr. Worth, we sure as shit better head for the nearest land."

"Not yet. We've been ordered southeast to look for an oil slick, wreckage, and survivors. "

"And I don't want to join them in the water." Jenks got it out between puffs. The Improved Model Navy Pump, as it was described in the Wilcox Crittenden catalogue, took three strokes to pump a gallon and provided no mechanical advantage at all: one had to haul the handle straight up from the body of the pump. Nick watched the bilge for a minute or so and said, "It's getting ahead of you fast, Boats. Let's get this cabin sole up and get a bucket brigade going."

Longo said, "Permission to start the engine, Skipper. If I shut the through-hull and pull the intake water hose off it, I can use the cooling pump on the engine to help pump."

"Do it."

AUGUST 2008

"DID IT, GRANDPA? Did you get ahead of the leak?"

"No. We couldn't even hold our own. There was access to the bilge through the engine box and through a hatch in the sole at the aft end of the main cabin. There was no way anyone could crawl down there to look for the leak without drowning. That's when we discovered that the beautiful teak and holly sole was screwed down onto a plywood subfloor that was screwed to the deck beams. It would have taken a week to dig out all the glued-in plugs to get at the screws holding the teak down so we could get at the plywood and the screws holding that down."

"How'd you get it out? I assumed you did, because you're here."

"With an axe. Works every time."

MAY 1942

THEY GOT A FOUR-MAN bucket brigade going up through the main hatch: one man filling a bucket from the engine room bilge and handing it to a man on the bottom of the main hatch ladder, who handed it to a man near the top, who handed it to a man in the cockpit who dumped it into the cockpit scuppers and handed it back while steering as best he could between buckets. They gave up on the useless pump in the head, but even with the engine pump helping, no matter how fast they bailed, they couldn't slow the accumulating water at all. The leak was gaining on them fast.

Once Nick, Longo, and Jenks had the cabin sole ripped up, the problem was obvious. The sound head had been torn out by the force of the collision with the log, so that most of the two-inch hole was wide open to the sea and water was coming in as if from a fire hose. Jenks grabbed a bath towel someone had hung above the cabin heater hoping it would dry, jumped down into the bilge, and pushed the towel into the gaping hole in the hull. As long as he held it in place with both hands the geyser stopped, but the second he moved his hands the water pressure pushed the towel out of the hole. He shoved it back in and held it while he said, "We need to either plug this from the outside, or make something to hold a packing or a plug in place from the inside."

Nick asked, "What have we got to make a packing from? Do you have any oakum, Boats?"

Still holding the towel in place with both hands, Jenks replied, "The hole's too big. Oakum will just fall through. What we need is a paint- or grease-soaked rag to act like a gasket under a piece of plank we can screw down. But we can't do that as long as that damned sound head shaft and lever are sticking out of the hole." The sound head was hanging under the boat and the shaft and lever to which the boden cable was attached stuck up through the hole at a steep angle.

Nick stepped down into the bilge beside Jenks and reached around him to grab the shaft. "Solid as a rock. The casing and some of the screws are obviously still attached." They were both kneeling in water almost to their hips and had their arms immersed in it to above their elbows. Nick said, "Jesus, that water's cold."

"Tell me something I don't know," Jenks replied. "I don't think anyone can dive under the boat and back those screws out. You'd get about a half a turn before your balls froze off."

Nick, deep in thought, mumbled, "I think it's called hypothermia."

Still holding the towel in place with both hands, Jenks replied, "That's something I didn't know. I do know that my balls are about to freeze off, but I'm glad you know the proper scientific name for it, Mr. Worth."

"I'll get her heaved to on the port tack to get the hole as high as possible. Joe, spell Boats holding the towel in place so he can warm up."

When he came back below, Slade, bottom man in the bucket brigade, said, "I think we're holding our own, Skipper. Maybe gaining a little."

Nick said, "Good" as he pushed past him, then said to Longo, who was now trying to warm up in front of the cabin heater, "We've got to get rid of that sound head before we can do anything else." Jenks was once more holding the towel in place.

Longo kept his teeth locked to keep them from chattering as he replied, "A piece of pipe and a hammer or the back of the axe. Need to cut the wires and the cable, too. I'll get something." He dropped the blanket on a bunk and moved aft to the engine compartment where his kept his tools and spare parts.

Nick stepped down into the bilge and as he reached down for

the towel blocking the hole said, "Get out of here, Boats, I'll take over."

Longo came back with the two-foot piece of pipe he used on wrenches to break rusted bolts loose, a pair of electrician's pliers, and a three-pound sledge hammer. Jenks asked him, "What are you going to do with that shit, Longo?"

"I figure we can cut the wires and the cable, then put the pipe against what's left of the head and use the hammer to knock it off."

Jenks said, "Forget that. You'd probably knock off a couple of feet of plank with it. Cut the wires but leave the rest of it to me." He went forward into the fo'c'sle and came back with an oversized wood chisel. Longo had cut the wires, but no matter how hard he squeezed them, the pliers couldn't cut the steel of the cable. "Get out of there, Joe." As Longo climbed out, Jenks dropped down into the bilge alongside Nick and said, "Let me get this between the flange and spacer block, Skipper, then do your best to stop the water while I chop the damned thing off."

Nick was cold, wet, and miserable but he noticed that was the first time Jenks had ever called him Skipper. He kept the towel in place as he said, "Forget it, Boats. The hole isn't the only thing that's leaking. If it was, we'd be gaining on it faster. I think the caulking got knocked loose from a couple of planks. Feel along the frame aft of the hole. Is it still sound?"

Jenks knelt next to Nick and did as instructed. "Shit, the frame feels splintered and I don't think the planking is fair anymore. It's bulged inward. That damned sound head is probably trying to twist itself out of the boat and take a couple of planks with it. If it lets go we'll have a hole no one can bail against."

"Here. Your turn on the towel, Boats." As Nick climbed out of the bilge he yelled to Slade, "What holds the lever on the shaft, Peter?"

"A couple of set screws with slot heads. They're recessed. You'll need a small, flat-head screwdriver."

Jenks asked, "Why don't we just saw the damned thing off even with the plank?"

"Because we need it to hold the sound head so it doesn't tear itself out of the boat along with the planks it's still attached to."

Nick went into the fore cabin where they had tossed the remains of the cabin sole and the table that had been fastened to it. While he pawed through the woodpile he asked Longo, "Joe, do you have a half-inch drill? That's what the diameter of the shaft on the sound head feels like. We have to plug the hole and support the head and the planks around it at the same time." He found a piece of plywood maybe a foot and a half square. "This might do it." He dropped down into the bilge and found that the plywood was just too long to fit between the frames, but would span almost four planks. "Thank God they put that thing where they did." The sound head had been centered in the only gently curved area of the wineglass hull. He handed the plywood up to Longo, who was waiting with a hacksaw in case they had to cut the shaft. "Here, cut about here. Don't we have a wood saw?"

"No. This is it. Here's the screwdriver for the lever screws."

Once he had removed the lever and pushed it out of the way, he reached for the towel. "I'll take over, Boats."

As Jenks climbed out he said, "That plywood isn't going to fit tight against the curve of the hull. We'll need some sort of gasket. I'll take care of it." He went into the aft cabin and covered a towel with the thick axle grease Longo used as a universal lubricant. He pawed through Longo's toolbox and found that the biggest drill they had on board was three-eighths of an inch in diameter.

Once the board was fitted, they drilled the hole for the shaft at the approximate angle and then Nick and Jenks carved it to fit with the narrow blade of a pocketknife and a rat-tail file. In the meantime the rest of the crew bailed madly against the leak.

They took one man from the main hatch bucket brigade and started a second one up through the main cabin skylight. One man filled a bucket while a man on deck hauled it up, dumped it, and dropped it back down.

Meanwhile Nick and Jenks worked on the plywood. While one of them carved at the hole for the shaft, the other held the towel over the sound head hole in the bottom. With the engine pumping and the two bailing teams, they could slowly gain on the leak. But when they had to move the towel to test the fit of the plywood they would lose ground rapidly. It was a race between the Rube Goldberg repair and the in-rushing water, and they were still losing it.

The water was over the cabin sole by the time they got the board fitted. By then they had to stand on the towel in the hole to hold it in place and take a breath and go completely underwater to check the plywood's fit. Once that was done they had to take turns diving under to put the greased towel gasket in place and fasten the plywood down with screws salvaged from the cabin sole.

It was another two hours before they got the boat bailed out as best they could and found that their leak problems were far from over. Several of the seams in the surrounding frame spaces were also leaking, the caulking having been knocked loose. But *Fourteen Boat* was no longer sinking, and by keeping the engine running and bailing for thirty or forty minutes every hour they could keep her afloat. Whether this would be true once they started to move was not yet known.

The cabin was a mess. Everything was sopping wet from the slopped and splashed water. With the cabin sole shredded they could only move through the boat awkwardly by hanging onto the furniture and stepping on the deck beams and the bits of sole remaining around the edges of the gaping hole.

They nailed the top of the table across two beams in front of the galley stove so Slade would have someplace to stand while he cooked, if he could get the stove to work.

Nick went into the aft cabin to calculate his best guess as to their position while Jenks and two others got reduced sail on the boat. They'd start with just the reefed foresail and the storm staysail.

Everything in the aft cabin was soaked too. The plotting sheet on the engine box lid that was lying on Jenks' bunk looked like a spitball someone had tried to unfold. Fortunately the logbook was damp but not destroyed. It, the sextant, and the chronometer were on the shelf right under the deck over Nick's bunk where they had some protection. The lid on the clock had been closed and it was still running.

When *Fourteen Boat* was moving again, Jenks called down the hatch from the cockpit, "Which way should we steer? You want to go north toward Greenport or west toward Atlantic City, Mr. Worth? Where's the nearest land?"

"About an eighth of a mile—straight down. We've been ordered to head southeast to look for an oil slick and survivors, remember? Steer 125 magnetic."

"Shit, Mr. Worth, that was before we hit that fucking log. Who knows how long that half-assed repair is going to last?"

"You have to go out..."

"I know, damn it," he said to Borg who was on the wheel. "Steer 125." As he turned to trim the sails for the new course he muttered, "This is a big fucking mistake. That college boy is going to drown us all."

Nick came out of the hatch and quietly replied with a very slight chuckle in his voice, "I heard that mutinous utterance, Boats. If the leak gets worse we'll just bail harder and take turns holding towels against it. I hope we don't have to because that bilge water sure gets ones mind off sex, doesn't it." Then he hardened his voice, "Now knock it off and get the boat sheeted to steer 125."

He went back below to draft a message telling Greenport what was happening. But they could not send it because the radio was soaked, too. Borg would have to completely disassemble it, clean the salt water out of it, dry it, and then hope it would work.

AUGUST 2008
"DID IT, GRANDPA?"

"Eventually Borg got the receiver working but we were almost to the Jersey shore before he could send."

"I didn't mean that. I meant did it get your mind off sex?"

"You're hopeless. I'm going to talk to your father about having you transferred from that den of sin you are now attending to a convent of the Sisters of Perpetual Guilt or some such."

She laughed, then asked, "Did you find the oil slick and any survivors?"

"We found the slick and some floating junk: a ladder, some bits of splintered wood, a ratty old life jacket, but no survivors."

"Was it from the log ship?"

"Probably, but we never found out. The oil slick would have drifted faster than the logs. The log ship was never heard from again."

They didn't speak for a long time after that as the miles clicked by.

FOURTEEN

AUGUST 2008
"**Did you go back to Noank,** Grandpa?"

"No. The wind clocked around into the northwest and filled in to about Force Five while we were searching for the oil slick. Long Island would have been a dead beat. Heeled down, the water would have been on the low side where it would hurt her stability, and while we were on starboard tack, the pressure on the patch would have been increased. I decided on the Jersey coast because it would be a reach across the wind so the boat would be more on her feet and the loads on the hull would be a lot less than they'd be if we were hard on a Force Five wind.

"She was starting to leak more and more. While we had her on the wind and healed down when we were searching, we could see that the problem was more than just water coming through our hinky repair of the sound head hole and some caulking that had worked loose. A couple of the planks were splintered. If one of those let go it would be all over. We ran the engine, sailed and bailed all the way and nobody got more than an hour's sleep in one piece in the five days from the time we hit the log until we sighted the Barnegat Light House."

"Didn't they send you any help?"

"We could hear them calling us, but couldn't reply. They sent a cutter to our patrol area, but by then we were well on our way to New Jersey.

MAY 1942

NICK WAS STANDING AT THE GALLEY counter trying to plot their position without destroying any more of the sodden paper chart laid out on it than was necessary. The position points he was plotting every eight hours were so agonizingly close together that there was no point in plotting them at four-hour intervals.

Langdon, straddling the hole in the cabin sole, had filled a bucket and was guiding it upward as someone hoisted it up through the skylight. Water splashed on Nick and the chart. Another bucket had come down as he was filling the first, so Langdon crouched, filled the second bucket, and guided it upward so the motion of the boat wouldn't spill most of it before it was dumped overboard. It was a never-ending procession of deep knee bends.

For the hundredth time Nick counted how long it took a bucket to disappear: about five or six seconds. At two gallons per bucket that was maybe twenty gallons a minute, far better than the useless pump behind the toilet. The three-man brigade bailing from the engine compartment bilge was even faster. Together with the engine this allowed them to get enough ahead of the leaks so they could take a short break every hour or so to have a cup of the stew that Slade concocted when he wasn't bailing. All the other food, like everything and everyone else in the boat, was sopping wet.

But the cold and the wet wasn't their only problem; there was also their hands. Lifting the wire handles of the buckets and the rope handles they had rigged to every other container they could find had covered their palms with blisters that broke and were replaced by even more painful blisters in the new skin trying to form beneath them. They wore out every glove on board and then wrapped their hands in lengths of cloth torn from towels. The gloves and toweling helped to protect their hands somewhat from the constant abrasion, but also kept them painfully wet with salt water.

They were within fifteen miles or so of Barnegat inlet when Borg, who had been working on the radio in the fore cabin for four days between shifts at bailing, came into the main cabin and proclaimed, "It works. I just got a reply from the Cape May Coast Guard Station. They're sending out one of the motor yachts from the inshore patrol with an auxiliary pump."

Nick scribbled their position on a scrap of paper. "Send this off and just say, 'Am leaking but coping. Will welcome the pump.' Then grab some chow and take a break."

Borg took the paper by the corner with two fingers so it wouldn't dissolve before he could read it.

AUGUST 2008

"**BOY, WERE WE BEAT.** The last day and a half we had to run both bucket brigades full time to stay even, because the engine ran out of gas. With sailing the boat, it kept us pretty busy."

"Nobody ever gets much sleep in a small yacht on an offshore passage, I suppose, but that had to be worse."

"I know that kind of tiredness. Been there, done that. This was exhaustion, something far beyond mere tiredness. It's a combination of prolonged lack of sleep, extreme discomfort, and silently repressed fear. The kind of fear you can't admit because if you do you'll panic.

"There's no way to run an urgent bucket brigade without slopping water over everything. The cabin heater crapped out when salt water found its way into the burners and fuel supply. The only sources of heat were the constantly running engine, until it ran out of gas, and the galley stove. How Slade kept that working I'll never know. The hot meals he concocted out of canned goods—Spam, canned vegetables...all the other food was wet and ruined—and the gallons of black coffee he made were our most important weapons in the battle with the leaks that we fought along with our battles with exhaustion and a fear I can only admit now, many years later. He also did what he could for our hands, although it wasn't much. The combination of constant wetness, the lifting ropes, and the handles of the buckets, pots, and paint cans we used turned our palms into bloody masses of broken blisters."

"It took you five days to sail, what, a hundred and fifty miles or so?"

"More than that with the search and all. We wound up going on just the foresail. If we used the main it made the boat work and leak more. Trying to stretch the gas, we only ran the engine fast enough to keep the pump spinning. It and the foresail pushed us along at maybe two or three knots or so. We even reefed the foresail if the wind picked up and the hull started to work very much."

"How did the crew deal with it?"

"Oddly enough, it made us more—I guess the best word is kind—to each other, not less. You'd think it would make everyone irritable and mean, but it didn't. Everybody became more solicitous of the others. Even Jenks. Toots, I have never been so beat in my whole life as I was then."

He paused in thought, then continued, "I just finished reading a book on the war in Italy and it talks about the combat exhaustion of infantrymen. This was the same thing. The most aggravating factor in that kind of fatigue is not the sleeplessness or the discomfort, or even the pain. It's the constant fear of instant death. The fear that none of us dared to mention was that something could tear loose at any minute and drown us all. Controlling constant terror, holding it at bay so you can function, is the most exhausting thing there is. The only good thing about it is that a frightened man with a bucket is the most efficient bilge pump there is."

"But you made it."

"Yes, but as I keep telling you, you have to remember that at the time we didn't know we were going to make it, although everyone now knows that we made it."

MAY 1942

THE COAST WAS A BLUE LINE on the horizon when the forty-foot Chris Craft Double Cabin Cruiser found them and two older men with a gasoline-powered pump came aboard. The pump could barely stay even with the leaks so a second one was sent over. Only when that was running could they finally stop bailing. *Fourteen Boat*'s crew dropped wherever they could find a spot that wasn't awash in seawater.

The Chris Craft's crew consisted of a doctor and his wife, a lawyer, the manager of the local gas company, and two of his employees. They were all well over fifty, had been friends and fishing buddies for years, and had signed up for the Coast Guard Auxiliary the week after Pearl Harbor. The twin-screw Chris Craft took *Fourteen Boat* in tow and sent over two more men. Nick and Jenks got the sail off of her with their help before they collapsed on the cockpit seats opposite each other, wrapped in the dry blankets the other skipper had also sent over.

Finally Jenks said, "Shit, Skipper..." and Nick replied, "Yeah, shit..." Then they both laughed.

They towed her through the momentarily calm but notoriously rough Barnegat inlet and across the bay to a boatyard in Toms River. A submerged cradle on the marine railway was waiting for them and they dragged the schooner out of the water. An over-age retread Navy lieutenant, now in the Coast Guard, was waiting for them. He returned Nick's salute when he came down the ladder from the dripping hull, then held out his hand to be shaken as he asked, "Uneventful trip, Ensign?"

Nick held up his scab-covered palms and avoided the handshake. "Yes, sir. No U-boats, no survivors, just sailing around trying to keep the boat from falling overboard." Nick filled him in as they watched the crew hand their sea bags down the ladder, then climb down after them. "I hope that's the last bucket brigade they have to do for a while."

The crew boarded a waiting bus to be taken to the Coast Guard Station as the yard foreman, a carpenter's mate, and Jenks, who had been surveying the bottom together, climbed aboard the boat. Nick and the lieutenant followed them, and while the other three were looking into the bilge he pulled his sea bag and shore uniform from the hanging locker at the foot of his bunk. Everything was soaked; that woolen uniform would definitely never fit him again. He tossed it all into the cockpit as the other three climbed around the hole where the cabin sole used to be.

The carpenter's mate asked, "Jesus, Ensign, how did you keep her afloat?"

"One bucket at a time."

"Besides the hole where the sound head used to be, at least three planks are splintered, a lot of the caulking's gone, and we're going to have to sister some frames. That must have been some log."

The lieutenant asked him, "How long will it take to get her ready for sea?"

"At least a week, probably two. Besides the hull repairs, we have to dry out the cabin, clean out the tanks, and replace or repair the electrical stuff that got wet. We'll just make a new sole out of tongue and groove stock. That's the easiest part."

"Make it so we can get it out without having to use an axe the next time."

"You planning on doing this regularly, Ensign?"

By the next day, they had all gotten two hot meals and a night's sleep. That morning Nick watched while his crew was issued new uniforms, a partial pay, and five days' liberty. It was afternoon before he could get to a pay phone. "Personnel, Miss Madison."

"Hi. We just got in yesterday."

"Are you in Greenport?"

"No, I'm at the Barnegat Coast Guard Station in New Jersey. We had a little problem with your brother's boat."

"My, God, what happened? Did it sink or get torpedoed or something?"

"No, nothing that exciting. She just leaked a little. It'll take a week or so for them to fix her. What are you doing for the next five or six days? Can you get off? I have to go to Brooks to get some uniforms. The base here doesn't have an officer's store. Could you meet me Under The Clock tomorrow afternoon?"

"Hold on. Let me talk to my boss."

He hung on the phone while the operator twice came on and said, "Please deposit twenty-five cents for another three minutes."

The operator was asking for yet more money when Amy came back and said, "It's all set. He didn't want to let me off at first, but I told him my hero had come home from the war so he'll let me go. Then I called my mother and told her I was coming down to Washington for a few days and bringing a friend with me."

Nick thought, but this time didn't say, "Oh, shit."

AUGUST 2008

"I ASSUME THAT BROOKS was Brooks Brothers, Grandpa, but how would she know which clock or even which city you were talking about?"

"Because back then the only Brooks Brothers was on Madison Avenue in New York and everyone in our generation, the generation before us, and the one after, all of us who grew up in the three-state area knew that Under The Clock was the lobby lounge in the Biltmore Hotel next to Grand Central Station. For forty years, until they tore the hotel down, it was the rendezvous for young people."

"All young people?"

"No, just young people of the better classes."

She knew he was trying to bait her into some politically correct statement he could tear apart, so she ignored the bait, and asked, "Was Madison Avenue named after one of my ancestors?"

"I have no idea."

"Did you want to go to Washington to meet her parents?"

"Hell, no."

"What did you have in mind?"

"Just what you think I had in mind. For once your dirty little mind has it right. Almost having to swim a couple of hundred miles concentrates the mind wonderfully once you're dry and warm again. I was hoping she'd go someplace with me and get married so we'd have a license to show some desk clerk."

"But she made you go to Washington to meet my great-grandparents instead. What a drag."

"Yeah. What a drag. But your grandmother had the bit in her teeth, and when she got like that I had no choice but to go along. That was the first of many times she did it to me."

JUNE 1942

THE LIEUTENANT LOANED HIM an old navy ensign's uniform that didn't fit at all and a cap that fell down over his ears until he stuffed the sweatband with toilet paper, and gave him a lift to the Baltimore and Ohio station the next morning. He scurried out of Penn Station and took a cab to Brooks before any of the MPs on duty could spot his odd getup. Particularly his shoes. He had spent the last weeks in sea boots and it wasn't until he dug them out of the soaked sea bag with the rest of his shore clothes that he realized what bad shape they were in. No amount of polish could keep them from squeaking and turning white with salt when he walked.

He was far better dressed two hours later when he walked into the Biltmore carrying a new Val Pak with a shoulder strap. Brooks had been more than accommodating, fitting and altering two uniforms while he waited and offering to mail the lieutenant's clothes back to him.

Amy was waiting for him at a small round table with a tea service on it. She stood when he approached but seemed somehow subdued and didn't kiss him with nearly the enthusiasm he expected. As they sat back down she asked, "What happened to your hands?" A medic at the CG Station had bandaged them that morning so he wouldn't get dirt onto the tender new skin that was just beginning to form.

"Blisters that broke and then new blisters formed on the skin under them that also broke. They're better already. I'll get rid of the bandages tonight." He held up his hands to show the already soiled bandages. "Tough to keep anything clean in this city. How are you, Toots?"

This did not sit well with her for some reason. "I'm fine. And don't call me Toots, okay?"

He wondered what was going on. "When did you arrive in the city? Have I kept you waiting long?"

She looked up at the ornate clock on the ironwork arch over the entrance to the lounge. "No, you're twenty minutes early, as a matter of fact. I came in last night and stayed with Linda Daniels, my college roommate. She and another girl have an apartment in Greenwich Village."

"Did you get the train tickets? I understand the New York to Washington trains are always full."

"We're on the 2:28. I got us a compartment. All the coach seats were sold out. Do you know a girl named Sharon Brant who went to Mount Holyoke?"

"Sure. We went out for a while my senior year. I'd go down there and she came up to Hanover for football weekends a couple of times."

"She's sharing the apartment with Linda. And you seem to have forgotten J-hop and a pledge formal or two. She remembered how you had this odd way of calling a girl Toots so that it wasn't insulting at all: it was endearing."

"Is this what this is about? A girl I dated in college years ago and how I call you Toots?"

"Linda said Sharon was more than a little fast in college. Was she?"

"That's none of your damn business, but for your information I always found her to be a perfect lady."

"So you say." She looked up at the Clock. "We'd better get going if we're going to make the train."

AUGUST 2008

"GRANDMA WAS JEALOUS?"

"Of course. Once they've selected a male to build a nest with, the females of every species become jealous and protective. If threatened they get instantly vindictive. Watch yourself, Toots. Once you've picked out a mate you'll find yourself acting the same way."

She smiled as she said, "I don't know if I like your calling me Toots either. Did she get over it?"

"Eventually."

"You don't hear girls called fast anymore. It meant kind of wild, didn't it?"

"Wild with a hint of promiscuousness. More than a hint. It was better than calling a girl a tramp, though. That's another word that's gone out of fashion, although Cole Porter wrote a great song about it."

"But you eventually made up, obviously."

"Not right away."

JUNE 1942

SHE WAS DEAD SILENT until they were in the compartment. He hoped she was cooling off but she started the conversation with, "I hope I'm not going to spend the rest of my life running into your old enamoratas. And I hope you'll behave like a gentleman with my parents. I know you aren't particularly pleased to have to meet them, although it's important to me.'"

They were sitting on opposite sides of the compartment, he by the door and she by the window, as far from each other as they could get. They glared at each other for a minute or two as he thought, *I don't need this trip or any of this shit. Forty-eight hours ago I wasn't sure I'd ever see her again and now I'm not sure that I want to. I'd better get this settled one way or the other right now.*

So he said, "Look, Amy, you're beginning to piss me off. First off, Sharon Brant was not my enamorata. What the hell ever that is. Second, I know full well how to behave in polite company, but I'm not going to pretend to be somebody else in order to impress your parents. If anything, they ought to go out of their way to impress me after my seeing how their asshole son behaves. If I don't come up to the high standard that he represents, tough. You'll just have to decide whose side you want to be on before we get to the next station because I'm ready to get off this damned train." He tore the bandages off his hands and tossed them in the waste receptacle in the corner.

"I hope your father isn't one of those insecure and overly aggressive types like your brother, because if he tries to prove it by his manly handshake, I'll start our relationship by knocking him on his ass." He stood up and said, "I have to go to the head," and stalked out.

He hoped when he returned that they would be able to change the subject but she wouldn't let it go. "My father is nothing like my brother."

"Good."

They were quiet for a while until she said, "The idea of you with another woman makes me almost nauseous."

"You'd rather I was such a hopeless case that no one would go out with me until you came along? And what about you, Toots? Am I the first guy to rescue you from a hopeless spinsterhood?"

"Of course not. I had plenty of dates and you won't believe the number of guys who find flimsy excuses to come to the Personnel Department."

"They've probably heard a rumor that you're fast."

"No one would ever dare to even think…" She saw his smile, paused, and then smiled in spite of herself as she said, "Oh, you." They stared at each other in silence until she finally came across the compartment and gave him a proper welcome-home kiss.

By the time it was finished she was sitting on his lap. "I'd better tell you about my parents and explain how Robert got the way he is. They didn't mean for him to grow up to be an ass…, a what you called him. They have money, old money. My great-grandfather was in cahoots with one of the railroad robber barons: Jay Gould."

"Look, Toots, my family isn't exactly broke. Well, maybe my father is. I hope he is."

"Where'd your family get its money?"

"My great-grandfather was a pattern maker in a foundry in Bridgeport. He only had a grade school education but he insisted his kids go to college. The American dream. My grandfather was a very successful surgeon who loved to sail and was a member of the offshore racing community for years. He was a very shrewd investor in his own right and among his sailing buddies were Bernard Baruch and a number of other Wall Street powerhouses. He got out of the market in '28 at the same time they did. Then he had the cash to pick up good stocks really cheap. He bought AT&T in 1933 for about ten bucks a share."

Amy kissed him again, then asked, "If it all went bust and you lost every penny, what would you do?"

"I've got a degree in chemistry and I've got pretty good mechanical skills. I'd get along. Don't worry."

"I'm not worried. I'm a really good secretary and office manager. We'd get along."

He kissed her this time. "Toots, could you get off my lap? My legs are going to sleep."

"Couldn't tell by me. Your circulation seems to be fine from where I'm sitting." Then she blushed and giggled. "That just popped out. Does that make me fast?"

"Yup. But that's all right. As you know, I like fast women: the faster the better."

She moved to the seat next to him while avoiding looking at his lap as he quickly crossed his legs. She took a deep breath, let it out, and then said, "About my parents. If through some stroke of bad luck they lost everything, they wouldn't be able to get along. Quite literally, they would die."

"They're older. I suppose it's to be expected that they wouldn't be as agile as a couple of kids like us."

"No. They've always been like that, even when they were young. Their whole life has been about protecting their money and the place in the ruling class that comes with it."

"They're conservatives?"

"They're not conservatives, they're reactionaries. As reactionary as Nicholas and Alexandra. All they care about is holding onto what they have and keeping the Great Unwashed that they profess to love in its place. And its place is as far from them as possible. Unless they're servants, of course. They're quite conflicted about servants. When I was a little girl I was fascinated by cooking. Still am, to tell the truth. But I was not allowed to set foot in the kitchen for fear that if I learned to cook I would become someone's servant. They'd rather I starved to death than take a job as someone's servant. I mean that quite literally."

"How do they feel about your job?"

"They hate it. My mother sees it as just another of the awful things I've done since I was a little girl. Did I tell you that I was an awful tomboy? My brother terrorized me every chance he got, and my mother let him do it. I think because she hoped it would civilize me. It just made me worse."

"When did you become the perfect, if a bit fast, young lady I have come to love?"

She kissed him again. A long, lingering one. Then she leaned back and said, "In boarding school. They shipped me off to boarding school when I was ten. Didn't need the tomboy act once I was out of my brother's clutches."

"Did he? You know…"

"Lord, no. If he'd even tried I'd have taken a ball bat to him and he knew it. No, it was just day in and day out meanness. Pokes, jabs, insults, taking and breaking my stuff. The more I liked something, the more likely it was to either disappear or be accidentally broken. "

"I wish I had thrown the bastard off the dock. So they probably expect you to bring home a member of the Great Unwashed, and I'm it?"

"Yup. And my mother told me to bring an evening gown because we have to go to a reception at some embassy. They're probably hoping to trap you into some gross social error to prove their superiority."

"Should I slurp my soup so I don't disappoint them? Or maybe goose one of the ladies at the reception?"

"That would be good. They'd like that. No, just say as little as possible and be on your best behavior."

"Why the hell are you dragging me there, Amy?"

She thought about it before saying, "Because I'm proud of you. You're quite a catch, Nicholas Worth, and I want to show them that their hopeless tomboy daughter who has become what my mother calls 'a factory worker'—you have no idea how much my parents despise factory workers—can land someone like you."

There was a Lincoln limousine waiting for them at Union Station driven by a chauffeur who had been with the family for years and called her Miss Amy. It made Nick feel as if he had wandered into *Gone With the Wind* by mistake. His life was utterly disjointed. Seventy-two hours before he had been out in the Atlantic bailing for his life with six men who were the backbone of America. Now he was sitting in a limousine with "Miss Amy" heading for what he was sure was a mansion in Georgetown. The thaw continued as she snuggled up against him and said, "Don't be nervous, darling. My parents will love you."

As if anything here could make him nervous after all that had happened to him in the last few months.

FIFTEEN

"**How was your reception** by Grandma's parents, Grandpa?"

"Cool, definitely cool." He closed his eyes and tried to recall the details that over the years he had tried to forget. Finally he said, "They say that odor is the strongest stimulant of memory. Well, whenever I walk into a room that's heavy with tobacco smell I think of my mother-in-law.

"I don't think very many people back then actually noticed the smell because just about everyone smoked. Cigarettes were about fifteen cents a pack, if people could get them. There were some off-brands that smelled worse than the others that were usually available. Wings. Spuds was another one, but as I recall Wings were the worst. But all cigarettes were unfiltered and powerfully addictive. They were made with raw tobacco, not the sissified stuff they use today. It's no wonder that lung cancer and emphysema are killing off my generation. The secondhand smoke alone was lethal and almost impossible to avoid. It was just an accepted fact of the environment, like light and darkness.

"Jenks smoked Wings, of course. But Jessica Madison, Amy's mother, smoked nothing but the best: king-size Pall Malls. And she had no trouble getting them in Washington. She was like my father and his Yalie friends: they were the only people I met in all those years who actually didn't realize that there was a war on. The ultimate in selfishness.

"Didn't Grandma smoke?"

"No. She said her brother had forced a cigarette on her once when she was about twelve and she had a coughing fit that lasted all day and half the night. We had to be the only couple in the country where neither smoked."

"Her mother wasn't impressed with you and your new Brooks Brothers uniform?"

"Not hardly."

JUNE 1942
"MOTHER, THIS IS NICHOLAS WORTH."

Jessica Madison elegantly shifted her cigarette from her right to her left hand, but he held up his raw, battered palms and said, "I'm very glad to meet you, Mrs. Madison, but forgive me for not taking your hand."

She stepped back and asked Amy, "Whatever happened to him?"

"It's sort of a war wound, Mother."

She obviously wasn't interested in that line of conversation. "You didn't tell me you were bringing home a young man, dear." There was an accusatory tone to the statement.

Amy held up her left ring finger. "Nick and I are going to be married."

Mrs. Madison looked from her daughter to her potential son-in-law. She took a deep drag and let it out through her nose as she looked him up and down and then turned back to her daughter as she said, "Your father will be along any moment. We can discuss this later." She turned and led them from the entrance hall into the living room as she changed the subject. "We're going to a reception at the Danish Legation tonight. You did bring a gown with you, didn't you, dear? And I hope the young man has a dress uniform if he's going to go with us."

"Mrs. Madison, this *is* a dress uniform."

"I meant an evening dress uniform. Does he at least know what that is, Amy?"

AUGUST 2008

"**Wow, Grandpa.** I guess it was definitely a cool reception."

"That woman, in all the years I knew her, she never once spoke directly to me if she could find a way to avoid it. This is probably an awful thought, but the best thing I can say about my mother-in-law is that she died young. Those cigarettes she used as a weapon to intimidate anyone she didn't approve of destroyed her heart and lungs. She liked to make sweeping gestures with them. It's a wonder she didn't set someone or something on fire."

"How about Grandma's father?"

"He wasn't a bad guy. At least he talked to me. He and Grandma were quite close, but he did everything he could to avoid aggravating his wife, and she was very easily aggravated. He kind of stayed on the fringe of things. He smoked a pipe. The contemplative sort. The first time I got him alone I asked, quite formally, for his daughter's hand in marriage. We were in his Packard coupe. Jessica, the mother-in-law from hell, insisted on riding in the Lincoln alone with Grandma to try to talk her out of everything: marrying me, working in a factory, living at Marion's, everything."

"Did he grant his permission or did you elope?"

"Yes to both. He asked me a lot of questions about my education, my family, how I intended to make a living after the war, that sort of thing. He didn't ask about what I was doing in the war. It turned out Brother Bob had given both of them an uncomplimentary earful about me. We were stopped at the light on the corner of Embassy Row, in front of the Ritz Carlton. I remember it like it was yesterday; he was wearing a soup and fish. 'I don't think you and Amy have known each other nearly long enough to take such a big step. But I know there is a war on.'"

"I asked him if that meant he had no objections and he said, 'No, I have no objections but I can't say the same for my wife.'"

"Well, Grandma obviously ignored her mother's objections or I wouldn't be here."

"She almost didn't."

JUNE 1942

THE DANISH LEGATION had an undefined semi-official status and had been housed in the British Embassy ever since the Germans had forced the Danes to close their own embassy when America entered the war. Nick and his future father-in-law were waiting at the curb when the Lincoln pulled up and Amy climbed out without waiting for the chauffeur to open the door. Her face was flushed, and without waiting for her mother to get out of the car she grabbed Nick's arm and headed for the door. All she said was, "That woman," as she struggled to get her breathing back to normal. She was wearing a light blue full-length gown with spaghetti straps and a moderate décolleté set off by a simple pendant with a diamond centered in it. She looked very beautiful.

As they walked down the hall toward the crowded ballroom, Nick asked, "What happened?"

"What didn't happen? My brother had her all primed. He called me again last week wanting me to quit my job and move into Manhattan to work for him. He got quite nasty and accused me of becoming just another sluttish factory girl. So I told him we were engaged and to leave me alone. She knew all along I was bringing you to meet them. She said I was just a sailor's plaything and as soon as you found someone you liked better you'd dump me." They stopped in the arched doorway to the crowded main room and through clenched teeth she added, "I'd like to kill them both. They've been in cahoots to make me miserable my whole life."

They started to move into the room as a waiter offered them champagne from a tray of crystal flutes. They each took one; Amy downed hers in two gulps and took a second as Nick looked across the room and saw a woman coming toward them. She was easy to spot because she was half a head taller than any other woman in the room. Nick, being like most men, didn't notice that her gown was identical to Amy's. He did, like most men, notice that because she was somewhat more robust than Amy, the same décolleté was more daring. Remembering what had happened Under The Clock, Nick thought, *Oh, shit.* He was very glad to see her safe, but sincerely wished it hadn't been at this moment.

"Nicholas. It is you, isn't it?"

"How are you Elise? I am so glad to see you safe. I've been worried about you ever since the Germans invaded Denmark."

"The Secret State Police," she used the full German name for the Gestapo, Geheime Staatspolizei, "were a bit angry with us, weren't they. All in all, that was a pretty nice day, though, wasn't it? Exciting. And who is this lovely person?"

Amy was on her third flute, sipping it this time, and was eyeing Elise and her gown. "Amy Madison, this is Elise Gottlieb. Elise and I met at the 1936 Olympics, went sailing together, and then got in trouble with the Nazis for crashing a party."

"It's Elise Christiansen now. I'm with the Legation."

Amy said, "I like your gown." Then she turned to Nick and said, "I don't feel well. I'm going home. Why don't you stay here and practice your German with Elise of the many last names." With that she turned and stalked out of the room.

Elise was genuinely perplexed. "I seem to have made the young lady angry and I have no idea why, other than the unfortunate coincidence of our gowns." It was only then that Nick realized that their gowns were identical.

"She has had a very bad day, believe me. She's my fiancée—at least, she was until a few minutes ago; now I'm not so sure."

"Then go after her, Nicholas. Don't lose her. Once things are better, call me at the Legation and the three of us can have a meal together. I want a chance to apologize for any pain I might have caused her."

"She's the one who should apologize. But she has had an awful day. I already said that, didn't I?"

"If she is important to you, Nicholas, go after her."

As he turned toward the door he said, "I'll call you."

"Yes, call me. I want to properly meet this person who is important to you."

Amy was just climbing into the Lincoln when he came running out and got in after her. "What's the matter, was Elise already booked for the night?" she snapped.

"Do you realize how much like your mother you sound? How about we stop so I can buy you some cigarettes to wave at me? Elise and I spent one day together six years ago."

"But it was a pretty exciting day that she obviously enjoyed and so did you. I'm sick of meeting one of your doxies after another."

She was getting to him so he hit back. "Especially if they're wearing the same gown and filling it a lot better. Is that your definition of a doxy?"

"What a hateful thing to say. Get out of this car right now."

"Well, you ought to be an expert on hateful, coming from that hateful, dysfunctional family of yours." He leaned over and said to the chauffeur, "Take me back to the house so I can get my Val Pak, then I'll get a cab to Union Station and never have to see anyone from the lunatic Madison family again. They're all alike."

They both sat in silence for the rest of the trip.

The next train wasn't until midnight so he had over two hours to wait.

He was just getting up to head for the gate when Amy came hurrying across the crowded station obviously looking for him. He considered ducking through the gate and never seeing her again, but instead waved at her. She was still wearing the light blue evening gown with a three-quarter length car coat over it. Without preliminary she asked, "Can we talk?"

He checked his watch. "My train leaves in twelve minutes."

"Always the navigator. Not ten minutes or fifteen minutes, precisely twelve minutes."

"Closer to eleven now. What's to talk about? I don't like your family and they don't like me. Oil and water. Those who have things and those who do things. This can't work."

"You sound like you've been thinking about this while you sat here. Did it occur to you that I don't like my family either and they don't like me? And your father is no prize either. Face it, Nick, we both come from dysfunctional families."

"I had my mother and my grandfather."

"And I have my father. I told him what happened while my mother was on the phone gleefully reporting to my brother how she drove you off. He gave me the keys to the Packard and told me to come get you."

"I don't want to go back there."

"I don't blame you. Neither do I. I threw my clothes and stuff in the car. Where do you want to go?"

"I don't want to go anyplace with you if you're going to keep having these fits of jealousy. I have never even thought of being anything but completely true to you from the moment we met, but I can't spend the rest of my life with someone who, for absolutely no reason, does not trust me."

Tears started but she fought them back. "I'm just so terrified of losing you. Every time you go out in that silly little boat... The idea that even if you do come back I could still lose you... Everything I've ever valued, my mother and brother took away or spoiled, and now they're trying to drive you away, too." She took a couple of deep breaths, then continued, "When you're at sea, every moment of every day I'm terrified of losing you, and everything in the whole damned world seems to be trying to take you away from me any way it can."

"No one but you can drive me away from you, Amy, and as far as my not coming back from a cruise goes," he shrugged, "there's a war on, you know. Neither of us can do anything about that except take our chances and hang in there until it's over." Until that moment he had not even considered how difficult his sea duty was for her. He had thought that she just went to work every day and waited for him to come back without realizing how agonizing that waiting was for her.

She sniffled. "I'm just so sorry for behaving like such a bitch, and for being such a mean-spirited bitch to your friend Elise."

He thought about it for just a second. "Well, I guess this relationship has reached the decision point. We either walk away from each other right now, or…"

"Or what?"

"You know what. Do you want to walk away?"

"No. Of course not. That's why I came after you."

"Then come on." He grabbed her hand and walked over to an information booth for service men run by the USO. There was a gray-haired lady working behind the counter. He asked her, "Could you tell me where is the nearest place to get married?"

She smiled, "You have no idea how often I get asked that. There's a three-day waiting period in D.C. and Maryland, but not in Virginia. Do you have a car?"

When they both nodded yes, she continued, "There's a Justice of the Peace in Bowling Green who will perform the ceremony any time of the night or day. It's about forty miles straight down 301 in the center of town. It's across from the courthouse. You can't miss it. And congratulations and good luck. My husband and I eloped in 1917 just before he left for France. We had twenty–four years together. He was at Hickam Field." Her eyes went glassy as she leaned over the counter, kissed Amy, and whispered something in her ear.

As they walked out to the car he asked, "What did she say to you?"

"Every day. Enjoy every day because it's a gift." Then she handed him the keys and said, "You drive. I've got a splitting headache from that champagne." He got in and leaned over to unlock the passenger door for her. As she got in she tossed her coat behind the seat, then slid across and kissed him. As she moved back she caught him looking down. "Do you still think Elise fills one of these dresses better than I do?"

"You fill it just fine, Amy.

AUGUST 2008
"WHAT WAS HICKAM FIELD, GRANDPA?"

"They don't teach you kids any history anymore, do they? Hickam Field was the Army Air Corps base in Hawaii. The Japs clobbered it at the same time they hit Pearl Harbor. Her husband was probably professional Army."

Amy thought about it, then asked, "You were completely surrounded by the reality of that war, weren't you?"

"You didn't have to go far to meet someone who had lost someone. And just about everyone had someone close to them who was in the service and could be killed or maimed. It concentrated our minds wonderfully. Now war is something that happens on TV to other people between sporting events and reality shows that really aren't about reality at all. I heard a paratrooper from World War Two say that it was something he'd never want to live through again, but he wouldn't have missed for the world. None of those people watching McNamara's spectator wars on TV have any idea just how"—he searched for a word—"urgently alive we were. The paratrooper had it exactly right."

"Urgently alive. Is that why you and Grandma got married so urgently?"

"Exactly. As I said, our minds were wonderfully concentrated by what was happening all around us, and what could happen to us any day. Not just to others, to us."

"When you were in harm's way."

"Exactly."

JUNE 1942

THEY GOT TO BOWLING GREEN at about three in the morning and sat in the car alternately dozing and necking until, at about six, an elderly man came out of the house to get his paper. Nick talked to him for a moment, introduced him to Amy, and then they followed him into the house.

They had been invited to get cleaned up and have breakfast before the ceremony, so Amy had finally gotten out of her evening gown, had a bath, and put on a light gray fitted suit that would be her wedding dress. Nick got cleaned up in a downstairs bathroom, shaved, and put on a fresh shirt. They had just sat down to breakfast with the Justice of the Peace and his wife when another couple came in. He wore the pinks and greens of an infantry lieutenant and she, like Amy, wore a traveling suit, except hers was very rumpled.

The lieutenant explained that he was stationed just outside of town at Fort A. P. Hill and expected to ship out any day. His bride had arrived the night before from Ohio after a circuitous two-and-a-half day train trip. They had been high school sweethearts.

AUGUST 2008

"THE JUSTICE OF THE PEACE and his wife were wonderful people. They invited the lieutenant and his bride to join us for breakfast."

Amy asked, "Pinks and greens?"

"The Army officer's dress uniform had a belted green jacket and light grayish trousers that were called pinks."

"I think I've seen them in old movies."

"The justice and his wife had two sons who had enlisted in the Marine Corps the day after Pearl Harbor. Their eldest child, a Navy nurse, was in the Philippines. We could tell they were worried sick about her."

"I've always been fascinated by your wedding picture. On the mantel behind you and Grandma there were three framed pictures but I could never make out who they were."

"The justice's wife took the picture of us standing in front of the fireplace in their living room. The pictures were of their kids. Anyway, we had a double wedding. Then the four of us went out and bought wedding rings at the local jewelry store and had lunch together. We never saw the other couple again."

"What happened?"

"Your grandmother kept in touch with her for a few years, but he didn't make it back from Europe. Eventually she remarried and we lost contact."

"God, you seemed to know a lot of people that didn't make it back."

"It would have been pretty hard not to know someone who didn't make it back. By the time it was over there were about a half a million killed and missing, plus another six hundred thousand wounded. And it was a much smaller country then, only a little over a hundred million people total. But just about all of those casualties were yanked out of one generation—mine. It decimated us."

"Where did you go on your honeymoon?"

To lighten the conversation he chuckled and said, "Honeymoon? That's funny. We were considering Biarritz, but it was always so crowded at that time of year. Paris was booked up at the moment with German tourists, and I really didn't feel much like a luxury ocean cruise. It was impossible to get a hotel room in D.C., so we decided that two days in the transient officer's billets at Fort A. P. Hill would be très chic."

"I won't even bother to ask what went on there. Then what did you do?"

"Well, we had to take the Packard back to Washington before her mother reported it stolen, if she hadn't already. So while your grandmother was in one phone booth calling her father, I went into the next one and called Elise at the Danish Legation. I figured I owed her that. She was insisting that we meet her for lunch when Grandma came into my booth and said that we were supposed to meet her father for lunch at a swanky restaurant in Washington at one o'clock. So I invited Elise to join us."

"How did that go?"

"Surprisingly well. My father-in-law was very gracious, his wife was mostly silent, and Elise was very, very charming. Grandma and she hit it off right away. She gave her a gold Danish coin mounted as a pendant for a wedding present."

"Is that where that came from? I have it and wear it on special occasions. I knew it was old but I never knew the significance."

"As we were saying goodbye in the restaurant's entranceway Elise pulled me aside and asked me not to call her again because she was going to be away for a while on business and would get in touch with me when she got back. When I asked her what business, all she said was, 'There's a war on, you know.'"

"Did you ever find out what the business was?"

"Not for sure. Years later I read in a history book that two days before D-day the commander of the Panzer division that was closest to Normandy was murdered in his bed by his Danish mistress. The Krauts went nuts trying to find her. She was a tall, gorgeous, green-eyed blonde, but they never caught her."

"Did you ever ask Elise if she had done it?"

"Yup. After the war. All she said was, 'We all had our adventures and did what we had to do, didn't we, Nicholas?'"

"She came to the U.S. after the war?"

"Yes, and I'm proud to say Grandma and I sponsored her. She worked her way through med school, wound up teaching at U.V.M., married, and had two kids. I think she never admitted what she had done in the war because basically she was ashamed of it and didn't want anyone, particularly her kids, to know about it. A lot of us had secrets we carried away with us and never admitted."

"Did you, Grandpa?"

"Did I what?"

"Have a secret."

He was silent for a while before saying, "If I told you, then it wouldn't be a secret anymore, would it?" Then he closed his eyes to signal that the conversation was over.

SIXTEEN

THEY CHANGED TRAINS in Philadelphia and took a local that stopped in Toms River, where he would leave her. His new wife would continue on to New York and then to Stratford to go back to work. As they stood in the aisle holding each other, with tears in her eyes, Amy whispered, "You remember my regulations and forget the Coast Guard's. Those don't apply to us."

"I'll remember. We'll probably be back in a couple of weeks. I'll call you when I know more. I might not be able to tell you much on the phone, though. Loose lips sink ships."

"Call me anyway. Now go back to your damn boat."

He kissed her once more, then left.

They had made considerable headway. When he got to the yard, *Fourteen Boat* was in the water beside a floating dock and Jenks came up the walkway to the fixed pier to meet him. "How is she, Boats? She seems to be floating without anyone throwing water out of the hatch."

"She's once more fulfilling this first duty of a boat: to keep the fucking water out. How was your leave, Skipper, and how is the lovely Miss Madison?"

"Alas, the lovely Miss Madison is no more. She is now the lovely Missus Worth."

"No shit?"

"Yup, no shit. How was your leave?"

"Didn't take one. If I did, these yard guys would never have gotten the boat fixed."

Nick doubted that but let it slide. "What about the guys?"

"They all went home except Slade. Would you believe that Langdon took him up to la-de-da Larchmont with him because there was no way he could get to Oklahoma and back. I guess Langdon's folks treated him like royalty. That was one happy shit-kicker when they came back."

Jenks was calling him Skipper, and the rest of the crew had obviously become buddies. Maybe almost sinking wasn't all bad. "Where are they?"

"Borg's putting in the new radio. I hope it's more waterproof than the last one. Cookie is getting the galley straightened out and stowing his medical stuff. Longo has the engine torn down and Snow is helping him."

"What about the sound equipment?"

"Done, for what it's worth. They put big doublers inside the hull behind both heads. To rip them off now we'd have to tear out the whole bottom."

"Where's Langdon?"

"Up in the shed painting the dory. He has really shaped up."

"What dory?"

"The one he and I rebuilt from one we found in the back of the yard. It'll fit under the fores'l boom on the cabin top. If the boat ever decides to head for the nearest land—which happens to be a hundred fathoms straight down—we ought to have some alternate transportation."

"I was thinking the same thing and was going to get a couple of Carly floats."

"Those things ain't worth a shit and we both know it. But lots of Banks schooner crews have survived in their dories when the mother ship went down. Besides, *Fourteen Boat* isn't really a schooner unless she has at least one dory on board."

Nick looked down at the boat. "What happened to the skylight?" The peaked glass and mahogany structure was gone, replaced by a flat, solid hatch.

"Got rid of the damned thing. Never saw one of 'em that didn't leak like a fuckin' faucet. We could carry the dory upside down over it, but with that thing in the way we couldn't turn it upright if we had to haul anything or anybody in it."

"It's going to make the cabin dark, isn't it?" He almost wished he had turned down the leave and not left Jenks in charge. Almost, but not really.

"Maybe a little darker. There's still plenty of light from the ports in the cabin sides. I'll gladly swap a little light for a lot less water dripping in my supper."

"Let's go look at our new lifeboat."

Langdon had just finished painting it the standard haze grey and was cleaning the brushes when they walked into the shed. Nick had to admit that it was a very pretty little boat with its sweeping shear, widely flaring sides, and tombstone transom. "In a hard chance, would it carry seven guys?"

"Dories this size can carry two guys and a thousand pounds of fish. We can tow it alongside when we're getting people out of the water, too. That would be a lot easier than hauling them all the way up the schooner's topsides. And it's got lockers under the thwarts with a first aid kit, some K-rations, and a couple of jugs of water."

"Okay, Boats. You've sold me."

"How was your leave, Scott? You and Peter had a good time?"

"Wonderful. My parents and one of my ex-girlfriends were quite taken with him. That aw-shucks-ma'am Oklahoma cowboy routine of his really works. I may adopt it myself. How was yours, Skipper?"

Jenks interjected, "Miss Madison and Mr. Worth got married."

"You did. Well, congratulations. I didn't meet her, but from what Harry and Joe tell me she is one fine lady." He held out his hand, which, like Nick's, was pretty much healed.

They shook hands and then Nick turned to Jenks. "How soon will we be ready to sail?"

"Another three days, maybe."

"Then I guess I'd better find out where they want us to go."

AUGUST 2008

THEY WERE JUST PASSING THE SOUTH BURLINGTON EXIT from I-89 when Nick said, "We sailed in the afternoon four days later in order to get through Barnegat Inlet at the slack water before the ebb. It was a beautiful spring day."

"You didn't talk to your father?" She asked it not knowing why and then wished she hadn't.

"No, but I did sign the paperwork the lawyer had sent down by special delivery to get him evicted, along with a will leaving everything to my new wife. I had never had a will before, but having the boat almost sink from under me and getting married finally made an adult out of me. The difference between a child and an adult is that an adult is aware of his own mortality; a child thinks death is something that only happens to other people."

It made Amy think about her own attitude toward death so she changed the subject. "Did they order you back to Greenport?"

"They sent us to a patrol area about a hundred miles east of the Barnegat Inlet in the approaches to New York. There had been a rash of sinkings in the area but they didn't know if it was more mines, or if it was torpedoes."

"Did the Germans drop many mines?"

"They had U-boats specifically designed to lay mines. They had raised hell on the east coast of England at the beginning of the war before the Brits started regular sweeps of the entrance channels, and degaussing their ships."

"Degaussing?"

"The mines were set off by the magnetic field of a ship passing over them. So they would run a steel ship through a big electric coil to break up its magnetic field. In the spring of 1942 we were only starting to set up degaussing stations and get enough mine sweepers. As it turned out there was at least one U-boat working in the area. Closer in, there might have been some mines."

"You saw a U-boat?"

"No, but we saw its handiwork."

She drove onto the Burlington exit cloverleaf. "We're here. Do you know how to get to the hotel? We've got plenty of time to check in and have something to eat before the memorial service at seven."

"Stay on this street right through town and when you get to the end by the lake, turn right. It should be right there."

It was a few minutes before seven when Nick Worth and his granddaughter walked into the paneled room in the University of Vermont Faculty Club. There were half a dozen rows of chairs facing a table with an urn flanked by two framed photos. Elise's children and grandchildren were standing around greeting people. One of the grandchildren had a five- or six-year-old boy with her. Elise's eldest son excused himself from the couple he was talking to and came toward them. "Uncle Nicholas. It is so good of you to come all this way. Mutti would have been so pleased."

"No way I couldn't come. She was a truly great lady and a great friend. This is my granddaughter and chauffeur, Amy." When Amy turned to exchange greetings Nick saw that she was wearing her grandmother's pendant: the one with the Danish coin. His eyes started to grow moist, so he turned away and examined the photos on the table. One was of Elise in late middle years, still beautiful and grown stately. The other was of her as a young woman. The tears started to flow as he looked at the urn and whispered, "One more adventure, Elise. The greatest and final one."

He could almost hear her say, "Oh yes, Nicholas. And we both love adventures, don't we?"

The next morning they went to the Mallets Bay Boat Club and watched Elise's family climb into the club launch with her ashes. They would spread them on Lake Champlain, which she loved, and which was so much like the Lake of Constance where she had once sailed with her brother.

When they were in the Buick and headed back toward I-89, Amy was tempted to ask which woman, Elise or her grandmother, had really been the love of her grandfather's life, but she realized it was one of those questions that must never be asked. Instead she asked, "Yesterday you said that although you didn't see any U-boats on that cruise, you saw their handiwork. How was that?"

JULY 1942

THEY HAD A FINE SOUTHWEST SAILING BREEZE, a summer wind, over the quarter as they reached due east toward their patrol area. It was their second evening out when Nick came on deck with his sextant, hack watch, and pad. He would shoot a round of stars once the sun was down. There was a tugboat approaching from off their port bow, but a couple of quick eyeball bearings showed that it would pass well ahead of them. It was maybe seventy feet long—painted black, of course—and going as fast as it could by the looks of the huge bow wave that was pushed up against the old tires that hung around her gunnels. It wasn't very fast. Maybe eight knots or so. Not any faster than the schooner was, going under all plain sail with the fresh breeze over her quarter. Tugs weren't built for speed.

He was a bit early for nautical twilight and stood in the cockpit talking with Snow and Langdon, waiting for the sun to go down and the first navigational stars to appear while the horizon was still visible. When he had finished taking his sights, he went below, reduced them, plotted their position, and wrote up the log. He could smell steaks frying. They would have fresh food for the couple of days that the ice lasted, and the idea of a steak and a salad sounded really good. As he turned to go into the main cabin he heard a far-off dull thud, then another and another. Then Langdon yelled, "Skipper, we've got flashes to starboard. There's a red rocket."

By the time he said "rocket" Nick was in the cockpit in time to see it flicker out and fall toward the sea. "Hank, put the boat on the wind." He crouched behind the binnacle and took a quick bearing on the trail left by the rocket: about 140° magnetic. "See if she'll point up to 140." He grabbed the mainsheet and started hauling it in as Langdon ran forward to trim the foresail and headsails. Jenks came on deck, took a quick look around, and went forward to help him.

Borg was on the sound equipment and Nick yelled down the hatch, "Hear anything, Harry?"

"Something I've only heard on those records they played for us at the sub base: the noises of a ship sinking. They're about twenty degrees on the starboard bow. Should I send a report, Skipper?"

"Not yet. I'd just as soon sneak up on whatever is out there."

Longo was at the bottom of the hatch, ready to start the engine. "I'll hold off on the machinery then, Skipper."

"Yup, but be ready."

Jenks came back into the cockpit. "Speaking of ready, I'll get my depth charge key."

They sailed on close hauled to a fresh breeze in almost total darkness broken only by the red lights in the binnacle and over the chart table. The water rushing past made it feel as if they were going thirty knots. "Joe, turn off the lights. Hank, steer as close as you can by the feel."

Slade came on deck. "You want me to go up to the gaff jaws, sir? You may need Boats down here."

"Good. Take a pair of glasses with you. But be careful. Don't fall." As soon as it was out he realized how dumb it must have sounded, but he was afraid that the motion high on the mast would make him sick. Then he remembered that Slade was never sick when there was work to be done.

Everything was silent except for the sounds of the boat going through the water until Slade yelled down to them. "Skipper, there's some red lights in the water to starboard."

"Where and how far?"

Then Langdon, who was standing on the dory holding on to the fore boom, said, "I see them too. They can't be far, although it's hard to tell in the dark."

"Tell me when to tack to lay them, Langdon." Then he raised his voice. "Cookie, keep a sharp all-around watch. We may not be alone."

A few minutes later Langdon said, "I think we could lay them if we tacked now."

"We'll hold off a bit. I don't want to have to tack twice. Get forward ready to trim when we tack." He took the wheel as he said, "Snow, go forward and help him." A couple of minutes later he said in a voice loud enough to be heard on the foredeck, "Ready about." Then, "The helm is alee," and the schooner came through the wind and settled on the other tack as they trimmed the sails. Nick thought he had never sailed with a racing crew that did it any better.

Then Langdon called from the bow, "They're life jacket lights. There are people in the water waving."

Jenks appeared beside him. "The other two depth charges are where we can get to them quick if we need them, and so are the weapons. You want to get sail off of her?"

Nick called down the hatch, "Do you hear anything, Harry?"

"No, the sinking and breaking up noises have stopped."

He said to Jenks, "Leave her dressed. We'll let everything luff when we get there. I want to get moving again just as soon as we get them on board." Then he called forward, "How many lights are there?"

"Six, I count six."

"Let the heads'l sheet run when I tell you and then come aft to help Boats get them out of the water. Cookie, give it one more good look around before you come down, and get ready to play doctor."

There were six of them but one was dead of a gunshot wound. As Nick had suspected, they were the crew of the tug. Its captain said that a U-boat had surfaced and immediately swept the pilothouse with machine gun fire to keep them from using their radio. The dead man was the mate. He had been on duty at the wheel, but although he had been wounded he had managed to get one rocket off from a Very pistol before he fell down the ladder as the captain was coming up from his cabin. Then the sub had put three rounds from its deck gun into the tug at the water line. In minutes she had rolled over and sunk.

"How many in your crew, Captain?"

"Eleven. The other two guys in the pilothouse were killed right away, and I don't think the two on engine room watch got out. It's just us, I'm pretty sure. I took a head count as soon as we were in the water. There's one missing. He was probably below and didn't get out. Maybe he got hit by one of the deck gun shots." He finished by saying, "That's really the final insult, isn't it? When the Krauts don't think your ship is worth a torpedo."

"What was your ship's name, Captain?"

"*Redwing.* She was an old girl, built in 1920, but a good one."

"We'll do a box search for your missing guy." The search had already begun. "Go below and give my radioman what he'll need to report what happened. Where were you headed?"

"Out due south from the Vineyard. A tanker caught one in the screws and needs a tow. They'll have to send another boat."

"Tell Borg, the radioman, to get the report ready to send but hold off until we're sure the U-boat has left."

"I never thought of it, but it must be nice to be silent and nearly invisible in the dark."

"That's because we've put enough miles on our sails so they're not white anymore. I never thought I'd approve of dirty gray sails, but they do have advantages."

AUGUST 2008

"**Did you find any more survivors**, Grandpa?"

"No, just the five living and the one dead. Right after dawn a plane came out and helped us search. Around noon a cutter arrived and took the survivors and the corpse off our hands and then we went on to our assigned grid." He paused, then said, "Boy, do I have a headache all of a sudden."

"Are you all right?"

"Yeah. It will pass."

"Are you sure? We're almost to Barre. I could pull off and find a doctor."

"Don't do that. It's better already."

"You're sure?"

"Yes, I'm sure."

He sounded a little testy so she decided to leave it. "Did you have any more excitement?"

"Not that I remember. There was a reported oil slick that we never found. That's a really big ocean out there. And there was a report of a U-boat on the surface that someone made, probably the damned Air Corps. We never found that either. Maybe they heard that the mighty *Fourteen Boat* was coming and hightailed it back to Germany. We mostly just sailed around until the food and water got low. The weather was nice though. Summer was coming in. We were only in Greenport three days and went right out again."

"Did you get to see Grandma?"

"No. She would have had to take the ferry from Bridgeport to Port Jeff, and then the train all the way out to Greenport. A whole day each way. She couldn't take that kind of time off. They were hiring like mad to get production of that new Navy fighter, the Corsair, started.

The Jap Zero was cleaning our clock. None of the fighters the Navy was flying could match it. It was the Navy's own damned fault."

"The Corsair is the one that's on that display outside the airport in Stratford, isn't it? The one with those odd wings."

"Yeah, and both it and the Zero were designed there."

"Huh?"

"In the early nineteen-thirties the U.S. Navy decided that it needed a new fighter for the new carriers it was building. So they held a design competition and Igor Sikorsky and his guys submitted a low-wing monoplane. The geniuses of the Navy Department knew that no monoplane could beat a biplane in a dogfight because biplanes have a much smaller turning radius. So they bought Curtis Goshawk biplanes instead. They looked like a hopped-up Spad. Talk about preparing for the last war.

Anyway, The Japanese Navy was very interested in the Sikorsky aircraft and managed to get hold of a set of plans. That became the Zero. When the U.S. Navy finally wised up, they replaced the Groshawk with Grumman Wildcats that were still no match for the Zero. The later version, the Hellcat, was much better. Our advantages were the ruggedness of the Gummans and the skill of our pilots. But the Corsair could eat Zeros for breakfast. Old Igor was in on the design of both. At least that's the legend in Stratford."

He lapsed into silence and when she glanced over at him his eyes were closed and he did seem to be asleep this time. She touched the brake to swing onto I-91 and when he didn't respond she was sure of it and decided to let him rest. A while later he began to snore.

She drove on in silence thinking about all he had told her about the world of his youth, so hugely different from hers and yet so close in time. It wasn't just the difference in technology: that world without television, laptop computers, cell phones, and plastic bags. No, the people were different. So much more dedicated, single-minded, and yes, dangerous than the Americans of today. They were not the sort you wanted to get mad at you. They did what they thought was necessary, and if anyone raised questions or demurred they said, "Don't you know there's a war on?" and just shoved them out of the way.

They were just halfway in time between the Civil and Indian Wars and the early twenty-first century she lived in. She wondered why the Americans of her grandfather's generation were so little different from the people of the late nineteenth century, but were so hugely different from the people she lived among today.

They had no concerns about what any other country or any group in their own country might think of what they did. They had no time for second thoughts or recriminations or abstract legalistic arguments. Just get the damned job done. Don't you know there's a war on?

Then she realized that when you looked at them as nineteenth century Americans with all of their faults but without any twenty-first century hang-ups, neuroses, or society-induced doubts and fears, you understood why their war had taken less than four years and why they had won it.

She began to doubt that the Americans of her day could have won that war. If forced to it, they would have stepped into that war like a little girl trying to decide if she wanted to go swimming in water that might be a bit cold. And they would have said, "Well, if we must, but let someone else or someone else's children fight it, and tell them to try not to hurt anyone."

A quote she had read somewhere from General Sherman came to mind. "War is the remedy our enemy has chosen, and I say, give him all he wants." That was exactly the way her grandfather's generation had reacted to being attacked. Although they had been almost exactly halfway in time between Sherman and the present day, they were in reality his contemporaries and nowhere close to today's America. They had given their enemies all the war they wanted and then some. She didn't think the present generation of Americans could bring themselves to do that. She was sure her grandfather would say that halfhearted retaliation and desultory negotiations—McNamara's War—were how modern Americans reacted to being attacked. She could not quite bring herself to agree with him. Yet how could the American people have changed so much in seventy years, have become so different, when in the previous seventy years they had changed hardly at all?

She began to think about her thesis and if that was the theme on which she could hang everything her grandfather had told her about his time.

SEVENTEEN

AUGUST 2008

THEY WERE PULLING INTO BRATTLEBORO when he woke up. "Huh? Where are we? I must have dozed off." He shook his left arm from the shoulder. "Damned arm's gone to sleep.

"In Brattleboro. We have to get gas. Do you want something to eat, Grandpa?"

"No. But you get something. I'll stay in the car. I don't feel like moving around." The truth was his left leg had gone to sleep too.

"How's your headache?"

"Better. I think the snooze helped." He shook his arm again. "Doesn't seem to want to wake up."

"I'll fill up the car and grab a quick chicken sandwich. Can I bring you something?"

"Maybe a chocolate shake?"

JUNE 1942

THEY HAD ANOTHER THREE-DAY turn-around in Greenport and went right out again. It was summer now, and the weather couldn't have been better. The prevailing southwest breeze had settled in and it was an easy reach out to their assigned area.

They had been on station about a week when the Air Corps reported spotting and bombing a periscope and they were sent to investigate. They didn't find anything, but on the way back to their patrol area they found a lifeboat with sixteen people in it. Their ship, a freighter, had sailed from Bridgeport with a full cargo of pig iron and cartridge brass and was on its way to Halifax to join a convoy. It had been torpedoed the night before and had gone down so fast that there hadn't been time to send an SOS.

They took the five injured aboard and took the lifeboat in tow. All of the injured had broken bones from being thrown violently into things when the torpedoes exploded. There was one man who had the symptoms of a fractured skull. He was bleeding from the ears and nose and had a nasty gash on the back of his head. They handed him below and put him in Nick's bunk. It was all they could do.

Greenport told them to proceed toward a rendezvous with a cutter that would meet them early the next morning. By the time they had gotten the injured on board and rigged the tow the breeze had gone down with the sun, so after a thorough all-around sound and visual search, they started the engine and made their way across the sea that would have been flat if it weren't for the long, slow, ground swell.

It was almost midnight when Nick noticed that there seemed to be more engine vibration than usual. They normally only used it for getting in and out of harbor and to charge the batteries while running it in neutral. When becalmed on station they just drifted, looked, and listened. He was in the cockpit talking to the freighter's captain, whose broken wrist Slade had placed in a sling but hadn't tried to set. He looked down the hatch and saw that Joe Longo was already moving the motor box/chart table aside. "You felt it too, Joe."

"Yeah. It seems to be coming from the propeller shaft. I'd like to shut it down so I can get to the stuffing box, Skipper."

"Okay." As their motion died, the small breeze it caused died, too.

Longo took the large wrench he used to tighten the seals on the stuffing box that surrounded the propeller shaft where it went through the hull. He crawled down behind the engine trying to avoid the hot exhaust pipe and manifold as Hank Snow came aft to help him.

Nick leaned in the hatch and listened to the grunting as Longo crawled as far as he could into the narrowing space and then reached the rest of the way to get the wrench on the stuffing box nut. Snow helped him snake his way out. He stood and reported to Nick. "I got all there is to get on the nut but it doesn't feel tight the way it should."

"Is it leaking?"

"More than it should with the engine shut down, but not too bad." The packing was supposed to leak a little when the shaft was turning so the salt water could cool and lubricate it. "Let's start it up and see what happens."

While Longo crouched beside the engine and shone a light down the shaft tunnel, Snow started it. Almost immediately Longo said, "Oh, Christ. Shut it off."

He looked up and said, "The shaft's jumpin' around like a hula girl and the box is leaking like a faucet, Skipper. That two-bladed prop must have worn out the seals completely."

"We have to get these people to the rendezvous. Start it up and when the water gets high enough in the engine room bilge, pull the cooling hose off again and let the engine pump it overboard. We're getting good at this, aren't we? We'll run on power and hope the seals don't let go completely before a breeze comes up. In the meantime you guys try to figure out what we'll do if it does let go completely." Borg had been standing in the entrance to the main cabin watching. Nick said to him, "Get your message pad, Harry. We'll have to report that *Fourteen Boat,* also known as *Leakin' Lena,* is at it again."

AUGUST 2008

"**DID YOU HAVE TO BAIL** like mad again, Grandpa?"

He was trying to suck the milkshake up the straw while he held the cup in his right hand. His left arm lay on the rest between the seats. The shake was too thick to be easily pulled through the straw.

"No. Just before dawn it started to rain and a breeze came up from the east. We shut down the engine and Longo and Snow managed to stuff some grease-soaked rags around the shaft. It held until we got to New London and they hauled the boat." He placed the milkshake cup in the door pocket. "Your Grandmother managed to get two whole days off from work and take the train to New London. She showed up carrying another cake for the crew."

"Were you out of the water long?"

"Just one day and part of another. They couldn't find the original three-bladed prop. It had probably been tossed into one of the scrap metal drives everyone was conducting. Even little kids went around pulling their red wagons and collecting flattened tin cans.

"They called around and got a prop from another yard. Everyone agreed that the two-bladed one moving in and out of the shadow of the deadwood was probably what shook the packing loose. We spent two more days getting ready for sea. When I took your grandmother to the train in a borrowed car, the last thing she said to me was, 'You remember my regulations. You come back to me, sailor.' It was a good thing she said it."

"Why?"

He closed his eyes. He didn't answer.

JULY 1942

THEY STOPPED IN GREENPORT for orders and to pick up a new grid chart and codebook: they were changing them more often now. The next day they sailed. It was full summer now, and the prevailing southwesterly breeze carried them out to their assigned area. It was hot below during the day and the off-duty watch took to sunbathing on deck while laughing about the U.S.C.G. providing luxury sailing vacations.

AUGUST 2008

A FEW MINUTES LATER he started to talk to his granddaughter again but he didn't answer her question about her grandmother's farewell comment. Instead he said, "But the grand weather didn't last. I looked it up on Google a while ago. You can get weather information for the last hundred years at one of those websites. Did you know that? A tropical low formed just north of Cuba and came up through the Straits of Florida. It was too early in the season for it to become a full-fledged hurricane but it rode north up the Stream picking up moisture and building winds of maybe thirty knots or so. It wouldn't have been a problem if it hadn't bumped into another low coming across the U.S. that was sucking cold dry air down from Canada. The result was a classic nor'easter."

"I thought nor'easters only happened in the winter and brought a ton of snow."

"No, lousy weather can happen anytime. The 1979 Fastnet storm happened in August and formed the same way. A couple of different kinds of systems got together and combined into real trouble. The weather men call it a meteorological bomb."

"You mean like *The Perfect Storm*?"

"Yeah, although this one never became as hellacious as that one or the Fastnet Gale. It rained buckets but it never blew much over sixty knots or so. That was quite bad enough. It caught us flatfooted because we didn't have the weather forecasting equipment or the understanding of storm formation that we have now. It was only four years earlier that the Great Hurricane of 1938 clobbered New England without warning."

"What happened? If you don't want to talk about it, it's okay." She already knew what had happened. Or thought she did.

JULY 1942

BY THE TIME THEY RECEIVED ORDERS to run for shelter it was too late. It had started to rain hard late in the afternoon and they kept reducing sail in stages until, by ten o'clock that night when they were told to head in, they had housed both booms and were hove to under just the tiny foremast storm tri-sail that neither they nor anyone else had ever used before.

The wind was howling out of the northeast and the seas were starting to build into the biggest that Nick had ever seen. Because they were building so quickly they had a vicious steepness to them. The schooner was lying with her bow about sixty degrees off the wind and seas, but occasionally a bigger sea and a wind gust would occur together and the bow would be pushed around until they were lying ninety degrees from the wind in the trough of the seas. When that happened, *Fourteen Boat* would do a sickening roll until the lee deck was under water, the cockpit filled, and the crew on deck would have been washed overboard if they hadn't been tied on.

The cabin was as thoroughly miserable as only the cabin of a small boat offshore in a blow can be. Because the hull and deckhouse were being racked and twisted by the seas there was water coming in around all the tightly closed cabin ports, the hatches, and down both masts despite the leather boots that surrounded them on the cabin top. The hull itself was hardly leaking at all and Nick was glad that, despite all the misery at the time, they had found and solved all the hull problems.

They took thirty-minute, two-man shifts in the cockpit. At that point they thought no one could take more than half an hour of the screaming wind and the rain that it blew like buckshot. Nick and Scott Langdon were on watch at about three in the morning when the trysail blew out, not with a bang, but with a loud ripping noise as first one seam and then the others tore open. One second it was there doing its job, and the next only a few tattered, wildly flapping pennants were left. A moment later those were gone, too.

The boat fell off broadside to the seas and was rolled rail down. Only now, without the force of the trysail to help the rudder turn the bow toward salvation, the next sea broke completely over her. Nick freed the wheel and turned the stern to the seas before the next one could hit and roll her over.

The schooner came up on her feet and ran down the face of that next wave probably as fast as she had ever gone in her life. At the bottom she dug her bow into the next sea and Nick was afraid she would just keep going down. But John Alden knew how to design a bow, so she shook herself free and started to fight her way to the next crest. Then it was another breathtaking plummet down the face of the next wave that came up behind her. Every bit of Nick's concentration was focused on keeping her stern aimed straight at the next oncoming sea. If he was just a small amount off, the wave would be able to grab the stern, turn the boat sideways, and throw her on her side down the slope. Then, while she wallowed, the next wave would roll her over.

Jenks appeared at his side and shouted, "Don't let her broach, for Christ's sake." Nick ignored the useless advice as they climbed to the crest of the next wave and he glanced at the red-lit binnacle. He was steering about fifteen degrees west of south by the compass. That meant they were going about due south true: out into the Atlantic as the American coast fell away to the west. He thought *Good. At least I don't have to worry about running up on the bricks.* Then the feel of the next wave coming up behind washed everything from his mind except making the exact helm corrections to keep it squarely behind the boat.

They ran on through the dark and the torrential rain with him and Jenks taking turns steering. Neither could do it for very long and neither would trust any of the other crewmen to do it. There was absolutely no room for error. Each wave must be judged exactly right or they would all die. It was that simple and that difficult.

It was almost dawn and Jenks was steering, when there was a loud crack from above their heads and something heavy fell to the deck. Two somethings. One of them bounced overboard but the other hit the transom of the upturned dory and landed in the cockpit. Nick picked it up and realized that it was a piece of one of the insulators spliced into the upper section of the backstay that served as a radio antenna. The steel cable must have sawed into it until it finally split in half. That would allow an inch or two of looseness in the stay that supported the top of the mast. He showed it to Jenks and Langdon and yelled, "The insulator."

He tossed it into the foot well as he thought, *Screw it. The runners are both set up tight and it's a new mast. No one in his right mind would crawl across the after deck and out on the boomkin to tighten the backstay turnbuckle. If the top of the mast stays up, it stays up. If it falls down, it falls down.* He yelled at Langdon, "You can go below, Scott. Boats and I have got her."

"You want me to take a turn steering? It doesn't look easy. I steered a Star downwind in conditions like this when a brute of a squall came through the Nationals two years ago. "

"Maybe later. Get out of the wind and rain and get some rest in case we need you."

They did need him. By the next afternoon the seas were getting even bigger and steeper and Nick guessed they had entered the Gulf Stream.

AUGUST 2008

HE KEPT HIS EYES CLOSED as they rolled into Connecticut and he remembered that it was in the Gulf Stream where the accepted truth and the real truth diverged.

He was considering telling the true story just this once when Amy interrupted his thoughts. "I know what happened in the Stream, Grandpa. I asked Grandma once about your leg and she showed me an old newspaper clipping that said several patrol craft had disappeared in a violent storm. It said there had been a survivor from one of them who had been found alive after drifting in a lifeboat for twenty days. Grandma said that was you, and she was only telling me so I wouldn't bother you about your leg. The clipping was kind of sketchy. No boat names or much detail."

"There was a war on. Everybody kept his cards close to his vest, especially when reporting bad news."

"If you don't want to talk about it I understand."

He thought about it. She would need an ending for her thesis and the guys deserved whatever immortality it would give them. They, and all the other members of the Hooligan Navy, who had followed regulations and gone out but had not come back. But the story the newspaper had reported, the story everyone had accepted, had been better than the truth because it had been believable. Even after all these years it was better.

The decision made, he started to talk, still with his eyes closed. The light bothered his eyes. "Crossing the Stream diagonally with the wind blowing into its teeth made the seas even steeper and the conditions even worse while it pushed us to the east, so we stayed in the worst of the storm even longer."

"Grandpa, I don't need the details." She remembered her grandmother's admonition. "Why don't you rest a while?"

He kept his eyes closed but ignored her and went on, "The Gulf Stream helped me in 1936, but tried to kill me in 1942. It was like everything else in the sea: not evil or cruel, just totally uncaring. That's why one seldom gets the chance to make a second mistake at sea. It would just as soon kill you today as tomorrow.

"We must have been almost across The Stream by the next afternoon when it happened. The winds and seas were no better and probably worse. I had just relieved Langdon on the wheel when the hatch opened and Slade appeared with a jar of something in his hand. It might have been coffee or maybe hot soup. He had been trying to get us something warm any way he could. I never found out what it was. Langdon helped him over the bridge deck and it must have distracted me because I lost concentration as a particularly big wave at a slightly different angle hit the boat and slewed her around to port.

"It was all over in a minute. The wave pushed her down on her starboard side, the side with the momentarily open hatch. Before we could do anything, both masts were in the water. The sea poured over the combing, pushed Langdon through the hatch, and then followed him below as the next wave broke over her. *Tiger Lillie* was a game lady to the end, though. As she settled she came upright and Peter

Slade had the presence of mind to cut the dory loose. I don't know where he found the strength, but he flipped it right side up as it floated off the sinking schooner."

"And that's when you hurt your leg?"

"I had my feet wedged between the wheel box and the depth charges. It was the only way I could steer without having to hold on. When the boat went over I was thrown to starboard and my left leg came free but the right one jammed and got broken. The next thing I knew Slade was dragging me into the dory."

"Didn't any of the others get out?"

"No, they all went down with her. All of them."

"I'm sorry I brought it all back."

"Yeah." He was silent for a while then said, "You make sure you get all of their names right. One other thing I want you to do when you get your thesis finished, find any of their surviving families. That should be pretty easy now with the Internet. They had brothers and sisters and I want you to track down their kids or grandkids and send them a copy of your thesis. I want them to know what fine men they were, so they can be proud that they're related to them. Other than Peter Slade, they have no gravestones. Your thesis will be their only memorial."

"Where's Peter Slade's gravestone, Grandpa?"

"In Arlington, where it belongs." But he thought, *You owe them all, not just Peter Slade, better than this. You were their skipper, for Christ's sake.*

EIGHTEEN

AMY THOUGHT HE WAS ASLEEP, but he was remembering what it was like drifting in the half-swamped dory with a badly infected compound fracture of his leg, and Peter Slade dead beside him. He was so far gone that at first the destroyer crew that found him thought they had found two dead men.

He remembered only snatches of Slade talking to him soothingly as he used the small supply of drinking water that had been stored in the boat to wash the stinging salt off of the wound before sprinkling it with sulfa powder from the first aid kit. In a few days the sulfa was gone and the water was almost gone. Then all Slade could do was hold up his head and give him an occasional small drink until the water ran out.

If the destroyer hadn't been returning from Bermuda, he never would have been found. The ship's doctor amputated his right leg just below the knee and hoped that it was far enough up to remove all of the infection. They kept him sedated all the way in and for another week after the second operation to clean up the stump in the hospital in Newport News. By then, working back from the place where the dory had been found, it had been decided that *Fourteen Boat* had probably been overwhelmed while running before steep following seas and only the captain and the cook, who were probably in the cockpit at the time, got off. Everyone believed that and no one blamed him. No one would have believed the truth.

When he had finally been allowed to regain full consciousness he was as weak as a newborn baby and the pain was still intense, so he had taken the easy way and just concurred with their assumptions. As he healed he realized that it wasn't fair to the crew, but convinced himself it was too late to set the story straight, and if he had tried, no one, not even his wife, would have believed him.

He sat in silence hoping his granddaughter would think he was asleep while he debated telling her what had really happened. For all these years he had been lugging around his intense guilt about not telling how the crew of *Fourteen Boat* had actually died. They had not been below lying in their bunks, the helpless victims of the storm. They had died on their feet.

In 1942 no one had even heard of survivor guilt. Yet he felt that guilt, and still felt it, when he allowed himself to think about what had really happened. But it was more than just guilt over surviving. It was guilt sharpened by the knowledge that he had done an immense disservice to his crew by not insisting upon the truth.

But he cared what this Amy thought of him, just as he had cared what that other Amy had thought of him. Would she think he was an old fool telling preposterous war stories, just as he had feared her grandmother would think he was a young scoundrel telling preposterous war stories?

Perhaps he wouldn't be able to accurately remember the truth about the last day of *Fourteen Boat*'s life after repressing it for two-thirds of a century.

Then he told himself, *That won't wash. You can remember every fucking minute of those last hours.*

JULY 1942

THEY RAN ON BEFORE THOSE AWFUL SEAS for the next two and a half days without broaching while everyone, even those who stayed below, became more and more exhausted. Even lying in a bunk was grueling, and if a sort of sleep that was more like a stupor finally came, there was no rest in it with the constant cold dampness, fear, and violent motion. Just lying still was hard physical labor.

By the time the wind began to moderate as the storm moved off to the east, they were somewhere southeast of the Gulf Stream between Bermuda and Cape Hatteras. The seas were still running high but they were less steep and broke less often all along their crests as they had done twelve hours earlier. The rain hadn't stopped, but the torrential downpours were coming less and less frequently. Jenks was in the cockpit watching Hank Snow steer, and Nick was standing at the chart table trying to remember how fast and in what direction they had run for how long. He had made only a half-dozen sketchy log entries in the last four days. Most of them said only, "Still running about 180° True at about eight to eleven knots." They had lost the impeller of the taffrail log the first night and he could only make the crudest estimate of their wildly varying speed.

The only good news was that the top of the mainmast was still intact.

The backstay had been loosened a couple of inches by the loss of the insulator, but the two interlocking spliced loops had held so it hadn't made any difference to the rig. It made a great deal of difference to the radio, though. With the antenna section of the stay shorted out, the radio was dead and there was no way they could fix it. Even if they could invent some sort of replacement insulator, it would be impossible for someone hoisted up the wildly swinging backstay to do anything but hang on and throw up.

Jenks called down the hatch, "Skipper, I think we can get some sail on her. It's lightened up a lot and she's starting to wallow in the valleys."

"Better tighten the backstay turnbuckle first."

"Yeah. Hand me up a pair of pliers and a screwdriver out of Longo's tool box."

They got the small staysail on her to keep steerageway and ran on.

It was late afternoon before the seas had moderated enough so they dared to turn the schooner toward them and put her on a reach that let her quarter the seas while heading west. Until it cleared enough so Nick could get a fix, that was his best guess of how to find their way home, although home would not be Greenport or New London. It would probably be somewhere on the Carolina coast.

They got the foresail on her to help her fight through the high, leftover seas as the wind backed around into the northwest and kept backing as it moderated, even though it still rained intermittently. The storm was definitely moving off to the east where it would probably raise hell with the Atlantic convoys.

At two in the morning they tacked and set the main. By then the wind had backed enough so they could still sail northwest on a close reach. The motion was not pleasant as the schooner fought her way through the seas, but the press of sail steadied her so it was not nearly as violent as it had been while scudding before the wind under bare poles. Nick hoped that by morning twilight it would have cleared enough for him to get a fix.

It was still full dark when, as he taped a fresh plotting sheet to the chart table, Langdon and Snow went past him to relieve Jenks and Longo on watch. He put his sextant on his bunk, set the hack watch to the chronometer, and hung it around his neck. He put a pad and pencil in his shirt pocket under his oilskins and the thick turtleneck sweater he wore beneath them and climbed into the cockpit to see if it had cleared enough to be able to see the horizon and a few stars just before the sun came up.

As if to answer his question, the clearing ended and it started to rain hard again. He said, "Shit," pulled the hatch closed, and sat down on a cockpit seat to see which would come first, the end of the rain squall or the end of the twilight just before dawn that he needed to determine their position.

The squall won. They broke out of it just after the sun had climbed over the horizon blotting out the stars, and a watery sunlight raised their visibility from a couple of hundred yards to several miles.

And there on the surface, perhaps a half-mile away, was U-271, its black painted number clearly visible against the gray of the conning tower and the rest of the ship. It was stopped broadside on to them and there were four or five men crouching on the foredeck working on the diving planes. There was a logo, a dancing demon, painted beside the number.

It took Nick a second to react before saying, "I'll take her. Get the sheets. Jibe ho." He swung the boat's stern through the wind before Hank Snow could get the main sheet under control, and the mainsail came crashing over against the lower back stay but fortunately didn't tear it out of the deck.

Jenks appeared in the hatch and asked, "What the fuck...?"

Nick aimed the boat at the retreating wall of the rain squall. "U-boat, on the surface. Got to get back into the squall before... Oh, shit," there was a boil of water under the sub's stern. "They've seen us. Start the engine. We've got to get back into the rain squall."

They were now going almost dead downwind and the apparent wind that drove the boat under sail had fallen off and so had their speed. The engine started and Nick called, "All ahead flank."

Jenks appeared in the hatch with the BAR and a couple of magazines. The submarine was now swinging bow on to them and two men were wrestling a large machine gun up onto the front edge of the conning tower. Jenks pushed across the cockpit and dropped onto the after deck as he shoved a magazine into the gun and cocked the bolt. He waited for them to get a little closer as he mumbled, "Come on, you bastards. Come on. You aren't shooting unarmed guys in a lifeboat now." The men on the sub were hanging an ammunition box on the side of their gun when the BAR erupted and the upper edge of the conning tower below the gun and the gun itself were lit by what looked like a swarm of fire flies: the sparks of the striking 30-06 metal-jacketed slugs. The two men disappeared and the gun's muzzle swung up toward the sky.

The men on the foredeck dropped their tools and ran toward the conning tower as Jenks shifted targets. He blew two of them off the deck, and wounded a third who dragged himself behind the deck gun while the boatswain shoved his other magazine into the gun. Two of the men ran behind the conning tower and disappeared before he could reload. He yelled, "Ammo" as he squeezed off a couple of rounds at a head that appeared and then disappeared over the edge of the conning tower.

Nick swung the boat to starboard, up toward the wind onto a reach so it was now blowing from almost abeam. With the sails driving her, the engine running at full speed, and the leftover seas behind her quarter, *Fourteen Boat* was now going as fast as she could.

The U-boat was going at least twice as fast, but Jenks had blinded it. It was now moving up almost alongside them but about two hundred yards to port. *Fourteen Boat* might escape into the squall after all.

Longo handed all of the ship's armament up onto the bridge deck. Laid out like that it was almost a joke. Two steel ammo boxes, a .45 caliber pistol with two clips, and a half-dozen unloaded BAR box magazines. Jenks yelled over his shoulder, "Somebody start loading magazines."

Longo, still standing in the hatch, opened one of the boxes and found it contained a mixed bag of grenades. Lying on top were a couple of the pineapples one associated with hand grenades. But the others were gray painted cylinders with W.P. stenciled on them in white: Willy Peter—white phosphorous. He pushed that box aside, opened the other, and started loading a magazine with .30-06 rounds from it. Langdon grabbed another magazine and started loading as well.

Nick, who was watching the sub and trying to decide how best to elude it, saw the periscope rise. "The periscope. See if you can hit the periscope, Boats."

Jenks fired a half dozen single shots with no effect, then said,

"Shit, Skipper. With the boats bouncing around like this, Davy Crockett couldn't hit something that small." Then he saw that the wounded man had left the shelter of the deck gun and was dragging himself back toward the bridge. Jenks blew him off the boat with a single shot. "Krauts I can hit. Periscopes? No."

As Nick steered east toward the storm he tried to put himself in the mind of the U-boat commander. His smartest move would be to turn away until he was out of the range of Jenks' weapon, then finish off the schooner with a few rounds from his deck gun. The deck gun was useless this close because Jenks would kill anyone who tried to get to it. The U-boat had been designed for stealthy long range attacks on ships. Neither its design nor its crew's training had prepared it for a close-quarters gunfight with a crazy Marine armed with a Browning Automatic Rifle. Nick prayed they would move outside the BAR's range because that might give him time to escape back behind the curtain of rain. If *Fourteen Boat* made it, he would ride the squall all the way to Iceland if that's what it took to escape.

But he was afraid the Kraut captain might not behave logically. He had lost several men and was yet to get a shot off. His blood lust might interfere with logic. As the U-boat gained speed, its forward diving planes, which appeared to be jammed in the full dive position, pushed its bow down until the foredeck was awash almost back to the conning tower.

Blood lust won out over logic. The sub turned toward them.

AUGUST 2008

"GRANDPA? ARE YOU ASLEEP?" He hadn't spoken in quite a while.

"No. Just thinking."

"We're in Meriden, coming up on the exit to the Parkway. We'll be home in a half hour or so."

"Good. My headache is back."

"They buried Peter Slade in Arlington. Did I tell you that?"

"He must have been a fine man."

"He gave his life for me. The only way I could have survived that long was because he had given me most of the water. I owe the greatest debt there is to him."

"I don't think there's any way a debt like that can be repaid."

"There's one way a small payment can be made, though."

"How."

"With the truth. Such a debt can only be repaid with the truth. Boy, this damned headache isn't getting any better." Then he closed his eyes and she hoped he could get some more sleep.

JULY 1942

THE U-BOAT HIT THEM almost squarely amidships. But instead of breaking in half as the U-boat commander had probably hoped, a wave lifted *Fourteen Boat* so she rode up over the sub's submerged bow and stayed on top of the wave as it rolled aft toward the deck gun. The pressure on her sails kept her heeled away from the conning tower until the gun's muzzle hit her at the turn of the bilge. The gun barrel crashed through her planking and held her like a butterfly pinned to a board.

Most of *Fourteen Boat's* crew scrambled across the cockpit to lie on the side deck and look over the edge at the sub's superstructure. Longo and Langdon grabbed the two ammo boxes and the magazines before they could follow the pistol overboard. Slade had the presence of mind to cut loose the dory so it slid down the deck and flipped right side up as it bounced over the combing. Then the ripping sound of a machine pistol came from the conning tower and hunks of teak came flying off the toe rail. The BAR answered but didn't silence the machine pistol because as Jenks was reloading, it replied in turn.

The U-boat was still charging on like a wounded fighting bull but now its foredeck was fully submerged from the downward force of the diving planes and the twenty tons of *Fourteen Boat* lying crosswise wedged against the deck gun.

The gun battle between Jenks and the people on the conning tower continued as Hank Snow came sliding down into the cockpit with half of his head blown off. Nick thought, *This can't go on. They'll kill us all.* He stuffed three grenades in each side pocket of his oilskin jacket and looked around for the .45 but couldn't see it. "Boats, keep the Krauts' heads down."

"What are you going to do, Skipper?"

"Just keep their fucking heads down for thirty seconds or so."

Jenks jammed a fresh clip in the BAR and said, "You're the boss."

Nick said, "Now." The boatswain fired one spaced shot after another at the conning tower as Nick rolled over the side and slid down the schooner' topside and bottom to the sub's deck and ran aft as fast as he could through the waist-deep water.

He reached the steel rungs welded to the side of the tower just as the BAR went silent and what sounded like at least two machine pistols opened up from right over his head. Then he heard the sound of the heavy machine gun finally firing. It went on and on with no answer from the schooner as he fished a fragmentation grenade out of his pocket, pulled the pin, and holding the spoon down, climbed up the rungs until he could drop it over the edge of the steel combing. It went off and the machine gun instantly stopped firing.

Then he heard a grunt and saw a head appear and disappear as someone looked down over the edge at him. He pulled the pin on the first grenade his hand found and lobbed it over the edge. It went off without the loud explosion of the first one but with a bang and a blinding flash. A man screamed and climbed over the combing above Nick's head and jumped, still screaming, into the sea trailing a column of white smoke from his back.

Nick pulled the pin of a fragmentation grenade and this time climbed high enough so he could see the three mangled and burning bodies the grenades had caused and the open hatch in the floor of the bridge. Another man was climbing the ladder from the control room. He threw the grenade at him. It bounced off his head and fell past him into the control room. When it went off, he threw the two remaining Willy Peters and the last fragmentation grenade after it and sealed the fate of U-217.

The water was climbing up the side of the conning tower quickly now as the U-boat's propellers, the jammed diving planes, and *Fourteen Boat's* weight pushed it under and there was no one in its ruined and burning control room to stop it. Nick turned sideways to jump clear of the sinking vessel. As he jumped, his right foot slipped inside the ladder rung. He heard a crack and felt an ungodly pain shoot from his leg into every part of his body. He hung there with his leg bent almost double just above his ankle and his head in the rising water.

Afterward he had no memory of how he got his foot out of his sea boot and freed himself from the sinking sub. The next thing he knew Peter Slade was pulling him into the dory. "What happened to the others?"

"That big machine gun just tore the boat apart. The dory got away from me and I dove in to try to catch it. If I hadn't, it would have gotten me too. Lay still, Skipper, and let me look at that leg."

Nick pushed himself up to try to look over the dory's gunnels. "Where's the sub?"

"Gone, and *Fourteen Boat* with her. We're all that's left. Let me look at that leg."

AUGUST 2008

"**HERE'S WHEELERS FARMS ROAD, GRANDPA.** Just about home."

Yes, he would tell the truth now that the underwater exploration expedition had found U-217 and there would be proof of what happened. The TV show had been made last summer and had ended with the announcement that they were going to send out another expedition this year to further explore the wreck. Why hadn't he thought of that before? *Fourteen Boat's* lead ballast keel was jammed under the deck gun and they would find that the conning tower hatch was open and the control room beneath it was demolished and burned out. Then everyone would know what *Fourteen Boat*'s crew had done in those most desperate of America's times.

Then the pain of a headache like no other hit him.

He moaned softly as she swung from the Parkway onto the cloverleaf. "Are you all right, Grandpa?" He definitely wasn't the moaning type.

Very softly he said, "It feels like my eyes are being pushed right out of my..." Then he was silent.

A moment later, as she was avoiding merging traffic, she smelled urine. That definitely wasn't like her grandfather. That was one old man's problem he had never had. "Grandpa." Louder this time. "Grandpa." There was no response. She looked over and saw that his eyes were open and his jaw hung slack. She turned on the caution flashers and floored the accelerator.

When her mother and father got to the hospital, Amy was sitting in the Emergency Room waiting area, her head in her hands staring at the floor. She looked up at them through red, tear-soaked eyes and said, "He's gone. Oh Daddy, Grandpa's gone. I'm going to miss that old man. I'm going to miss him so."

EPILOGUE

MAY 2009

BY THE FOLLOWING SPRING Amy Worth was way ahead of schedule with her master's degree and ready to start applying for a place in a doctoral program in case she couldn't find the journalism job she wanted. She planned to take courses through the summer session and finish her master's in the fall semester. She had handed in her thesis the week before and now she went to her advisor's office to get her grade.

He was a small, almost delicate man, but quite handsome. She would have suspected he was gay if he hadn't always shown such interest in her legs. She had inherited her grandmother's legs, after all. As soon as she was seated across from him, he checked them out, then told her, "It's an A, of course, Ms. Worth. I've already turned in the grade. Well researched and documented and an interesting read as well. But I find it hard to believe that men would willingly go out into the Atlantic in the winter in little sailing yachts to confront warships."

"They went. It's all documented in the notes. The records of the Coast Guard, the Navy's Eastern Sea Frontier logs, and all of the other sources prove that they went."

"Oh, I know they went. I just find it difficult to understand why they willingly subjected themselves to that kind of discomfort and risk. There must have been ways to avoid it."

She gave him the answer she knew her grandfather's generation would have given. "There was a war on, you know."

"Huh? Yes." He didn't know how to deal with that so he changed the subject. "As a matter of fact, the thesis is so good that I'm sure we could get it published commercially as a book with just the changes in the format that you'd expect. It would be assured of a market with the current Greatest Generation fad and all that. Would you be interested?"

She thought, *A fad? Grandpa and his crew were one of the greatest generations all right, they were not just some fad, for God's sake.* The generations of Valley Forge and of the Twentieth Maine and Belleau Wood and "We shall prevail or Molly Stark sleeps a widow tonight" came to mind, but she only said, "Of course I'd like to see it published as a book."

"I'm sure the people at the University Press would be very interested. They've published both of my books. But I think we should start with some of the larger New York publishers. My literary agent can handle that. It will require considerable editing to get it from the somewhat stodgy format required of a thesis, into the format of a book, but I'd be willing to help with that."

Now that he had her complete interest, his tone changed slightly as he tried to sink the hook. "Of course, the publisher may want the author to be someone with a bit more gravitas than a master's candidate. That's particularly true of the people over at the University Press. They're terrible intellectual snobs. I'm sure they would want to list me as a coauthor."

She kept a straight face as she thought, *And they normally list coauthors in alphabetical order, don't they?"* His name was Albertson. *I only hope I can get out of here with my A without strangling this twerp.*

"Your name, of course, would also be on the cover and title page and you'd be given considerable credit for your work in the acknowledgements."

She bit her lip as she thought, *Oh yeah, but the closer we get to the publication date, the smaller my name will get on the cover, until it disappears completely. Not today, Charlie. Or should I say Earnest. It sounds like something my great-grandfather would have pulled.* But she said, "Oh professor, you've caught me completely by surprise. I'm just loaded down with course work for the next few weeks." The truth was her course work was just about finished and with the thesis done and graded she had almost a month free before the summer session started.

She continued, "Besides, if we were to publish it as a book there are a few loose ends I'd like to tie up first." That, at least, was the truth. Just before she had turned in the thesis she had gone one last time through the notes she had made right after that last trip with her grandfather. One thing had been bothering her ever since. She had come across his comments about the wreck of U-217 as they had looked at that videotape together. She hadn't mentioned the U-boat in the thesis because she didn't know what significance, if any, it had. "Can I get back to you on this book thing in a few days? To tell the truth, I knew it was pretty good, and hoped it would get an A, but I never thought anyone would talk about a book. I'd like to think about it."

With that she stood, thanked him again as she shook his hand, and got out of there.

As she walked out to the Riviera that still had that extra accelerator pedal, she said to herself, *Kindly Professor Albertson obviously liked your story, Grandpa. He liked it so much he will probably try to steal it. I think we need to copyright it quick.*

When she got back to her apartment, she brought up the finished thesis on her computer and made up a new title page that didn't mention the university or her advisor. She stared at the silver cup and the model of *Morning Glory* on her bookshelf as she thought about something to replace "A thesis in partial fulfillment of the requirements for a master's degree." She finally typed "Recollections of the Hooligan Navy" in its place.

She went online and Googled, "Copyright." This led her to the Library of Congress copyright website. She read the instructions, filled in the forms and, following the step-by-step procedure, uploaded the manuscript. She paid the fee with a credit card and a few minutes later received a verification, which she printed out.

She swiveled around and once more stared at the schooner model on her bookshelf as she thought, *I know your generation would have used a more direct way of dealing with that twerp, Grandpa, but I live in less desperate but far more litigious times. Now what about U-217? I'll have to get in touch with that guy at Woods Hole that explored the wreck and ask him if he ever found out what sank it.*

She still had the videotape. She had found it in the VCR when she helped her parents clean out her grandfather's apartment. She'd go online to the German Navy Archives and try to find a photo of U-217. She wondered what that thing painted on the conning tower was: the shape beside the number. She had thought it was either a shadow or the painted silhouette of a man, but her grandfather had been absolutely positive it was neither. How could he have been so positive?

The whole story of her grandfather's war would be incomplete until she knew where U-217 fitted. The more she thought about it the more convinced she became that, at the end, when he was talking about what was owed to his crew, he had wanted to tell her.

She continued to stare at the model of *Morning Glory* while she thought about it. Finally she turned back to her computer, and typed "German U-boat 217" into a search engine as she said aloud, "Don't worry, Grandpa, if there's more to your story I'll find it, even if I never tell another living soul."

Nevis, 26 April 2011

AUTHOR'S NOTES

This is a work of fiction but it is based on real events.

• The descriptions of the Bermuda Races of 1936 and 1938 are accurate, as is the description of the race along the coast from Block Island to Mount Desert Island, finishing in Gloucester that replaced the Bermuda Race in 1940. The weather in all three races was pretty much as I described it. However, in its reports of the '36 race the *New York Times,* for some reason, failed to mention that the schooner *Morning Glory* had won her class.

• The Berlin Olympics of 1936 happened, of course, as did the lavish party given on an island in the Wannsee by Joseph Goebbels for the delegation of gullible Americans, led by Charles and Anne Lindbergh. They swallowed every bit of Nazi propaganda and washed it down with fine German sparkling wine. The best sources for a description of this party and everything else that happened in Nazi Germany in the thirties are William Shirer's *The Rise and Fall of the Third Reich,* and *The Nightmare Years.*

• The Nuremberg Laws, which first took their nationality and then their humanity from the Jews of Germany, happened. When they were applied to all the Jews of Europe, only two countries resisted. It wasn't the French, the Poles, the Belgians, or the Russians. They found reasons for acquiescence. Such reasons and such people always exist.

Only the tiny Danish and Dutch nations, to their everlasting glory, resisted. When the occupying Germans announced that all the Jews in Denmark would be required to wear a yellow Star of David to identify them, the King of the Danes emerged from his palace wearing a star. In a few hours everyone in the country was wearing one. Before the Germans could round up the Jews of Denmark, as they did in those other countries, the whole nation conspired to sail them all, every one, across to Sweden in a single night. That magnificent escape actually happened. In what has to be the ultimate example of blockheaded Teutonic stupidity, the Germans retaliated by blowing up Tivoli, Copenhagen's magnificent amusement park.

 • The visit to the Tempelhof Aerodrome hosted by Goering for the Lindbergh delegation actually happened, as did the implied threat of the eight-engine transport plane being turned into an intercontinental bomber.

 • In a storm it was common practice for the schooners of the Gloucester fishing fleet to ride it out at anchor on the Banks. The storm that decimated the fleet in 1938 actually occurred and overwhelmed many of them.

 • In the thirties Army Air Corps fighter planes were divided into two subgroups: Interceptors and Pursuit ships, each designed to different criteria. The theory was that Interceptors didn't have to be as fast as the Pursuits because the incoming bombers would be coming toward them. The Battle of Britain showed that having two types of fighters for what were supposedly two different missions was a useless complication. Speed, maneuverability, and rate of climb were the keys in air battle. This obsolete theory, though, was the reason that World War Two Army Air Corps fighters were designated with a P and not an F. Hence P-40, P-38, P-47 and P-51. They were Pursuit Planes.

 • At the beginning of the war the Army refused to take men with flat feet. They were considered unfit for service and classified 4-F. Later they took almost anyone they could find.

 • The United States gave the British fifty old destroyers and ten Coast Guard Cutters in 1940, before Pearl Harbor. It left us desperately short of anti-submarine craft when we entered the war.

• "The happy time" of the German U-boats off the U.S. coast in 1942 happened. In February of 1942 alone they sank sixty-nine ships in the western Atlantic, many of them within sight of the American coast.

• The city fathers of Miami and other coastal cities refused to turn off the bright lights during the tourist season although they were silhouetting ships for the U-boats. Not everyone, it seems, knew that there was a war on.

• The Coast Guard's desperately organized picket line of yachts cruising fifty to a hundred miles offshore with orders "to observe and report the actions and activities of all hostile submarines" existed. Many of them were sailing yachts because they had far better endurance and sea-keeping ability than motor yachts.

• Eagle Boats existed and were designed by Henry Ford during World War One for anti-submarine patrol. They were not much good and the Navy didn't want them, so the Coast Guard got stuck with them.

• An Atlantic storm in December of 1942 wreaked havoc on those yachts of the picket line that did not reach harbor in time. The yawl *Ziada* actually existed, and as far as I know, still exists. She was on station off Nantucket when the storm hit. She ran off before it and finally arrived at the Ocracoke Inlet in North Carolina after covering 3,100 miles in twenty days.

• Arthur Fiedler, the conductor of the Boston Pops, volunteered and skippered a patrol boat in the Hooligan Navy.

• The incident of the German saboteurs happened exactly as Nicholas Worth related it to his granddaughter.

• The U.S. Congress, as has been true since the First Continental Congress, was of little help when it decided to involve itself in the details of a war. In its wisdom, it actually ordered that the boats of the auxiliary picket line that were over fifty feet long should be armed with a heavy machine gun and four three-hundred-pound depth charges. But they should be forgiven; 1942 was a time of desperate improvisation. Everything possible was done, not to win the war, that would come later, but to keep from losing it.

• In June of 1942 two small vessels were among those lost. The tug, U.S.S. *Gannet*, was sunk by torpedoes. Sixteen crewmen were lost. *YP-389*, a fishing vessel taken over by the Navy and armed for submarine duty, was sunk by gunfire. I combined these two incidents into the fictional tug *Redwing*.

• While searching for survivors of a torpedoed tanker off Ft. Lauderdale, a 38-foot cruiser of the Corsair Fleet encountered a U-boat whose diving fins had apparently been damaged by shots from the deck gun of the tanker; it was diving and surfacing repeatedly. It dove, then suddenly surfaced under the cruiser, lifting it clear out of the water. The sub dove again and the boat floated off. The cruiser limped back to port with several planks stove in and paint marks from the U-boat.

• If the reader is interested in the historical record of those desperate times, *The U-boat Archives of the Eastern Sea Frontier* is an hour-by-hour record of just how intense the U-boat war was off the U.S. coast in the opening months of World War Two. Another excellent source is C. Kay Larson's *The US Coast Guard Auxiliary in World War Two*.

16372102R00148

Made in the USA
Lexington, KY
19 July 2012